MURDER OFF STAGE

MURDER OFF STAGE

Mary Miley

**SEVERN
HOUSE**

First world edition published in Great Britain and the USA in 2023
by Severn House, an imprint of Canongate Books Ltd,
14 High Street, Edinburgh EH1 1TE.

severnhouse.com

British Library Cataloguing-in-Publication Data
A CIP catalogue record for this title is available from the British Library.

ISBN-13: 978-1-4483-1140-8 (cased)
ISBN-13: 978-1-4483-1141-5 (e-book)

All Severn House titles are printed on acid-free paper.

Typeset by Palimpsest Book Production Ltd.,
Falkirk, Stirlingshire, Scotland.
Printed and bound in Great Britain by
TJ Books, Padstow, Cornwall.

Praise for Mary Miley

About the author

Mary Miley grew up in New York, Pennsylvania, Illinois, and Virginia, and worked her way through the College of William and Mary in Virginia as a costumed tour guide at Colonial Williamsburg.

As Mary Miley Theobald, she has published numerous nonfiction books and articles on history, travel and business topics. As Mary Miley, she is the award-winning author of the Roaring Twenties mysteries and the Mystic's Accomplice mysteries series. When she's not home writing, she can be found in the fields or bottling factory at Valley Road Vineyards, the Virginia winery she (and a few friends) own, where everything she does would have been illegal in the Roaring Twenties.

marymileytheobald.com

ONE

Vaudeville kids grow up tough. Outsiders – we call them civilians – see only the razzle-dazzle of the stage: the glamour, the talent, the applause. They know nothing about the grinding reality as we haul our trunks to a different city each Sunday, check in and out of fleabag hotels and boarding houses, sleep on trains in second-class seats, and pretend a cheese sandwich between performances is dinner. It can be a bleak, rootless existence, but it does teach resilience and self-reliance. True, no vaudeville kid sees the inside of a school-room or eats a home-cooked meal, but we learn more than most adults will ever know about the world and its extraordinary cast of characters.

Don't think we're ignorant – vaudeville kids teach themselves to read and figure, usually in the dressing room between acts or on Sundays on the train. Nor do we lack for family. In fact, vaudeville works much like a big family, with folks looking out for one another in hard times like they did for me when my mother died. I would have ended up in an orphanage at twelve if Mother hadn't found me a slot with the Kid Circus, where they treated me like a long-lost sister. Friends made along the vaudeville circuit are friends for life. Even when schedules don't overlap for years, we can pick up right where we left off.

Which is exactly what happened when I met up with Adele Astaire in New York that autumn in 1926. We'd been like sisters when we were young, when our acts shared a booking for many months on the Orpheum circuit, and again a few years later on Gus Sun. Adele and her little brother Freddy had a dance and comedy routine their mother managed. I was always proud that my mother (stage name Chloe Randall) was a headliner in her own right, as well as our manager. I still hear her rich contralto at night, sometimes, singing me to sleep like she used to.

Adele and I hadn't seen one another in ages, but we'd kept in touch with the occasional letter, and I'd followed her stunning success with pride – and, truth to tell, a little envy – as she danced her way from Broadway to London's West End and back. Trade newspapers like *Variety* and *Billboard* kept me up to date. Just last year, she'd provided me with some crucial information when I was trying to figure out who had murdered a Los Angeles theater projectionist, and I'd told her then about how I'd left vaudeville for a fresh start in the world of moving pictures. As jobs go, assistant script girl was miles below glamorous, but I was almost as happy with my life in the rough-and-tumble of Hollywood's film industry as she was with her international acclaim.

'Did you really dance with the Prince of Wales,' I asked Adele as we made our way to the Morosco Theater near Times Square, 'or was that just your agent's invention?' We were heading out on a busman's holiday – two actresses spending an evening at the theater. She had conjured up tickets for *Rules of Engagement*, the Pulitzer Prize-winning hit of the season, even though it had been sold out for weeks.

'I absolutely, really and truly, honest-to-God did. Even taught him some new steps. And he's a reasonably good dancer. We met when he came backstage after a performance of *Stop Flirting* and later, he told everyone how much he liked it. A kind word from His Royal Highness filled the seats every night! We became rather good friends, and nooooo,' she giggled at my pointed look, 'not that kind of friend. Although he certainly made it clear that if I wanted a fling . . . He is quite amusing, and very charming to all the ladies, and I mean *all*. When we return to London in a few weeks for *Lady Be Good*, I've no doubt we'll see him again. And his brother, Prince George. Lovely man. Shy but a gem. It's a joy to work in London. They really make a fuss of us over there.'

I shook my head in amazement. 'You're incredible, hobnobbing with royalty!'

'And what about you, my dear? You've brought your own royalty along with you to New York, haven't you? Imagine being on a first-name basis with Douglas Fairbanks and Mary Pickford, the king and queen of Hollywood!'

In those days, I lived in Hollywood, at the edge of Los Angeles, where the motion picture industry had settled thanks to the perpetual sunshine that let cameras roll almost every day of the year. This trip to New York came about because of my job at Pickford-Fairbanks Studios, but I'd been in New York City before, as a child with my mother and later with my vaudeville act, the Little Darlings, so I knew my way around the Theater District.

'I work for Miss Pickford and Mr Fairbanks, Adele. I admire them tremendously, but I would never claim to be friends. Though I have to admit they've been very good to me. To all their employees, in fact. Counting the bodyguards, there are six of us employees on this trip and we're staying at the same hotel they're in – the Algonquin.'

'I'm surprised they're not staying at someplace ritzier like the Plaza. How do you like the Algonquin?'

'It's marvelous! And a great location, smack in the middle of the Theater District. Nicer than anything I saw in my vaudeville years, that's for sure. The Algonquin is where they stayed on their honeymoon back in 1920, so it's their sentimental favorite.'

'So who else famous have you met out there in California?'

'Well, I was at a dinner party at Pickfair once with Charlie Chaplin and his teenage wife, Lita. And I've seen lots of well-known actors and actresses at the studio or at parties, but they usually don't know me. I'm just a lowly script girl for one of the industry's smaller studios.'

'What's a script girl do, exactly?'

As successful as she was in vaudeville and on the stage, Adele hadn't acted in any motion pictures. I gave her a shorthand explanation. 'She's the director's right hand, a liaison between him and the film editor. You do know that the scenes in a picture aren't filmed first to last, right? It isn't like filming a play.'

'I'd heard something like that.'

'It's cheaper to film the scenes in groups that use the same actors or the same set rather than starting with the opening scene and ending with the final one. You can imagine how confusing that can get with the various clothing, hairstyles, props, weather and accessories. You can't have the heroine wearing a paisley scarf when she walks out of one room and a checkered scarf as she enters the next. The script girl monitors all that kind of thing during shooting to avoid errors in continuity, making sure those elements remain constant from scene to scene. She tracks wardrobe and makeup, keeps notes on each scene, and takes each day's film and notes to the editor.'

'Sounds important.'

'When it comes to making a picture, every job is important.'

'Don't be so modest! I'm proud of you, Jessie. Your mother would be proud of you, too. Who would have thought two little girls like us would come this far? Oh, here we are – the Morosco. I am so looking forward to seeing *Rules of Engagement* again. This time I can concentrate on the acting and staging instead of the plot.'

Adele's remark about my mother set off a warm glow deep inside my chest. I didn't often talk to people who had known my mother. When our families had been booked on the same circuit, our mothers had become quite friendly, often treating us kids like we were one big family. Though I have to say, there was no sisterly resemblance between Adele – tall, dark curly hair and ivory skin – and myself, with my short, fly-away auburn hair and freckles.

And I understood what Adele meant about watching the actors on stage. I'd done the same in my vaudeville years, taking in a particular picture or a stage show several times so I could study the actors' techniques. Watching an adult Mary Pickford play children's roles on the screen helped me perfect my own impersonations of children for the vaudeville stage, and that kept me working in kiddie acts until I reached my mid-twenties. No one could surpass Adele when it came to dancing, singing and comedy, but she wanted to improve her dramatic acting skills – her one weakness, if it could be called that. Observing the actors in *Rules of Engagement* might teach her something. In this business, you had to keep running just to stay in place.

We dispensed with the basics on our way to the theater, catching up on news of mutual friends. Adele's mother, Mrs Astaire, had been enjoying good health until a recent illness sent her to bed. 'Mother sends her love and hopes you'll be in New York long enough to call on her at our hotel. She's retired from active management now, but she often travels with us, nonetheless. It's hard to break such a long habit!'

Adele's dance partner and little brother Freddy was no longer little, nor was he called Freddy. Fred had grown into a brilliant choreographer, and now it was he who handled the business side of their career. 'I'm working for *him* now!' moaned Adele, but her manner was gay and I could tell she was happy with the arrangement. 'He's a tyrant. Every morning we rehearse until I think my feet are going to fall off. Critics loved our *Fascinating Rhythm* number, but are rave reviews good enough for Fred? No siree bob! He's constantly making changes, "improvements", he calls them, and then improving on the improvements! But it's heaven having afternoons and evenings free to do whatever I like!'

As we jostled our way through the throng clogging the theater's entrance, a number of people recognized Adele and called out to her, which turned even more heads and brought more greetings from strangers and acquaintances alike.

'Oh, look, it's Adele Astaire! Adele! Yoo-hoo! Over here! How lovely to see you again, my dear! You remember me – Rebecca Samuels from the Bishops' party?'

'Miss Astaire, um, geez, I saw you in *Lady Be Good*. You were wonderful! Could I have your autograph on this playbill?'

'Good evening, Adele. Do let me introduce my brother, Robert Hadley. Aren't you off to London soon? Tell Fred that Frances says hello and hopes to see him at the Gershwins' on Wednesday.'

'Evening, Miss Astaire. What is your seat number? Oh, good, we're just three rows back from you. Let's meet during Intermission for a drink.'

And so much more of the same that it was almost curtain time before we finally navigated the lobby crowd and reached the usher who escorted us to our seats.

'Second row center?' I marveled. 'Gosh, Adele, how did you manage that?'

'One of the benefits of having a Broadway hit. I can get tickets to anything, any time – free. Let me know what else you want to see while you're in New York.'

'If I have any evenings to myself, I surely will. I'm not here on holiday, remember.'

'What *are* you doing while you're here? Obviously, there isn't any script-girl work for you in New York City.'

'Miss Pickford asked me to come east so I could help with their correspondence and run errands for her and Douglas during the day. I'm used to doing a bit of everything – a real Girl Friday. My title at their studio is script girl for Douglas's pictures, but when he's not filming, I pitch in wherever I'm needed. A jill-of-all-trades, you might say.'

She smiled at that and squeezed my hand. 'It's so good to see you again, Jessie! You look great! And I love your hair – when did you bob it?'

'Last year, after I'd quit playing kiddie roles. I wasn't sorry to lose those tiresome braids; they were so childish. Of course, I wish I had a Louise Brooks sort of bob, all sleek and dark and mysterious, but it's the best I can do with this auburn mess.'

She gave a great sigh. 'It's been too long! Success is great but it sure gets lonely sometimes, doesn't it?'

'You, lonely? After that gauntlet we've just run?'

She lowered her voice. 'Oh, sure, I've got a lot of so-called friends these days – a hit musical brings an avalanche of attention – but vaudeville friends who knew me and Freddy and Mama back in the rough days, well, those are the ones who matter. With you, I can relax and be myself. No pretending. Oh, look! See that man in the front row, over there to the right?'

'The bald fella?'

'No, on his right. Tall. Dark hair and glasses.'

'Yeah, who is it?'

'Edward Ricks, *Rules of Engagement*'s playwright. You know, the Pulitzer Prize-winner. He's very involved with the stage production. I'm told he comes most nights to make sure every detail is perfect. I'm sure the director hates his guts – like Fred, Edward Ricks changes things all the time, even music – moving props, altering dialogue. Things that are none of his business. Drives everyone batty, as you can imagine. I've run into him at several parties. Bit of a snob. Maybe I can introduce you after the final curtain. Shhh, there go the lights . . .'

The audience hushed as the lights dimmed. A handful of musicians struck up an overture. When it had concluded, the curtain parted to reveal a battlefield trench at the Western Front, complete with liberal swirls of gunpowder haze produced, I knew from experience, by dry ice in buckets hidden about the stage. Drums and cymbals provided the sound effects of a distant battle. I'd heard a little about the story: a young soldier's encounters with a German officer and a French African soldier in a prison camp during the Great War change him in unexpected ways. That the horrors of trench warfare profoundly altered the men who served was not news to anyone; the kicker was that the war had changed everyone back home too. It was a highly acclaimed, serious work, one that would merit discussion afterwards about how we all struggle to live with what life randomly hands us, and I gave the first act my complete attention.

Intermission broke the solemnity an hour and a half later. 'What d'you think so far?' asked Adele as we stood and stretched our backs.

'Powerful,' I replied. 'Well staged. The acting is excellent. Especially Crenshaw.'

'Yes, he's very good,' said Adele vaguely, her attention focused over my shoulder toward the end of the front row where the play's author had been seated. 'Damnit,' she muttered. 'We're trapped here and there goes Edward Ricks through the side door. I won't be able to introduce you – oh, never mind. It's no great loss. The Pulitzer and the profits have swelled his head, and he's turned into an insufferable prig.' Just then her eye fell on a handsome gent across the aisle who spotted her at the same moment, gave an eager wave, and muscled his way toward us for a kiss on the cheek and an animated chat. Twenty minutes later, the play resumed.

During Act Two Scene One, the action shifted to a living room in a well-to-do American home. The lead, played by the handsome actor Allen Crenshaw, sat in an overstuffed chair, center stage right, as an elegantly attired woman, played by a lovely red-headed actress named Norah Rose, entered upstage left, through a door at the top of a flight of stairs. Crenshaw stood, looking up at her. There followed a vicious argument that degenerated into insults, at which point the hysterical actress pulled a pistol from her handbag and fired a couple of shots in his general direction. Crenshaw dropped to the floor in a graceless heap. He lay there, motionless. As a connoisseur of death scenes – I've played Ophelia, Juliet and Cleopatra in my career and fancy myself an authority on realistic death scenes – I judged it exceptionally good. None of the phony histrionics actors are prone to wallow in.

'That's odd,' Adele murmured in my ear. 'Ricks must have changed the plot again.'

'What?'

'Last month when I saw this, he was wounded in the leg and got up.'

Silence stretched for several seconds. The actress came down the stairs one hesitant step at a time. 'Geoffrey?' she said, using Allen Crenshaw's character's name. 'Geoffrey? Are you . . . what's . . .?' She reached the place where he lay crumpled on his back and dropped to her knees. 'Allen?' she said in a tremulous voice, reaching down and pressing his shoulder with her hand.

Then she let loose a piercing scream.

It wasn't until she used his real name that I realized she wasn't acting. Adele caught it too. So did a few others in the audience, probably all of them actors. A stagehand dashed out from the wings and crouched beside Crenshaw, lifting his head.

'Curtain!' he shouted over his shoulder. 'Get a doctor!'

The two ends of the curtain collided so fast that the heavy velvet shuddered. The audience erupted in alarm. Three men – presumably medical men – leaped from their seats and hurried toward the door leading to the wings. Seconds later, two policemen jogged down the aisle and disappeared through the same door. Some spectators bolted for the entrance, but most of us stayed glued to our seats, waiting to learn what had happened.

'Aw, it's just a publicity stunt,' said a man behind me. 'D'you remember when it happened a coupla years back? What was the play? *Secret Enemy* or *Forbidden Enemy* or something like that? It was doing poorly at the box office, so they staged a fake death on stage to get in the papers.'

'Well, *Rules of Engagement* isn't doing poorly at the box office,' replied the woman with him in a voice that expressed her disapproval.

'Maybe it's a joke,' offered someone else.

'Not funny,' said another.

'It couldn't have been a real bullet. He probably had a heart attack,' said a woman in front of us. 'Do you think we should go?'

Her companion shook his head. 'Not yet. They'll make an announcement shortly.'

He was right. A few minutes later, who should come out to calm the audience but playwright Edward Ricks himself? He parted the curtain and stepped to the very edge of the stage. He didn't need to motion for quiet.

'Ladies and gentlemen,' he began, his hands clasped in front of his chest. 'I'm very sorry to inform you that Mr Crenshaw has collapsed. Doctors are looking after him at this moment and, rest assured, a full recovery is expected.'

'Thank goodness,' whispered Adele.

The audience breathed a collective sigh of relief, and Mr Ricks gave a tight smile before continuing. 'Unfortunately, I must also inform you that the show cannot continue tonight. The theater will make every effort to refund your ticket price or issue you a replacement for a future date, even if we have to add another performance to the calendar. Please be patient as you leave. Every box-office window is being staffed now so you will not have to wait too long to make your individual arrangements, but if you prefer, you may return tomorrow. A thousand apologies for the inconvenience from the entire cast and from myself.' He signaled to the conductor to launch into a jaunty exit piece, then came down the stage steps to address those of us in the first few rows who were just beginning to file out.

'Excuse me, ladies, gentlemen,' he said in an authoritative voice. 'I am requested by the police to ask those of you seated in the first two rows to please write your name and address on this pad of paper before you leave, so that someone from the police can contact you in the unlikely event they need to ask some questions. I appreciate your cooperation very much.'

So it was a gunshot wound after all. Only a real bullet would necessitate police involvement. There would be no reason to question members of the audience if Crenshaw had suffered a heart attack or had fainted. As Adele and I worked our way toward Ricks, I noticed several people, presumably too important or too busy to bother with a police inquiry, slip out without leaving their names.

Edward Ricks spotted Adele and gave a feeble wave. 'Adele, my dear, what bad luck that you chose tonight's performance.'

He managed a wan smile. She introduced me as her friend from Hollywood. Ricks gave me a casting director's glance from head to toe and a dismissive nod.

Not much gets past a person who has spent her entire life on the stage: a quick once-over was all I needed to peg Edward Ricks's age at about forty-five. The dark toupee told me he was fighting that number; his fleshy jowls and the corset under his vest suggested he was losing the battle. He paid no attention to me.

'What happened, Edward?' Adele asked. 'Was it a heart attack? Or was he really shot?'

Ricks glanced about, then pulled her aside. I barely heard him over the commotion. 'He was shot. Somehow, the gun was loaded with live rounds.'

She gasped. 'Thank God he wasn't killed!'

'I just said that to calm the audience. He's dead.'

TWO

The shooting happened too late in the evening to make New York's morning newspapers, but rumors have a way of outrunning ink, especially in the Theater District. Newspapers splashed the killing across the front page of every afternoon paper in the city and throughout much of the rest of the country as well. Hearst and Pulitzer waged their usual slanderous war of words in an effort to exaggerate the scandal in ways that would outsell the other's papers. Dueling headlines screamed 'The Morosco Murder', 'Death at the Theater', and 'Shooting on Stage', and they carried titillating banners like 'Scorned actress shoots lover during second act' and 'Actress thought bullets were dummies' and 'Crenshaw sole casualty of *Rules of Engagement*'.

Late that morning, when Mary Pickford learned from her French maid that I'd been sitting yards away from the horrifying spectacle, she and Douglas Fairbanks waylaid me in the sitting room of our suite at the Algonquin as I was finishing my room-service breakfast. I was sharing the two-bedroom suite with the three other women who accompanied Miss Pickford on all her trips: her French maid, Jeanne; her makeup girl, Susan; and her wardrobe girl, Natalie. She used a local woman for her hair.

'Good morning, everyone,' said Miss Pickford, as she floated into the room where the four of us were gathered. 'Jessie, my dear, the whole city is talking about the terrible shooting last night at the Morosco. Jeanne said you were there. Can that be true? Is Allen Crenshaw really dead or just injured? I simply can't believe the nonsense I'm hearing downstairs.'

Mary Pickford had turned thirty-four some months earlier, but it was no exaggeration to say she looked half her age. Her flawless complexion and petite figure – she was just a shade over five feet, same as me, and she watched her weight like a mad woman – explained much of the spread. Her famous dark blonde ringlets subtracted a few more years from her actual age, and she was always careful to keep her fingernails short and unpolished and her makeup natural, and of course she never smoked or took a drink. At least, not in public. 'Our Little Mary', her adoring public called her or, 'The Girl with the Curls' or 'America's Sweetheart'. With a face recognized all over the world, Mary Pickford was more international phenomenon than film star. Some said she was the richest woman on Earth. She was certainly one of the most influential.

'I'm afraid he's dead,' I told her. 'At least, that's what the playwright told us.'

'Edward Ricks, the man who won the Pulitzer?'

'Yes. He was backstage with Crenshaw and the doctors just after the shooting occurred. I was in the second row center with Adele Astaire. We watched it all happen, thinking it was part of the show. We had no idea . . . not at first.'

'How horrible! An accident, of course . . . wasn't it?'

I shrugged. 'I guess that's what the police will have to figure out: was it a genuine accident or did the shooter want him dead? Did someone put real bullets in the gun that was supposed to be loaded with blanks? The actress who fired the shots, Norah Rose, looked as confused as the audience.'

'Well, she *is* an actress,' interrupted Douglas Fairbanks drily as he fiddled with his cufflinks, then held out his arm to his wife with a sigh of frustration. America's swashbuckling hero conquered by a stubborn cufflink.

'Whether or not she knew there were real bullets in the gun, I can't say.'

'Did you say you were with Adele Astaire?' Douglas asked.

I nodded. 'She's an old friend from vaudeville. Her mother and mine were fast friends, and we shared a billing on a couple of circuits when we were kids. I haven't seen her in years.'

'She and her brother got glowing reviews for their latest Gershwin musical. We'll have to make it a point to catch it while we're here, Mary,' he said to his wife before turning back to me. 'What's it called?'

'*Lady Be Good*,' I said, 'but I'm afraid it's not playing right now. She and Fred are having a bit of a rest before they take it to London in a few weeks.'

'Well, shoot! Maybe we'll get to London while it's playing

there. All right, Mary, my love, we'd better get moving or we'll be late. Jessie, you'll find a pile of invitations on the desk in our suite. Send regrets to all of them except the one on the top. And here's a list of gifts we need for tonight's reception. After you gather up those, you're off for the afternoon. All of you, be back here by six.'

As I finished my coffee, I telephoned Adele at the Hotel Astor. 'I've got work to do this morning,' I told her, 'but I'll be finished by early afternoon.'

'Great! I've had a telephone call from a police detective, and they want to ask me some questions about last night. I told them two o'clock. Can you be here by then?'

'Sure I can, although no one contacted me. Maybe they don't want to question me.'

'Never mind what they want. *I* want you with me. You've had practice dealing with the police, and I haven't. We'll give better answers if we're together, don't you think?'

Actually, I did. So after I'd written thirty-one regrets to people who had invited Mary Pickford or Douglas Fairbanks to a dinner, reception, party or show, and after I'd scrounged half a dozen stores for the scarves, perfume and sterling cigarette cases that Douglas wanted to give people tonight, and after I'd wrapped them in glossy white paper and tied them with shiny gold ribbon, the way Miss Pickford liked, I hoofed it the few blocks over to the Astor on Times Square where Adele and her brother had been staying throughout their Broadway run.

I dressed carefully for the occasion. Being questioned by the police required modest clothing in order to lend an air of respectability that would give them faith in whatever I said. Adele was right, I'd been around police a good deal in the past year or so. I'd been wary of cops all my life, but they didn't intimidate me any longer.

Since childhood, I'd carried a healthy distrust of the men in uniform who arrested my mother and me time and again on behalf of the Gerry Society, those pinched-face do-gooders who believed children under sixteen should be banned from the morally corrupt stage. The law didn't forbid all performance – it said kid performers couldn't move about on the stage. They could sing or recite poetry as long as they stood still, but they couldn't dance or take a step. Who knows what twisted logic was behind that? Gerry spies would sit in the audience and report to the cops any young-looking performer who twitched. My mother and I got arrested a number of times, particularly in New York where they enforced the laws more vigorously than in other states. She usually just paid the fine and we kept going. When that or bribery didn't work and we had to go to court, she'd make me up to look older, covering my freckles, using rouge on my cheeks and crimson lipstick, painting my fingernails with blood-red lacquer, and dressing me in a padded brassiere and – Presto! Twelve became sixteen and the judge would dismiss the case.

Then there were times after my mother died when I strayed into shoplifting to get along. Truth be told, I was a pretty good thief, able to stash small items from department stores or drug-stores in my pockets without getting caught. Hunger is a powerful motivator, so when there was no food around, I filched enough from a greengrocer's stand to stave off the gnawing in my stomach until someone bought me a meal or shared a sandwich. I got slapped a few times or lectured or prayed over, and twice spent a night in jail. Only once did I get roughed up pretty bad, and that was by some sick old cop who would have gone all the way if the matron hadn't appeared in the nick of time and pulled him off me. That's why I was shy of uniforms in general, police in particular. It was easier dealing with detectives; they dressed in their own clothes.

For my meeting with Adele and the detective that day, I changed into a sand-colored, two-piece suit with a crisp white collar and cuffs. Very professional looking. Very serious.

It wasn't like I went around searching for murders to solve. Naturally women can't be policemen or detectives, so the idea of investigating crimes or putting killers in prison never entered my head. Nonetheless, it seems I was good at it. A dear friend once told me that my curiosity lured me into trouble and my common sense let me escape. 'You notice things others miss,' he'd said during one of his rare introspective moods. 'And you have a way of sensing things, almost like a mind reader.' I had given that analysis considerable thought. I was certainly no psychic, but after spending a lifetime on stage watching for subtle cues, making decisions based on someone's tone of voice, picking up on a raised eyebrow or the lift of a chin, and absorbing the audience's mood through the pores of my skin, it was probably inevitable that I would become sensitive to details, especially the human kind. I think maybe I read people, not minds.

As I rode up the hotel elevator to Adele's suite, I congratulated myself that this was one death I would not have to worry about. The police would solve this without me. I'd help, of course, by answering any questions they posed, but I suspected there was little Adele or I could say that would amount to much. We'd seen only what everyone else in the audience had seen; a little closer maybe, but we knew nothing more than the rest.

'Oh, thank heavens you're here!' cooed Adele, fluttering like a beautiful butterfly as she opened the door to her magnificent suite. Dressed in a gauzy, pale green gown with a handkerchief hem, her feet were bare and her dark brown hair had been curled on only one side of her head. Her huge eyes sparkled. Adele Astaire would have dazzled in a flour sack dress.

A maid peered out of the doorway to the adjoining bedroom. 'Miss Astaire, please hurry and let me finish your hair. Those police will be here any minute.'

'Go on, go on. I'll entertain myself,' I said, wiggling my fingers like a farmwife shooing chickens.

'All right. I'm coming, Georgia. Make yourself comfortable, Jessie. I'll only be a few minutes.'

No hotel suite was too good for the favorite star of New York's favorite musical. *Lady Be Good* producers were certainly keeping Adele and her brother in luxury. I squinted my eyes and took in the whole scene, from the grand piano at one end to the marble fireplace at the other, to the three sparkling chandeliers that dangled in between. On the walls hung paintings that looked like they'd been stolen from a museum. And the view of the city from that huge window! I wondered if Mrs Astaire had a room this nice.

'I'm a bundle of nerves,' Adele said as she re-entered the living room, fully dressed and coiffed. 'I'd offer you a cocktail but under the circumstances . . .'

'Yeah, let's hold off until the detective has gone.' Although, if he were anything like Carl Delaney, my detective friend back in Los Angeles, he'd appreciate sharing a drink with us, never mind the irksome Prohibition laws. It hadn't taken me more than a short walk down a single Manhattan street to realize that New Yorkers flouted the federal laws with brazen contempt. In one block alone, I passed two speakeasies, two drug stores dispensing 'prescription' liquor, and one 'kosher wine' retailer. No one had to even cross the street to buy liquor.

We had only a few minutes to review our impressions of the play when the buzzer sounded. The maid opened the door and relieved the visitor of his fedora and coat. 'Detective Benjamin Quinn, madam,' she announced as she escorted him into the living room.

Let me say up front that no one could be in a room with Adele for ten minutes without falling in love with her, and Detective Quinn was no exception to the rule. He looked about my own age – a bit young to be a detective, I thought – and seemed more nervous than Adele. 'Miss Astaire,' he began, clearing his throat and pulling off his dark-rimmed spectacles as if to get a closer look. 'Thank you for agreeing to see me. I . . . we . . . the New York City police appreciate your willingness to help us with this investigation, with this tragic, um, occurrence.'

'Certainly, Detective Quinn. I am happy to do whatever I can. And this is Miss Jessie Beckett,' she said as she directed him to the chair opposite our sofa. 'She was beside me at the theater last night. I was sure you'd want to question her as well.'

'Certainly,' he said, with so little conviction that I realized he had come to interview Adele not because he thought she could be of any real help, but rather because he couldn't resist the opportunity to spend a few minutes in the presence of the celebrated performer. 'Pleased to meet you, Miss Beckett.'

As we settled into our seats, Adele turned to her maid and requested tea. I studied Detective Quinn as he took a small notepad and pencil stub out of his breast pocket. He wore street clothes, a brown pin-striped sack suit with a double-breasted jacket and wide trouser legs – the sort I associated with flashy people like gangsters and theater folks – and brown shoes with the sort of spit-and-polish shine that men learn in the military. Quinn was lean. His face was long, serious, and clean-shaven, except for a wisp of a mustache, and he wore his hair short in the army way. He was of an age to have spent the end of the

Great War in the trenches, as so many of our boys did, including my own detective friend, Carl Delaney. It occurred to me that the police force was a natural career choice for many of our returning doughboys. They understood discipline and had learned first-hand how civilization collapses into chaos when law and order disappear.

'How can we help you?' asked Adele. Only someone who knew her as well as I did would have seen how tense she was, playing her part in a formal style entirely foreign to her normal lively, gay manner. I spoke up to take the spotlight off her.

'Detective Quinn, this has been such a shocking death, and we want to help in any way we can, of course, but I'm afraid we are wasting your time.'

'Not at all, ladies,' he said rather pompously. 'Not at all. This is a simple case that turns on one simple question: who put two live rounds in the stage gun? We know who shot Mr Crenshaw – hundreds of people saw Miss Norah Rose do it. She claims she didn't know the gun was loaded with live rounds. If that's true, we have a murderer to catch.'

It might have been a simple case, but simple didn't mean easy. This would be more complicated and harder to solve than Detective Quinn believed. I kept my thoughts to myself, but wondered about his experience.

'Let's just begin with a few questions, shall we, ladies? How well did you know the deceased, Allen Crenshaw?'

'I didn't know him at all,' I said, turning to Adele so she could take her turn.

'I knew him casually. I'd see him now and then at parties.'

'How often?'

'Oh, I don't know . . .'

'Twice? Five times? Ten times? A score?'

'A dozen times, maybe.'

'And what about Miss Rose? How well did you know her?'

'Not at all,' I said again, reinforcing my own irrelevance.

'Not well,' said Adele. 'She is a casual acquaintance who's fun to talk to at parties.'

'And what did you talk about at these parties?'

Adele leaned back in the chair, her nervousness forgotten now that she was on familiar ground. 'We're in the same business, detective, so it's natural we should talk about the theater. The stage, the crew, the publicity, the music, the playwright, the advertising, the reviews, the other actors . . . everything about the play and the players.'

'What was her relationship with Mr Crenshaw?'

Georgia came in from the tiny kitchen with a tray of tea and shortbread. Adele paused to pour. As she handed the detective his cup, she returned to his question. 'I don't like gossip, detective, and I don't spread it. All I can tell you is they were rumored to be romantically involved some months ago when the play first opened. Gossip said they'd parted ways since. I have no idea whether or not the rumors are true. I haven't seen them together in months. Except on stage, of course.'

He looked at me, but I shook my head and helped myself to a cookie. I had nothing to add here. He turned back to Adele.

'You don't know if they were friendly or antagonistic toward one another?'

'I'm afraid not.'

'You don't know whether Miss Rose held a grudge against Mr Crenshaw after they . . . uh . . . "parted ways"?'

'I do not.'

'A grudge strong enough to lead to murder?'

'I cannot say.'

'What was Mr Crenshaw's reputation in the theater world?'

'He was widely regarded as a superb actor. A natural.'

'I meant, what was his personal reputation?'

'Like most actors, he had a large ego.'

'And a reputation as a playboy?' the detective prompted.

She paused, reluctant, I thought, to say anything negative about the deceased, then admitted, 'That's true.'

'Did you like him?'

Adele bristled. 'I never experienced any unwelcome advances, if that's what you're insinuating.'

'I'm only asking for your opinion of him.'

'Well, then, I didn't care for him, if you must know. I avoided him when I could.'

'You knew he was married?'

She stirred her tea and nodded. 'Of course. His wife Marjorie is a friend. I haven't seen her in months, though.'

'Is she an actress?'

'Yes, but not as successful as her husband. I don't think she's working at the moment.'

'You say you haven't seen her lately?'

'No. Allen – Mr Crenshaw – began attending social events with Norah Rose or other lady friends I didn't know. I felt sorry for Marjorie. She deserved better.'

'Are they estranged?'

'You'll have to ask her that.'

'I plan to.' Detective Quinn made a few notes and turned to me. 'Would you be able to describe the scene where Crenshaw was shot?'

'Certainly,' I said, glad to be of some use. 'He was alone on the stage. He delivered a monologue. The actress – Miss Rose – entered upstage left, through a door. She delivered her lines and removed a gun from her handbag. She fired two or three shots which knocked him backwards against the wall, then forwards on to the floor. I thought at the time it was quite unlike the usual campy death scene where they clutch their heart and stagger about the stage for several minutes – this was highly realistic. He just slumped to the floor. But I didn't consider the possibility that he'd actually been shot until Adele whispered something about how, when she'd seen the play previously, he'd only been wounded.'

Adele confirmed that her recollections were the same as mine. I wondered how many of the first two rows of spectators Detective Quinn planned to interview. No doubt he had recognized Adele's name on the list and chose her because of her theater connections. She would have more knowledge of the actors than most other audience members. And I couldn't help but notice how his eyes rarely left her face. Another admirer for Adele's overflowing collection!

'Do you know anyone with a grudge against Crenshaw?' By now he knew not to bother me with these questions. Adele thought carefully for a moment before answering in the negative.

'No one who would feel so aggrieved that they would kill him. As I mentioned, he had a large ego and could be rude, even insulting, especially when drinking. But that could be said of most people. Some people took offense at things Allen did or said, usually when he was in his cups. But killing him? I can't think of anyone who hated him as much as that.'

The detective spent another fifteen minutes asking increasingly irrelevant questions and drinking a second cup of tea, until even he could think of no way to prolong his stay. I saw Adele's eyes narrow and her face took on a crafty expression. She was up to something. As I stood there, watching with amazement, she cast her line into the river, hooked her fish, and reeled him in like the expert angler she was.

First she stood, signaling an end to the interview. Quinn took the hint and got on his feet.

'I hope Jessie and I have been helpful, Detective Quinn,' she said. 'You must not hesitate to telephone if you think of any further questions. Did I understand you wanted to speak with Marjorie Crenshaw?'

'Uh, yeah . . .'

'I think I can help you there. I know Marjorie well enough to assure you that she will not want to talk to the police under the present circumstances. But if I accompany you, I can smooth the way. She'll open the door to me, and I can persuade her to cooperate. I also know that she's likely to be home now. If we go straight to her apartment from here, we can have a helpful conversation and then perhaps you and Jessie and I can go directly to an early dinner.'

That raised my eyebrows. 'Um, Adele, you must've forgotten . . . I think I mentioned that Mr Fairbanks and Miss Pickford are expecting me back at the Algonquin at six.'

Detective Quinn's jaw dropped. 'Douglas Fairbanks?' he asked.

'Of course,' said Adele. 'You knew they were in New York, didn't you? It was in all the papers. Jessie is one of their assistants. She will be a great asset at an interview with Marjorie, since she has worked hand-in-glove with the Los Angeles police department for years now, solving any number of murders. Haven't you, Jessie?'

'Um, well, I helped a little . . .'

'Isn't she modest? Jessie cracked the Serbian murder spree that occurred last year, one of them in New York City – you remember that one, don't you, detective? The Serbian cook who was gunned down in a restaurant right here in the theater district?

She solved that one and linked it to four other revenge killings. Caught the murderer red-handed too. You probably remember her name from the newspapers.'

Quinn looked at me with a mixture of doubt and awe. Suddenly I was *someone.*

Time for me to squeeze in a word edgewise. 'I'd be happy to go with you to Mrs Crenshaw's, but I'll have to hot-foot it to the Algonquin immediately afterwards. I couldn't stay for dinner.'

'Oh, what a shame. Well, the detective and I will have to have dinner by ourselves. You won't mind that, will you, detective?'

The wide-eyed detective couldn't believe his luck. A lowly police detective dining with the toast of Broadway? He would be delighted to drive us to the address that Adele provided. His Ford was parked a block up from the hotel entrance. We descended in the elevator and waited at the curb while he fetched the motorcar.

'What on earth are you up to?' I hissed as soon as he was out of earshot. 'That poor man is moonstruck. He'd walk off the Brooklyn Bridge if you asked him to.'

She flicked her fingers impatiently. 'I want to solve a murder, like you. But I can't do it alone; I don't know how. You've got to help me.'

'The police can solve this murder just fine by themselves.'

'Hell, no, they can't. The theater world will chew up that poor detective and spit him out. You saw how green he was. Without us – without you – he hasn't a chance.'

THREE

Adele did not exaggerate. Detective Quinn would not have made it past the dragon-like doorman at Marjorie Crenshaw's building without her. When the doorman rang up to Marjorie's apartment and announced the visitors, we heard a long pause as he listened, then responded, 'Yes, madam. Certainly.' With a grim expression, he replaced the receiver and directed us to the elevator where a colored boy rode us to the fifth floor.

'Why, Adele . . . this is . . . certainly unexpected,' she said looking past Adele to Detective Quinn and me standing behind her. The small black poodle in her arms gave a yip. 'Hush, Fifi, darling. They're friends. I think.'

'Marjorie,' Adele crooned, taking the woman in a loose embrace so as not to crush little Fifi. 'I am sooooo very sorry about Allen's death. A note of condolence seemed inadequate considering the circumstances, so I wanted to come by in person and express my sympathies. As fate would have it, I was in the audience last night, and my first thoughts were of you, my dear.'

'Thank you, Adele, you're always so kind.'

'Let me introduce you to Detective Benjamin Quinn from the police, who came to question me and my friend, Jessie Beckett, this afternoon. As witnesses, we feel obliged to help the police as much as we can, so they can learn what happened last night and bring the guilty party to justice. The detective mentioned that he was on his way here, and I thought it would help if I were here with you when he asked his questions. For support. Of course, I'll slip away if you prefer to see the detective on your own . . .'

'No, no, do come in. All of you. It's been quite a shock; I don't have to tell you.'

Adele's prediction had been right on the money. Marjorie Crenshaw seemed relieved to have a friend with her during the detective's questioning. My presence received no further explanation, and evidently, Marjorie didn't think it needed one. I wondered whether she realized that she was a possible suspect in her husband's death.

'It was a horrible shock to me, too, Marjorie. Thank God you weren't there.'

Marjorie Crenshaw was an attractive woman of middle years, probably the same age as her husband, but that made her too old for all but the most insignificant of theater parts. Legit, vaudeville and moving pictures were all hard on women. Men could play leading roles well into their fifties – just look at Douglas Fairbanks, still playing the dashing young hero at forty-three – but women? Women aged out at thirty. Except for Mary Pickford. Marjorie had tried to hang on to her youth by bobbing her hair, flattening her chest, and sporting a straight-waisted day dress that looked like something a young flapper had bought off the rack, but her makeup failed to camouflage the wrinkles at the corners of her eyes and upper lip. I was all sympathy – I, too, had aged out of my vaudeville career at twenty-five when the kiddie roles dried up.

Marjorie Crenshaw lived comfortably, if not luxuriously, in a small Midtown apartment she had furnished with an old-fashioned, chintz-covered sofa and matching chairs and lighted with Tiffany-style lamps. The corner Victrola and upright piano made me think she sang as well as acted; the radio against the wall provided a modern touch. Depositing Fifi on a plush cushion, she offered us coffee or tea, and when we declined, situated herself beside the little dog. 'Make yourselves at home,' she said with a sweep of her hand to indicate the chairs.

Detective Quinn wasted no time, plunging past the preliminaries straight into the interrogation. 'When was the last time you saw your husband, Mrs Crenshaw?'

She fidgeted with Fifi's collar for a minute before admitting what we all knew. 'It's been several weeks. Four or five. I'm afraid he doesn't live here any more. As a matter of fact, he hasn't lived here for the past year.'

'Are you divorced, Mrs Crenshaw?'

She cleared her throat delicately. 'As Adele knows,' she began, with an apologetic glance toward Adele, 'I wanted to avoid the scandal of a divorce, so no, we are not divorced.'

'Do you have any children?'

'We were not blessed with children.'

Meaning she would probably inherit all of her husband's estate, large or small. An interesting bit of news.

'Does Mr Crenshaw have his own separate residence?'

'I believe so.'

'Where is that?'

'I'm not sure. His agent will know.'

'And what happened the last time you met? Where was it – here?'

'No, it was at a restaurant. Alfredo's. Two weeks ago, I believe, or three. Allen wanted to see how I felt about him moving back home.' I saw the surprise on Adele's face when Marjorie made that remark. 'The tragedy of all this is that Allen told me he had finally come to his senses and wanted to reconcile. And now it's too late.' She took a handkerchief out of her sleeve and dabbed her eyes. Adele reached across the coffee table, squeezed Marjorie's hand, and whispered, 'I'm so sorry.'

She regained her composure and continued. 'Allen rang me on the telephone this past Tuesday to beg me to take him back at once. He said he'd grown up. He said he'd been out of his mind to think there was another woman who could take my place. His little flings meant nothing to him, he said. I told him I'd have to have a few days to consider . . . but then I called him back the very next night and told him all was forgiven.'

'You're a brick, Marjorie,' said Adele.

'He was planning to move back home on Monday. And now he never will.' She stifled a sob and swallowed hard.

'Did your husband have a will, Mrs Crenshaw?'

Her eyes narrowed. 'A will? No, of course not. He didn't expect to be murdered, did he?'

'Did your husband have any children?'

'I said we didn't.'

'Did he have any children from any other relationships?'

Her 'No' was as frosty as a winter morning.

'Then you'll inherit his entire estate?'

She gave a dismissive snort. 'Some estate! Debts, you mean.' A sudden frown crossed her brow. 'You can't inherit debts, can you? I won't pay any of his debts!'

'I'm not a lawyer, Mrs Crenshaw, but I believe your husband's lawful debts will have to be paid out of his estate, reducing whatever he leaves to you.' *Un*lawful debts, such as gambling debts or private loans, were another matter. 'Were you aware of any money problems he was having?'

'Well, none specifically. I just know he was living above his means, as they say. I assume he owed money around town.'

Quinn scribbled some notes before continuing. 'Were you aware of any other problems? Female problems? Gambling? Drinking? Drugs? Serious arguments? Anything that would make someone want to kill him?'

Her lips tightened and her eyes narrowed to dangerous slits. 'That little alley cat, Norah Rose, had her claws into him for a while. I heard she didn't take it well when he cast her off. She was the one who shot him. Why haven't the police arrested her?'

'We're questioning her, ma'am. She did indeed pull the trigger, but she may not have known there was live ammunition in the gun.' Marjorie's eye-roll expressed quite clearly what she thought of that notion. 'Were there any other people who might have wished ill on your husband? Any enemies?'

'There may have been some other girlfriends I wasn't aware of, but otherwise . . . no. Everyone liked Allen. He was a charmer. He didn't gamble, he didn't drink or use drugs, and he'd had several raises thanks to the success of *Rules of Engagement*. And we were going to be happy again . . .' She dabbed her eyes once more.

'Poor lady,' sighed the gullible Detective Quinn when we were back in the elevator.

It was a little after four o'clock, too early for a meal, so Adele arranged to meet Detective Quinn at her favorite Italian restaurant in the theater district at eight. 'We'll discuss the case there,' she said coyly.

'You are such a flirt!' I cried, after he had dropped us back at the Astor.

'He's sweet. No ring – fair game. And who knows what we can come up with over dinner? The solution to the crime perhaps?'

'Well, consider this while you're solving the crime: your friend Marjorie had no need of her handkerchief.'

'What do you mean?'

'She kept dabbing her eyes, but she wasn't crying. Her eyes weren't wet. And that's some convenient story about Allen moving back in next week. Do you think that's true, or is it something she wants to put out to the public to raise her reputation?'

'Gosh, I don't know.'

'Obviously Detective Quinn swallowed every word she uttered. She was convincing, I'll grant you that, but she's an actress. Unemployed, maybe, but an actress trained in delivering convincing portrayals. I'd take nothing she said at face value. Were the Crenshaws really planning to reconcile? Allen Crenshaw isn't around to tell us otherwise, is he?'

'That's true,' she admitted.

'And she made Allen sound like a paragon. No drinking, no gambling, no drugs. I thought you said he had a nasty temper when he was drinking.'

'That's true too. Maybe she said that because the detective was in the room and she didn't want to admit to illegal drinking. Although I noticed a decanter and glasses on the sidebar.'

I considered the lay of the land for a few moments. 'I wonder what the stage manager at the Morosco would have to say about the bullets. I'm sure Detective Quinn has interviewed him already – or he will be doing so soon.'

'I know the stage manager. Bill Levine. He was stage manager at a theater where Fred and I were performing *For Goodness' Sake* a few years ago. I saw his name in the program last night and remembered him.'

'Well, here's an idea. Since we're so near the theater and it's only four thirty, let's drop in and see if we can talk with him. I'd like to hear what he has to say about the gun.'

Adele clapped her hands like a child about to be handed an ice-cream cone. 'I knew you'd want to help solve this murder!'

Why not? I had the time. We had nothing to lose by pursuing this a little way. Besides, as my detective friend Carl Delaney once said, I was good at this investigative work. Thinking of Carl made me recollect the importance of keeping the local police informed, so I added, 'And you can tell Detective Quinn whatever we learn from Levine when you see him at dinner tonight.'

FOUR

When we reached the Morosco Theater, the cab driver asked for an autograph instead of his fare. Adele gave him both, plus a big smile. By then, the sun had dropped behind the skyline, rinsing the color out of the city streets and dousing the air with gray chill. The Morosco would not wake up fully for another two hours, but backstage was starting to hum like a beehive. For two girls raised in the theater world, getting inside posed no problem. We went straight to the stage door and talked our way past the bent old man serving as gate-keeper. Within minutes, we had tracked Bill Levine to his basement office, a dimly lit space crammed from cement floor to low ceiling with debris. He remembered Adele. Who didn't?

'I know you're up to your neck with trouble,' cooed Adele, 'getting the understudy up to speed and handling the police, but my friend Jessie and I wanted to ask you about last night, if you can stand a few more quick questions. We were in the audience and are helping Detective Quinn with his investigation.'

Bill Levine was a big, gruff man with ruddy cheeks that suggested he kept a bottle close at hand. Questions were unnecessary. He was happy to answer his own.

'Sure, hon, I've got a few minutes for you anytime. But if the cops think they're gonna pin this on me, they got another think coming.' He threw up his hands. 'What did I do yesterday? I did what I always do, every damn night the same. I took two blank cartridges out of this here box,' and he reached into a desk drawer, retrieved a red and white cardboard box marked STANE, and shook it. It was half-full of cartridges. 'I took this revolver,' and he reached for a gun sitting on a stack of papers like a paperweight, 'and I loaded it. And no, there are no live cartridges anywhere in my office. Or anywhere in the theater, for that matter. And yes, I know every inch of this place. Then I walked to where Norah makes her entrance. Come on, follow me. I got nothing to hide.'

He led us through a labyrinth of narrow passageways cluttered with racks of costumes, piles of scrap wood, tin buckets, and sacks that bulged with undeterminable contents, up some flimsy stairs until we reached the spot where Norah Rose made her entrance in Act Two, Scene One. I breathed in the familiar scent of backstage: fresh paint, musty lumber, flop sweat, and even the faint rot of old costumes. Most actors and musicians wouldn't show up for another hour or so, but backstage bustled with electricians fiddling with lights, seamstresses repairing costumes, and cats keeping the rats at bay. An assortment of cleaners lugging brooms and mops scurried past us, flattening themselves against the wall for the big man to pass.

'Oh, Mr Levine,' interrupted one nervous boy who caught up with the stage manager. 'The dry-ice man is here and—'

'Same place as yesterday,' he growled at the lad, and then to us, he continued. 'Right here.' He patted the empty shelf. 'I always lay it right here so she can pick it up as she enters. I'll do it again tonight.'

'What do you think happened?' Adele asked.

Levine shrugged. 'No way someone could have substituted live ammo in my box. You saw how they were all alike. I showed that to the detective this morning. Anyone trying to substitute something different, I'd've noticed. Anyone making a substitution would have to have done it after I loaded the revolver and set it on this here shelf.'

'How much time elapsed between when you laid the gun on the shelf and Norah picked it up?'

'Maybe an hour, maybe two.'

I stifled a groan. During that long a time, any one of dozens of people backstage could have made the switch. I tried a different line. 'Mr Levine, was there anyone here who had a grudge against Crenshaw? Any actors, any stagehands, crew?'

'That detective asked me the same question and I told him this: lots of people didn't like Crenshaw. His understudy, Ted Youngerman, thought he shoulda had the role to begin with; Norah Rose got dumped just a coupla weeks ago; the drummer would like to kill him – forget I said that. And then there's the guy's long-suffering wife, Marjorie. But hey, not liking someone doesn't mean murdering him, you know?'

It did to someone.

'You know Marjorie Crenshaw?' asked Adele.

'I know who she is. We worked together on a production eight or ten years ago when she played a scorned wife. Prophetic, huh? She came by yesterday morning with a package for Crenshaw. Don't think she remembered me. She asked for his dressing room. Now, I know what's up between those two, so I didn't think it was a good idea to tell her where his dressing room was, so I took the package from her and put it there myself.'

Adele and I exchanged glances. Marjorie had neglected to mention that minor detail when we talked this afternoon. 'Do you know what was in the package?'

'I'm no snoop. I put it on his dressing table. Probably still there, if you wanna look.'

We did.

As leading man, Crenshaw had the largest and most convenient dressing room; nonetheless, it was hardly bigger than a closet. There was a miniature sink in one corner (a luxury I'd never had in all my years in vaudeville), a lighted dressing table and two chairs, and a rack of costumes he'd never wear again. Bottles of hair goo, brushes and open pots of greasepaint stood on the dressing table, and a half-smoked cigarette lay in the ashtray, giving the room an eerie sense that someone had just stepped out and would be back in a minute. The shelves on one wall were crammed with jars and boxes. A package wrapped in brown paper lay at the edge of the desk, unopened.

'Shall we?' I asked Levine.

'He won't object now.'

The package was about the size of a hatbox but heavier than if it had held hats. I tore the brown paper away gingerly, hoping the police wouldn't consider this tampering with evidence.

'A box,' commented Adele. 'How pretty.' And old. It was enameled on the lid and edged in dull brass. An antique, perhaps. I lifted the hinged lid. Inside were papers. A few letters, some still in their envelopes. Adele and I exchanged glances.

'You gals can have a go at reading those, if you wanna. I got work to do.'

'I'm sure you do, Mr Levine,' said Adele. 'This is going to be a tense performance.'

'Everything's gonna go off just fine tonight. It's awful, of course, what happened to Crenshaw yesterday, but the show must go on, eh? Luckily, Youngerman stepped right into the role without a hitch. This afternoon the director ran him through a few scenes. He's got 'em all down pat. Amazing. We'll be fine.'

'I'll stop by your office when we leave and tell you what we find,' said Adele.

'Tell the cops. I don't care.'

FIVE

The next day ran me ragged with errands for my two bosses, fetching purchases, delivering gifts, arranging interviews and photo shoots, and responding to fan mail and invitations in between answering the telephone. The others worked just as hard as I did – Miss Pickford's makeup needed freshening half a dozen times during the day and her New York-based hairdresser stood ready to plump those famous ringlets at a moment's notice. Who knew when some nervy photographer might push up close and flash a picture? The slick motion-picture magazines that had recently sprung up like weeds would pay a small fortune for a photo of Mary or Douglas, especially an unflattering one, so they couldn't risk looking anything less than their best at every moment. Fame brought an exhausting lifestyle with it.

'Don't breathe a word of this,' I told Adele later that evening when we met at her hotel, 'but some of those famous curls are fake.'

'No fooling?'

'She pins four or six curls to her own when she goes out.'

'I'd kill to have skin like hers. What's her secret?'

'No magic to it. She wipes off her face powder with a cotton wad dipped in almond oil, then pats her skin with witch hazel.'

'I'll start tomorrow! She's a wonder,' Adele sighed, and I had to agree. Mary Pickford had been my idol since my introduction to her pictures when I was a kid. Knowing her had only deepened my respect.

Adele went on, 'I'm so glad she gave you the night off.'

'I wasn't expecting it, but it's a welcome break. I hope your hosts won't mind you dragging me along to their party unannounced, as it were.'

'Heavens, no. They'll welcome your fresh face. And wait 'til you see their penthouse! Glorioski!'

'When we get back, maybe we can tackle those papers.'

'I had a look earlier. I didn't read them all, just sorted through them. There are some official documents, some letters – some years old, others recent, judging from postmarks.'

'From women? Like love letters?' That sounded promising.

'Some from women,' replied Adele. 'Others from men. No names I recognized.'

'They can't be love letters. Why would a girlfriend send a love letter to the address where her boyfriend's wife lived?'

'If she didn't know he had a wife?'

'Maybe. But if Marjorie did somehow get hold of any love letters to her husband, surely she'd have saved them – they'd be great evidence in a divorce suit. She wouldn't return them to her two-timing louse. My guess is Marjorie was cleaning out Allen's desk and decided to deliver the contents to him at the theater. Sounds like a pretty feeble excuse to get inside . . . maybe it was a ruse to get inside and switch out the bullets. What do you think?'

'Makes sense. But according to Bill Levine, she didn't get very far inside.'

'He didn't see her get inside. That doesn't mean she didn't.'

'Anyway, you can have a look at the papers later.'

'I'll take them home with me tonight and go through 'em when I get the chance.'

'Good idea. Ah, here's Fred now. He's coming to the party with us, of course.'

With a squeal and a big hug, Fred Astaire lifted me off my feet and twirled me around until my head was spinning. 'It's little Baby, little Baby! What a sight for sore eyes!'

It was the same Freddy I'd practically lived with during many months of our childhood, the exact same age as me, who'd shared more meals and hotel rooms with my mother and me than I could count, and who'd patiently taught me Adele's part of their bride-and-groom-on-a-cake routine so I could fill in for her that time she caught the measles. His receding hairline made him look older than his years and more serious, but I'd recognize those ears from a hundred yards.

'I'm not Baby any longer,' I laughed when he finally set me on my feet. 'These days I'm Jessie.' The nickname my mother called me had long since gone the way of the dodo, but it had been pretty useful in those early years when my name changed as often as my stage acts. In vaudeville, people tended to call you by the name you were using in your act, and during my career, I had a dozen. During my Shakespeare period I was called Juliet, then Becky Jordan when I was one of the Jordan Sisters. During my Kid Kabaret years, I was billed as Sallie Angel – I *hated* that one! – and for a season I was Jo Baker with my 'twin brother' Joey, and then Sophie with the Dancing Dollies. For my last years on the stage, I went by Carrie Darling, the second Little Darling in that family song-and-dance act. Now I was Jessie, after my murdered cousin, a name I intended to keep.

'You'll always be Baby to me, doll.'

'How's your mother feeling today?' I asked him. 'Adele told me she's been doing poorly since last week.'

'I just came from her room. She ate some chicken broth and drank a pot of tea, so that's good. At least she's feeling stronger. She knows you're here and wants very much to see you, but . . .'

'But not today. I understand. I'll be here at least two weeks, so maybe later, when she's up to visitors.' I'd hate to leave New York without having the chance to reminisce with my mother's old friend.

'Sure thing, doll. Now, I want to hear all about your recent escapades, what you've been up to these past coupla years, eh?'

'Not on your life, Fred,' interrupted Adele. 'Get your glad rags on. It's party time and we're already late. You can quiz Jessie in the taxi. Now, shoo!'

With an eye-roll at his bossy big sister, Fred vanished into the adjacent bedroom. Adele took over the interrogator's role while we waited. 'Tell me about your fella. I want to hear everything!'

So I told her about David Carr going to prison for two and a half years for doing nothing worse than hundreds of other men were doing, men who got a slap on the wrist for the same sort of thing, and how that witch Maybel Willebrandt and her federal goons – the ones they call prohis – had it in for him from the start, and how he hadn't killed anyone except in self-defense, and how he'd meant to go straight and leave bootlegging in the dust but how opportunities just kept falling down in front of him, and then I mentioned that he had put his Hollywood house in my name because he loved me so much (although he'd never quite said those exact words). Oh, he did the things they got him on all right – insurance fraud and tax evasion – but there were so many people out there who did worse and never saw the inside of a cell. It wasn't fair. 'Life isn't fair, Baby,' my mother used to say. How right she was!

And everything I told Adele was the truth, minus a few details that made David look too much like a gangster. You had to know him to understand that he wasn't as bad as his description made him sound. I confessed that I hadn't heard from him in months but that I wrote him every week and worried about him, locked away for so long with real criminals. What would it do to him? Would he be the same when they released him? I tried not to think about that.

'What about your detective friend?' she asked. 'The one who helped you solve those murders.'

'Carl? He's a good friend. The best.' She raised her eyebrows, but I had nothing more to add. To be perfectly honest, I wasn't sure how I felt about Carl Delaney, and even thinking about those feelings seemed disloyal to David. I liked Carl. I liked him a lot. And I pretended not to know that he was crazy about me. But I'd given my heart to David Carr and I wouldn't desert him now just because he was incarcerated for Prohibition crimes.

As if on cue, Fred re-entered the room and hijacked the conversation.

'How do I look?' he asked, performing a graceful pirouette that ended with a fingertip flourish.

'Good enough to escort two knockout flappers,' answered his sister. 'Vamos.'

I'll say this for the Van der Ladens, they certainly knew how to entertain. Their elegant apartment – one of several scattered about the globe, I was told – was chock-full of glamorous guests, not to mention a dozen musicians playing from a balcony over-looking the river and a score of waiters busily peddling fancy drinks and an out-of-this-world array of delicacies I was eager to sample. Any guest of the Astaires was welcome at their humble abode, and since Fred went about introducing me as his child-hood sweetheart who currently worked for Mary Pickford and Douglas Fairbanks, I was accepted into this glittering assembly as an equal. The favorite topic of conversation – no surprise –

was the Crenshaw murder. And who better to fill in the blanks than the two women who had been sitting in the second row?

Well, turns out there *was* someone better, and he arrived shortly after we did. Edward Ricks himself waltzed in around eleven o'clock, having come straight from the evening's performance of *Rules of Engagement*. He had scarcely time to hand his hat and scarf to the butler before a bevy of admirers surrounded him.

'How did it go tonight?' several asked. 'How did Youngerman do?'

Ricks chuckled and held up his hands as if to ward off blows. 'Patience, my friends, patience. Let me get a drink – oh, thank you,' he murmured as someone handed him a glass of champagne. 'Just what the doctor ordered.' He downed the contents and gave a satisfying sigh before continuing. 'I just had to be there. In fact, I've been at the Morosco all day, working with Youngerman and the rest of the cast and crew to make sure everything was shipshape for tonight, and our efforts were not in vain. Young Youngerman, as I call him, is a natural for the role,' he said, pausing for a ripple of laughter at this meager display of wit. 'As tragic as Crenshaw's demise was, the play itself will not suffer. Youngerman rose to the occasion as only a brilliant actor of his caliber can. I believe he will turn out to be Crenshaw's equal, if not surpass him. Naturally, I was most anxious about Act Two Scene One when the shooting occurs. As the scene approached, the tension in the theater soared to epic proportions, but everything went off smoothly and the audience gave an audible sigh of relief when Youngerman clutched his wounded leg and carried on with the dialogue.'

He nodded graciously at the effusive compliments and excused himself to speak to our host and hostess. Half an hour passed before he wandered over to Adele.

'Jessie was sitting beside me at the performance last night,' she told Ricks. 'We're helping the detective with his investigations.'

'Really, now, are you? Two charming young ladies dabbling in crime-solving? How is it going, after only two days? Are they going to pin it on poor Norah, or have they discovered who it was who switched the bullets?'

'Detective Quinn is hard at work. Has he interviewed you yet?'

'He has not. That is his mistake. I think it not immodest of me to say that my own theories should provide him with some leads to consider.'

'Such as?'

'Well, look at it this way. If Norah is to be the chief suspect – and mind you, I'm not suggesting she's innocent or guilty – but if she's to be the chief suspect, one must ask why, if she wanted Crenshaw dead – and here I presume her motive would be his cutting off their relationship – if she wanted the man dead, why on earth would she shoot him in public, in full view of a thousand pairs of eyes? Why not shoot him in his apartment? Or in a dark alley? Or at night as they walked through Central Park? There must be hundreds of better ways, more discreet ways, to murder someone other than shooting him on stage.'

'You make a good point,' said Adele.

'I always do. It's obvious that poor Norah is being used. Framed. The question your detective should be answering is, who substituted live rounds for the blanks?'

'And do you have any ideas?' I asked.

He seemed to notice me for the first time. His eyes traveled up and down for a short minute, evaluating my value. Evidently I passed muster, for he smirked. 'Of course, my dear. As one who has spent nearly every day at the Morosco since rehearsals began, I know every corner of that theater and every actor and stagehand. And all their foibles. Has your detective questioned the stage manager? Bill Levine is an obvious suspect, I should think.'

'Why is that?'

Ricks looked down his nose at me as if I were a simpleton. 'He hated Crenshaw.'

Adele and I exchanged glances. Neither of us had picked up on that when we talked with Levine. 'There was bad blood between them?'

He glanced around, as if to make sure no one was eavesdropping on our conversation, and lowered his voice. 'Bill Levine is drinking again, although he thinks no one has noticed. He couldn't stay away from the hooch. The man has no willpower. Crenshaw noticed. And threatened to tell the director. He'd have been fired, for sure.'

'He told you that?'

'Not exactly. I, um, overheard part of an ugly quarrel between the two men that took place in Levine's office. I chose not to intervene. Besides that, Levine was nursing an old grudge against Crenshaw from a previous episode. Crenshaw had worked with Levine years ago, when Levine was stage manager at the Excelsior and Crenshaw had some minor role in a musical there. I forget which musical. Anyway, Levine's drinking caused some trouble – don't remember details – and it was Crenshaw who ratted on him and got him fired. Bill Levine isn't the sort to forgive and forget, and it was looking like history was about to repeat itself, so yes, he had a damn good motive. Now I'm not saying he did it or anything, but if your detective hasn't pursued that line of investigation, you gals better see to it he gets on the right track, and quick about it.'

SIX

'You're a dear, Jessie, for making time for an old lady.' Despite the afternoon hour, Johanna Astaire greeted me at the door wearing her dressing gown and no makeup and glided into the living room of her hotel suite, located several doors down from the larger, two-bedroom apartment her children shared. Indicating an overstuffed slipper chair, she reclined on a matching settee and draped a throw dramatically across her legs.

'I'm so glad you're feeling well enough to have a visitor,' I said. 'I'd have stopped by sooner but Adele warned me off. It's been lovely seeing her and Fred again.'

'I only wish you could have been in New York earlier when *Lady Be Good* was still playing. They were wonderful!' she sighed. 'Forgive a proud mama for saying it, but I have never seen a finer performance in my life. Critics and audiences raved.'

'Maybe I'll get the chance to see the show in London. Will you be going with them next month?'

She fingered the fringe on her throw. 'I hope so. The children want me there, desperately. If I'm strong enough to make the crossing, I'll go with them; otherwise, I'll join them there later. London is a marvelous city but, honestly, if I seem hesitant, it's because the climate is so damp and cold that my doctor says I may have to remain home this winter. Not here in frigid New York, of course, but in Florida or someplace sunny and dry. But enough about me. Adele tells me you are working for Mary Pickford! My favorite film actress, to be sure.'

'Miss Pickford? Yes, I do work for her sometimes but mostly for Douglas Fairbanks. I've been a script girl for their film studio ever since I left vaudeville.'

The doorbell rang.

'Would you get that for me, dear? It's room service. I've ordered a high tea like they do in England. Such civilized customs they have over there!'

In came a waiter with a rolling cart of delicate tea sandwiches, tiny fruit tarts, little iced cakes and, of course, a silver teapot filled with piping hot tea. As I poured her cup and my own, she continued.

'I heard you washed out.'

Ouch. Johanna Astaire had always had a sharp tongue. Well, what she said was true. No reason to sugarcoat it.

'I'm afraid that's right. I played in a variety of kiddie acts after my mother died, some singing, some dancing, some acting, some acrobatic. Whatever came along. My last act was with the Little Darlings, a song-and-dance family act, kinda like the Seven Little Foys. Because of my size, I was able to play one of the older kids until I was twenty-five, but when that act split up, I was out of work for good. I thought I could get another gig easy as pie, but it turns out I'm a "jack of all trades, master of none", as the old saying goes. Good at a lot of things, great at nothing. I aged out of what I was best at – being a kid. So when I got into some trouble and was recovering from a broken leg, I was lucky to have vaudeville friends who recommended me to Douglas Fairbanks for a job. He gave me a chance and here I am.'

'Chloë Randall . . . Now there was a talent. A rare talent, your mother. What a voice! And what poise. Incredible stage presence. She always had the audience in the palm of her hand. A *real* beauty.' She gave me a calculating stare to let me know I didn't quite measure up to my mother's talent or looks. I'd forgotten about that cruel side of Mrs Astaire. Memories flooded back. A fierce stage mom, talking up her own children, talking down the competition. Pushing Fred and Adele mercilessly in rehearsal after rehearsal, ignoring tears and exhaustion, determined to make them into headliners. Toasts of the town. Broadway stars. Only now did I remember my mother telling me that Adele's mother yearned to be on stage herself, but lacked the talent. She used her children to reach the fame she couldn't get herself.

'Tell me about my mother,' I said, trying to steer the conversation in a more pleasant direction. It wasn't often I had the chance to talk with someone who had known my mother. And known her well. 'You were good friends. Tell me something about when we used to travel together.'

Her gaze moved away from my face to the window as her thoughts drifted back in time, until I thought she had forgotten

I was there. Then she began. 'There was one time . . . Orpheum Circuit . . . you kids were maybe six or eight. We had jumped from somewhere to Memphis, and Chloë's trunks had gone on to New Orleans by mistake. She bluffed the manager at the Monday morning call wearing her street clothes, and he slotted her in the second-best position. She wasn't headlining then, but close. She figured the trunk would catch up to us before that evening's show. Of course, it didn't, and she was out of a costume. I offered her one of mine, but she was a tiny thing, too small for my clothes. Nonetheless, it was all she had, so we pinned my gown up in back and at the hem and it looked pretty good, from the front at least.'

She smiled to herself, still looking out the window, as if she were alone in the past. 'It was a lavender gown. Lots of spangles. One of my favorites. Anyway, Chloë came on stage and began to sing. And you remember how she moved when she sang. There was no way Chloë could sing without her expressive movements, she could never stand like a statue while she performed. So the pins in back didn't hold.' Mrs Astaire put her hand to her mouth and giggled at the memory. 'One by one, they popped, and my gown started to sag across the front. I watched from the wings, horrified. Then she stepped on the hem and pulled out several pins there. By now, the audience, at least the first few rows, could see her costume was wilting, and when the weight of the sleeves pulled apart the pins in the collar, the dress drooped like a sack.'

She was laughing now, and so was I. Pausing to catch her breath and dab her eyes with a handkerchief, she continued.

'Chloë looked like a little girl playing dress-up in her mother's gown! It was hilarious. Any other performer would have been mortified. Anyone else would have run off the stage, but not Chloë. She started to laugh at herself. You know, Jessie, no one can laugh at you if you laugh at yourself first. They laugh with you. My, my, what a scene that was! I began laughing too, from the wings. And with a wave of her hand, she stopped the music in the middle of her song, hiked up the sagging fabric, and told the audience exactly what had happened with her lost trunk and the pins. She made the story so funny; the audience was rolling in the aisles. They loved her. I'm sure many thought it was part of her act. In fact, later on, I advised her to make it part of her act, but she never did. My, my, what a night that was! I'll never forget it.'

Nor would I. I hadn't heard that story and the telling of it gave me a precious glimpse of the mother I'd lost at twelve.

Mrs Astaire seemed energized by the telling and with me egging her on, went on about the times they had put us kids to bed and slipped out for a drink, the ways they fobbed off lecherous men who assumed all vaudeville women were cheap and easy, the troubles they had finding boarding houses clean enough for children yet cheap enough for their thin wallets, the lean times when they would lend each other a few dollars to stretch food to payday, the sharing and repairing of costumes so our acts looked fresh, their worries about their children's lack of schooling, and their efforts to teach us to read and figure during the Sunday train rides to the next city. I realized that there were some hard times I hadn't been aware of, so cleverly had my mother shielded me from knowing we were poor. I could hear the envy in Mrs Astaire's voice, that my mother became a headliner while she could only watch from the wings as her children danced their way to the stars.

Her voice grew hoarse from all the talk, and I realized somewhat guiltily that I'd overstayed my welcome.

I stood. 'This has been a lovely visit, Mrs Astaire. I'm so grateful you could make time to see me, and I hope you will be fully recovered soon. And thank you so much for the delicious tea.'

'I'm happy you could spare the time for an old lady,' she said, and I took the hint.

'Heavens, Mrs Astaire, you're not old! Just fagged out from your illness. You'll be up and at 'em any day now.'

'Do me a favor, dear,' she said, reaching for a short stack of envelopes on the table beside her. 'Mail these at the desk when you go down.'

'Certainly.' As I took four or five envelopes from her, my eyes fell on the address of the one on top. It was addressed to Mr Allen Crenshaw! Confused, I stuttered, 'Oh, um . . . did you, I mean . . . did you intend to send a note to . . . I thought you knew. Didn't Adele tell you that Allen Crenshaw had been killed?'

She looked puzzled for a moment, then her frown cleared. 'Oh no, my dear, that's a different Allen Crenshaw. It's his uncle.

They had the same name. I was writing my condolences on the death of his nephew.'

'Oh, I'm so sorry. I misunderstood. I didn't mean to pry, but I couldn't help but see . . .'

'Quite all right. You made the logical assumption. I knew the elder Allen Crenshaw twenty years ago when he married one of my friends – she was a friend of your mother's too – by the name of Cyrene Hayes. A vaudeville singer, like your mother. She left the stage to marry Crenshaw. An astute move on her part, since he was a very wealthy older man. Owned a big furniture company here in New York. She died a year or two ago. I don't know Allen Crenshaw so very well, but thought I'd send a note of condolence anyway. He and Cyrene were terribly fond of their nephew, since they had no children of their own. He was like a son to them. Mind you, I never met young Allen Crenshaw, never even saw him on stage, but I knew the connection. I recognized the name, of course, from the newspapers when he was killed. Cyrene and Allen wanted their nephew to go into the furniture business, but the dazzle of the footlights proved stronger than a desk in a corner office. I expect the nephew, if he'd lived, would have inherited the business.'

It was like LA Detective Carl Delaney had stepped into the room beside me and was whispering in my ear. Who inherits the business now? Who is next in line for the fortune? Follow the money, he would say. Follow the money.

'Did young Allen Crenshaw have brothers or sisters?'

'I know what you're thinking. Who inherits the furniture company? Cyrene and Allen had another nephew. A confirmed bachelor, if you get my meaning. I think his name is Wesley Crenshaw, or maybe Weston. Anyway, Cyrene liked the lad but old Allen would have nothing to do with him when he turned out to be a nancy-boy. Probably cut out of the will. I wonder if there's anyone left in the next generation to inherit.'

'Do you know what Wesley is doing now?'

She pondered the question for a moment. 'Last I heard, he was living here in New York and working in the garment industry. Since Cyrene passed away, I haven't kept in touch with the family, so that's stale news. I don't really know.'

SEVEN

G reen is my best color. Any shade of green, dark or light, lime green, sage green, even olive green. Green doesn't fight with my auburn hair, and it brings out the color of my eyes. My favorite gown is emerald green. It has bugle beads and a fringed drop-waist, and although it's two years old and the scalloped hemline comes a bit higher on my knee than you see in the fashion magazines today, I love it for its color and because it came from the time I was impersonating a missing heiress. It carries good memories and gives my confidence a boost – something I needed for the dinner Douglas and Mary were hosting that night. In any case, it was the only fancy dress I'd brought with me to New York, so there was no trouble deciding what to wear.

I had spent hours with the Algonquin Hotel's chef and staff, transforming my two bosses' vision into reality. It was to be a very special dinner with very special guests, including genuine European royalty. Miss Pickford wanted to host the meal in the privacy of their own suite, away from any reporters and their flash bulbs. Their suite had a large dining room but its table would seat only eight. We would be ten, so I arranged for a replacement table and chairs, then sat down with the chef, a highly skilled Frenchman who knew more about the couple's culinary preferences than they did themselves. Since his menu was certain to make the society columns in every New York newspaper, he needed no urging to lavish his attention on the meal.

Ever the homebody, Mary Pickford would have preferred to spend the evening quietly with her husband, listening to music and dining in private on the balcony, but boisterous Douglas Fairbanks was at his peak in a crowd. He adored socializing with his movie-mad fans, and was particularly energized when the company consisted of distinguished people from other walks of life, as it would that night when the guest list included New

York's flamboyant Mayor Jimmy Walker and his wife, current Broadway darlings Adele and Fred Astaire, and Queen Marie of Romania, who was visiting America for the first time with two of her children, Prince Nicholas and Princess Ileana. They all accepted the invitations I had sent – no one, to my knowledge, had ever turned down an invitation from America's Sweetheart and her swashbuckling husband. Because of my long friendship with the Astaires, this lowly script girl was included in the dinner too. I penned all the invitations, including the one to myself – something to keep in my box of special memories.

It wasn't my first time to dine with my famous employers. I had once been invited to a large dinner party at Pickfair, the Hollywood mansion that Douglas bought his wife when they married. That event was attended by Charlie and Lita Chaplin, Mary's sister Lottie Pickford and brother Jack, who were film stars in their own right, and many big-wig directors, producers and stars. It was a noisy collection of pretentious film people vying for top billing, but it was great fun! And through it all, Miss Pickford and Douglas Fairbanks presided graciously, without an ounce of arrogance between them. It was their habit to treat their employees like colleagues and to respect the abilities of others, regardless of their station in life. No wonder: both had come from desperately poor backgrounds – genuine rags-to-riches examples – and they knew better than most that the lowliest stagehand could become a star director overnight. Or vice versa. Miss Pickford acknowledged our similar backgrounds, commenting more than once about the hardships of itinerant theater life that had made us both stronger, and Douglas treated me as if I were his younger sister rather than the hired help, always supportive of my investigations. All that aside, I was keenly aware of the honor of being included in this evening's affair and determined to walk the line carefully . . . not too familiar, not too obsequious. It's touchy being in a room where everyone else is rungs above you on the status ladder.

I was proud to introduce the Astaires to Miss Pickford and Douglas, and delighted that they were soon chatting away like old friends. Mary had arranged it so we three arrived half an hour before the other guests in order to have some time to swap stories about the old days and how much the New York theater world had changed. 'Mother reminded us that we once shared a vaudeville stage with you, Doug, about fifteen years ago,' said Adele. 'She said you were headlining and that we had the dreaded opening act spot. I'm afraid I don't remember it – I was only a youngster – but Mother's memory is never wrong about this sort of thing.' Douglas professed himself delighted to know that they had once played for the same audience.

When the French mantel clock struck eight, our attention shifted.

'I've never met royalty before,' I said a bit nervously.

'Nothing to it,' said Adele with a dismissive wave of one hand. 'Here's how it works. As official host, Douglas will introduce us to Her Majesty. Being American, I don't curtsey—'

'Good girl,' said Douglas, an ardent American.

'—but some do. I prefer to give a gentle nod of my head.'

'Entirely appropriate,' he said.

'You let her speak first, then talk to her like she was anyone else.'

'I hope she knows some English. My Romanian is a bit rusty!'

Adele giggled. 'Her English is probably better than yours or mine. She's an English princess, Jessie, born and raised in Britain. Her grandmother was Queen Victoria.'

'So she's cousin to the current king,' put in Fred, not to be outdone by his sister when it came to knowledge of British royalty.

'Why is she visiting America?' I wondered aloud.

Douglas shrugged. 'All I know is that Romania was a staunch ally during the Great War, and I'm told she was largely respon-sible for that. That's good enough for me!'

His remarks reminded me that he and Mary had, before their marriage, spent countless hours at rallies selling war bonds in support of our troops in France. Naturally he would look upon the Romanian queen as an ally in that patriotic cause.

'And she is much loved by her people, Douglas,' added Miss Pickford.

The doorbell chimed. Douglas's bodyguard, who doubled as butler, admitted a good-looking, middle-aged man I recognized from newspaper photos, Mayor Jimmy Walker, and his wife, Janet. I blinked with surprise when I saw Walker's flamboyant midnight-blue dinner jacket with its satin lapels and colorful striped bow tie. No wonder the press had nicknamed him Beau James! His wife was a plain Jane beside him, dressed in pale gray silk the color of her hair. She wore no jewelry save for a simple gold wedding ring, while her husband sported three large rings, two with diamonds. I was put in mind of a drab little wren perched next to a tropical bird. It must have escaped the mayor that none of us were New York City voters, for he launched almost immediately into political topics we outsiders knew little about. It seemed he expected praise for some recent subway expansion and for keeping the fare at a nickel. Mary and Douglas feigned polite interest. Feeling sorry for the wren, I asked whether they had any children, and was rewarded with a wide smile and the story of the little boy and girl they had adopted.

The doorbell chimed again and the butler announced the arrival of Queen Marie of Romania and her two children.

If a casting director had wanted to find a woman to play the part of a queen, he would need look no further than Queen Marie of Romania. She looked like she was born to the role – which of course she was. And rigorously trained for it, for such regal deportment did not come about by accident. I imagined she'd spent long hours as a young girl gliding about the room with a book balanced on her head.

And what a head! She had a mop of curly auburn hair – very near the color of my own! – that had been skillfully arranged to look unarranged, and intelligent, sky-blue eyes. A tiara decorated with enormous baroque pearls rested comfortably among the curls, matched by long ropes of graduated pearls that hung from her slender neck. She wore a mid-calf ivory silk gown trimmed in fur that could have come from nowhere but a Paris salon. Fortunately, she bore no resemblance to her grandmother, dour old Queen Victoria, whom I knew only from pictures. No, this queen was beautiful. If she ever needed a paying career, I knew right where she could find it.

Introductions went just as Adele had predicted. Douglas, ever the charmer, kissed Her Majesty's hand. I made my nod to her and shook hands democratically with Prince Nicholas and Princess Ileana. The princess, a pretty girl of about seventeen, was rendered almost speechless when introduced to her favorite film idols. Her older brother tried to act nonchalant, but anyone could tell he was as impressed as his sister.

'I loved *Zorro* and *Robin Hood*,' she gushed when she could find her voice. 'And the *Thief of Bagdad* was amazing! However did you make those carpets fly?'

No one was kinder to his young fans than Douglas, who spent several minutes explaining some of the secrets behind the unique action scenes that were filmed in a mocked-up Arab marketplace. We had only recently finished *The Black Pirate*, so he told her about the difficulties they had to overcome in order to film in two-color Technicolor, as well as the tricks behind the daring scene where he slashes a line with his knife and swings upward to the main topsail, then plunges the knife into the canvas and slides down the topsail, holding on to the hilt as it severs the canvas in two. He promised he would send a copy of the new film to their palace in Bucharest as soon as he returned to Hollywood.

EIGHT

While Douglas entertained the young people by revealing some of his film secrets, their mother the queen was telling us about her arrival in New York. 'Despite the stinging rain, our welcome was so enthusiastic, we were speechless. The whistle of the steamers alongside our own ship, the roar of the guns, the white smoke against the gray fog, the voices cheering . . . and you, Mr Mayor, graciously meeting us at the dock. Such an honor!'

Mr Mayor said the correct thing, as politicians do.

In the last minutes before the guests arrived, Miss Pickford had chosen seating arrangements: the queen sat at Douglas's right and the mayor at her right. That meant four on each side, with me between the young prince and princess and across from Fred, who kept sending me tiny winks when he thought no one was looking. Waiters who could have stepped out of a British castle served the soup course, a cold consommé, as talk ranged from President Coolidge's recent speech in which he had celebrated American prosperity by noting that there were now twenty million motorcars clogging American roads, to the women's vote that had only recently been established in America. It turned out Queen Marie was the darling of international suffragette circles and a tireless supporter of women's rights in Romania as well as in other countries of Europe. Prince Nicholas, on leave from Great Britain's Royal Navy so he could escort his mother on her American tour, told me about his service during the past two years as a lieutenant on a light cruiser, courtesy of his mother's English heritage. Mayor Walker's opposition to Prohibition stimulated a vigorous discussion as he held forth on the foolishness of the dry laws and the many ways he and New York's citizenry were flouting them.

'I myself visit the so-called speakeasies frequently,' he told Prince Nicholas.

'But no one will arrest the mayor, surely. Are not other citizens afraid of arrest?'

'There's no one to arrest them,' boasted the mayor, as waiters brought in the filleted trout amandine fish course. 'Well, almost no one. There are a few federal agents, some call them prohis, who conduct the occasional raid for appearances' sake, but for the most part, liquor is served discreetly in restaurants and speakeasies without any fuss. Anyone unlucky enough to be arrested is released after paying a modest fine. The courts would be choked if they attempted to try all the cases, and frankly, no jury of New Yorkers would convict anyone anyway, so trials would be pointless.'

I didn't attempt to tell the young prince that the authorities were not so blind in all parts of our country. Witness poor David, serving his two and a half years.

'I cannot help noticing, Mr Mayor, that tonight's affair is free of alcohol,' the prince said.

I said nothing, waiting for our host or hostess to explain. When they appeared not to have heard the prince's comment, I spoke softly to him. 'It is Mr Fairbanks who chooses not to serve alcoholic beverages. Nor does he serve them at his home in Hollywood. He feels spirits are detrimental to his health.' I knew that Mary Pickford went along with her husband's wishes, at least when he was present, hosting affairs like this one where exotic fruit drinks and flavored waters were served, but no alcohol. Many a time I'd been with her when she enjoyed a glass of wine or a highball without Douglas's knowledge.

It wasn't until the waiters brought out the main course, Douglas's favorite beef tenderloin with potatoes au gratin, that the conversation came around to the Crenshaw murder. I knew we wouldn't avoid it; it was too much in the newspapers to have evaded the sharp eyes of our royal guests. And it was the prince who raised the inappropriate subject, so we had no choice but to rehash the details.

'Such a shocking thing to happen!' exclaimed the prince.

'And Jessie and Adele were right there in the front row!' put in Douglas. I gave a weak smile. The young man's eyes grew wide as he turned toward me.

'Yes, well, it was actually the second row,' I said stupidly. Who cared which row we were in?

'What happened? Were the newspaper accounts accurate?'

'Pretty much.'

'Was it an accident or a murder?'

'That hasn't been determined yet.' I gave an uneasy glance in the mayor's direction and leaned over the table toward Adele to entreat her help. 'I'm sure the police will have all the answers soon, don't you think, Adele?'

But that wasn't enough to satisfy the prince's curiosity.

'Jessie and Adele have been helping the detective assigned to the case,' said Douglas. If I'd been sitting closer to him, I'd have kicked him under the table. That's all we needed, for the mayor of New York to hear about our amateurish, unorthodox investigation! But Douglas hadn't finished. 'Jessie's a whiz at solving murders. Why, back home in Hollywood, she figured out who murdered a prominent film director and a WAMPAS Baby Star last year, and later exposed the man who had killed an actress, which saved the person who'd been wrongly convicted from the hangman.'

'Don't forget that awful person who killed the Serbian projectionist and the other Serbs in San Francisco and St Louis,' added Miss Pickford. 'And one was killed here in New York. You remember that, Mayor Walker, don't you? The murdered man was dining in a restaurant and the killer disappeared through the back door like a ghost. It was in all the New York papers. All about some feud that happened back in Serbia before the war, wasn't it, Jessie?'

Mayor Walker nodded gravely, as if he knew all about it.

'Ah, yes,' signed Her Majesty. 'The Balkans . . . always exporting violence.'

By now, Prince Nicholas was looking at me and Adele with new respect. We were not going to get out of this conversation without going through all the details, so I stifled a sigh and described our evening at the theater when Allen Crenshaw had met his maker.

'The detective assigned to the case interviewed Adele and me the following day. When we realized he wanted to interview Mrs Marjorie Crenshaw, Allen Crenshaw's widow, Adele figured we could help him get in to see her.' I looked pointedly at Adele, signaling her to take it from there.

She caught the cue. 'I knew Marjorie Crenshaw from previous

theater work, and I was able to encourage her to talk with Detective Quinn. She told us that she and her husband had been estranged – he was not the most faithful of men – but that he had left his other woman, begged his wife's forgiveness, and was planning to move back into their home. Of course, that was her story, and with her husband dead, there was no way we could know if it was true. He had recently ended his romance with the actress Norah Rose, so perhaps it was.'

I smiled to myself at Adele's careful choice of words. She would never have said 'mistress' or 'affair', not with a seventeen-year-old, gently brought-up princess at the table. We had to tread carefully.

'Norah Rose was the one who shot him, right?' the prince asked Adele.

'She was the one who shot the gun, yes. But I know Norah, and I cannot believe she has it in her to step on a spider, let alone kill a man, never mind his ending their romance. Someone else wanted Allen Crenshaw dead, and that person exchanged the blanks for real bullets in order to throw the blame on to Norah. That's our theory, anyway.'

'Whom do the investigators suspect?' he asked eagerly.

'Norah's romance with Crenshaw ended abruptly, so some think that was motive enough for her. She says she broke it off with him, not the other way around, but I don't believe her. Nonetheless, she isn't a suspect, not in my book. Marjorie Crenshaw had a motive – he had humiliated her more than once with his dalliances with actresses and chorus girls . . .' Here Mayor Walker found something highly interesting about his water goblet. I couldn't help but glance at his wife, poor thing, who was equally busy pushing cherries around her dessert plate. Her husband's own reputation for chasing chorus girls was legendary. 'And she told the detective she hadn't seen him in days but that was a lie. Jessie and I learned that she had visited the theater the very day he was killed, to deliver a package. She had the opportunity to switch bullets, assuming she knew how to load a pistol.'

'So she's the main suspect!' said the prince.

'She's one that the detective is considering, but there's also the understudy, Mr Youngerman, who was primed to step into the role the minute Crenshaw died. Actors have been known to get up to all kinds of dirty tricks to secure a good part, and the lead in *Rules of Engagement* is one of the most desirable roles on Broadway.'

Mary Pickford nodded. 'He pretends to be very sorry about Crenshaw's death, but everyone in the theater world knows that bad luck for the star is good luck for the understudy.'

Adele went on. 'Another suspect is the stage manager, Bill Levine, who had a grudge with Crenshaw going way back. When we talked to him, he said nothing about his previous run-in with Crenshaw, several years ago when Crenshaw complained about his drunkenness to the producers of a play they were both involved with, and Levine was fired. It seems Levine had started drinking again, and Crenshaw was threatening to expose him once more. A second incident like that would ruin his career for good.'

With a glance, she passed the story back to me. 'Like Adele, I can't imagine Norah could have done the murder. Even if she wanted to kill him, why on earth would she choose to do it herself and in front of an audience, with all the risks that entails? Why not hire someone to ambush him in a dark alley where no one would see? Or slip some arsenic powder in his coffee? And another thing – how did Norah get to be such a remarkably good marksman that she could fire the pistol from clear across the stage and hit Crenshaw in the heart with one shot? That was an amazingly accurate shot even for someone familiar with pistols; or it was very good luck. And with murder, I've learned not to put much stock in luck.'

I stopped abruptly. It occurred to me that Norah had fired two shots. The stage gun was always loaded with two blanks. The script called for two shots. Someone had substituted two live rounds, but where had the second shot landed? Why hadn't anyone noticed it lodged in the wall behind where Allen Crenshaw had been standing? I looked at Adele, who seemed to have the same thought. We needed to get back to the Morosco Theater as soon as possible and look for that slug.

'I wish I could have been there,' sighed the prince. 'I wish I could see that play. What is its title?'

'*Rules of Engagement*,' said Douglas. 'It won the Pulitzer for drama last June.' Noting Queen Marie's blank look, he explained,

'The Pulitzer Prize is an American award that recognizes exceptional work in each of several categories, such as drama, journalism, fiction, and so forth. If you like, I can get you tickets to any performance.'

'Could you? For me too?' breathed the princess, her eyes sparkling with excitement. 'Could we, Mother?'

'I can get as many as you like, my dear,' said Douglas. 'There is a performance every evening except Sunday, and two on Saturdays with the matinée. But of course,' he turned to the queen, 'I don't know how long Your Majesty plans to be in New York, and I'm sure you are very busy.'

The queen's schedule collapsed at the assault of her eager children. 'What are itineraries for, except to be changed?' she acceded graciously. 'Thank you, Mr Fairbanks. It seems we would be delighted to see this prize-winning play tomorrow night, if tickets can be procured.'

Tickets were procured with a single telephone call. Six tickets in a box overlooking the stage: three for the Queen and her children, two for Mary and Douglas, who had not seen the play either, and one for me, because, as Douglas insisted, I deserved to see the second half.

NINE

The following night, Douglas sent his limousine to the Plaza where the Queen and her son and daughter were staying. The chauffeur had been instructed to bring them to the back door of the Morosco Theater where they could enter discreetly. We met them there, along with the play's director, Ira Belkowitz, who escorted our distinguished party through the backstage maze, past dumbfounded actors and stagehands, and up the stairs to the theater's finest box. We did not enter the box until the lights had dimmed, when the audience could see no more than our dark figures groping for our seats. Few would have recognized the Romanian royals. Everyone would have recognized Douglas and Mary.

It was an interesting comparison, watching Youngerman in the role I had seen Crenshaw play a few short days ago, and I had to admit, the understudy had risen to the occasion. He perhaps lacked Crenshaw's self-confidence but that would come with time. On the whole, I agreed with the critics who awarded him high marks. At intermission the director sent up a tray of champagne and some delicate finger sandwiches, and who should come knocking at the box door but Mr Pulitzer Prize himself, Edward Ricks! Ira Belkowitz must have alerted him to the presence of these dignitaries.

The slight crease between Douglas's eyebrows told me he was piqued at the playwright's cheek in barging into his box uninvited, but ever-gracious Mary Pickford welcomed the man as if she had expected him and introduced him to their royal guests. She praised the first act and complimented him on the Pulitzer. 'Douglas and I have long thought that the film world needs something similar, an award that could be given out each year for the best film, the best actor, the best actress, the best director, and so forth. He and Charlie Chaplin want to start up such an award.'

'That's a wonderful idea. And it would provide a great service to the film industry by recognizing exceptional works and thereby encouraging others to greater heights. For example, my current project is a highly innovative work that pushes the boundaries of playwriting to bold new horizons. I've had to become thoroughly immersed in the scientific world, exploring the mysteries of our universe with some of the most brilliant minds of our century in an effort to bring a new dimension to the humble stage. It will generate controversy, I don't doubt – lesser minds have always striven to strangle new ideas; just look at the art scene and Dalí and Picasso – but I relish the debate that expands the dramatic arts.'

This soliloquy was greeted with an awkward silence, which Ricks filled with a question directed at Queen Marie. 'And what do you think of my little play thus far?'

I winced at the man's crude fishing for compliments. What else could Her Majesty say? After a few remarks about the understudy's acting ability and how the protagonist's character had been altered by the gruesome realities of trench warfare, she asked, 'Did you base your characters on anyone in particular, Mr Ricks? Men you knew who served in the trenches? Or does your knowledge come from personal experience?'

'In a manner of speaking. I came to know several young men whose experiences and characters inspired my creation of Lieutenant Hanson. However, I rely mostly on my robust imagination and deep knowledge of human nature when forming my characters.'

'Did you serve in the war yourself, Mr Ricks?'

It was a question I had never thought to ask. Edward Ricks was in his mid-forties, beyond draft age, and the war had ended eight years ago. Surely the queen could see that he was too old to have served.

'Well, yes,' he said, eyes downcast in a display of modesty I thought overplayed. 'But not in the trenches. As you know, America didn't come into the war until 1917, so some of us, some of the more idealistic of us Americans, volunteered in Canada or Britain in 1914 or '15. I don't like to talk about my service, but I joined the Royal Navy and served aboard a light cruiser.'

The prince perked up. 'Capital! What ship was it?'

Ricks looked surprised, but he answered smoothly enough, 'The HMS *Aurora*.'

'Did you see much action?'

'Everyone saw action. We were in the thick of it during the Battle of Dogger Bank in early '15. No place on earth could be colder than the North Sea in January.' He shivered dramatically. At that moment, the lights flickered. 'Excuse me, Your Majesty,' he said with a bow. 'I must get back to the wings to make sure all goes smoothly during the next act. We come to the scene where, well . . . I need say no more. My presence seems to give the actors confidence and reassurance.' He bade a good evening to Her Majesty and the prince and princess and then to Miss Pickford and Douglas, calling those two by their first names as if he were their equal. He glanced in my direction but left me off the list.

TEN

My morning errands for Miss Pickford and Douglas included a stop at Chic Chapeau on West 46th, a stone's throw from the Morosco, so I seized the opportunity to duck into the theater before I headed back to the Algonquin with Miss Pickford's new blue hatbox in hand. Adele was not with me – she was struggling through her morning rehearsal with Fred – but the stage-door guard recognized me from my previous visit when I'd been with her and he let me pass, pointing the way toward Bill Levine's office where I could request permission to access the stage. Rounding a corner, I nearly collided with Detective Benjamin Quinn, who was just leaving the stage manager's office.

'Whoa! Miss Beckett!' he said, doffing his fedora. 'Fancy meeting you here! Or should I say, what brings you back to the scene of the crime?'

I didn't spend a lifetime in vaudeville without learning how to deliver a credible ad lib during a crisis, like when the dialogue faltered or a piece of scenery crashed to the floor. 'Lovely seeing you, detective. What luck to find you here!'

Bill Levine stood, arms folded, glaring at the two people who were interrupting his work. I focused first on him.

'Mr Levine, would it be all right if I got up on stage for a few minutes? I'll be gone in a flash.'

'What for?' he growled.

'Didn't you tell us there were always two rounds – blanks – in Norah's gun?'

'Yeah, what about it? The script calls for two shots to be fired.'

'And Norah no doubt did as she always did and fired those two shots, right?'

'So?'

'I remember hearing two distinct shots being fired that night, although it might have sounded like three. Definitely not one.'

His puzzled frown told me he had no idea why this mattered.

'The shots can be mingled with the drum crescendo. The orchestra plays some suspenseful music that rises to a drum roll, and that cues Norah to fire her gun. More drama that way. Or so says Ricks the Great.'

'That's right! I remember that music. Anyway,' and here I turned to the detective, 'I wondered why no one noticed the second bullet that should have been lodged in the wall behind where Crenshaw was standing. I want to see if I can find it.'

'So what if it's not there?' Levine asked.

Detective Quinn had caught my meaning. 'Then where did it go? By all accounts, Norah pointed the gun at Crenshaw, the proof of which is that she hit him once. But not twice. And she didn't point toward the ceiling or the floor. The police on the scene that night found no slugs lodged in the wall. I wonder where it went.'

'Can we take a quick look, Mr Levine?'

'What the hell, go ahead. Just make sure it's quick. And stay out of everybody's way.'

There was no one anywhere near us when Detective Quinn and I mounted the steps to the stage. A glance at the smooth, gray wall behind where Crenshaw had stood was all it took to see that the second bullet wasn't lodged there.

We divided our efforts, Quinn to the left, me to the right, and started to search the stage walls beyond that bit of gray scenery, imagining all possible trajectories that the bullet could have taken and tracing them to the spot where a bullet could have struck. After fifteen minutes, we switched places and repeated the effort, just in case one of us had missed something.

'You know,' Quinn mused aloud from around a scenery corner, 'Crenshaw's apartment was broken into.'

That was interesting news. 'When?'

'Police can't say. Other than it happened after his death.'

'So it could have been late that night he was killed or the next day.'

'Probably.'

'You're thinking that someone wanted him dead so they could search his apartment? That's odd. They could have done that while he was alive. Anyone would know that he was at the theater every night and the apartment would be empty. Did you see the place?'

'Yep. The beat cop called me as soon as he heard from the landlady.'

'How did she happen to go into his apartment?'

'Says she went in to check on the place after she read about his death in the papers.'

'Check for what?'

'In case he'd left a lamp on or the water running, she said. Pretty lame, if you ask me. Probably just snooping. But she gave us the tip and, as soon as I was notified, I went right over.'

'Did you find anything missing?'

'Not that I could tell. The place had been searched but not vandalized, if you know what I mean. Drawers messed up, left open. Closets rummaged through. Boxes dragged out from under the bed and emptied. Somebody was looking for something particular.'

'Was every room, every closet, and every drawer searched?'

'What do you mean?'

'Was any place left undisturbed?'

'Not really.'

'Then I'm guessing the thief didn't find what he was looking for. If he had, he'd've stopped searching and there would be parts of the apartment that were undisturbed, right?'

Quinn grunted.

'I wonder what it was.' I wondered if his wife Marjorie would have an idea. It was worth asking Adele to give her a call.

We continued our search until at last, the detective spoke up. 'It's no good, Jessie. There's no slug anywhere. And yet we found two shell casings in the gun.'

'And the audience heard two, at least Adele and I did. The drum roll might have masked them but there were definitely two, or maybe three. What about . . . I'm wondering . . . I'm afraid I don't know much about how guns work, detective. We only ever used toy guns in vaudeville.'

'Yeah, that's what they shoulda been using here. What lunatic insisted on a real pistol?'

'No doubt the director or the playwright wanted authenticity. In any case, I was wondering if you could tell the difference between a blank and a real bullet. I mean, after they were shot.'

He considered the question for only a second. 'No, not really.

Except for the slug, all you'd have is the casing and that would look the same for either. The police on the scene that night found two casings in the pistol for evidence. You see, a cartridge is made up of the casing, the primer – gunpowder – and a bullet. Or, if it's a blank, then no bullet. It sounds the same though. Maybe a little louder.'

'Then Norah's gun could have had one real cartridge and one blank, right?'

'I guess it's possible, but why on earth would anyone switch one round and not both? That would have given her only half the chance of hitting the target.'

I had no answer.

ELEVEN

The Morosco was less than a five-minute walk from the Algonquin Hotel, so when Detective Quinn and I left the theater, I asked him if he wanted to come back to the hotel with me and have a look at the papers that Adele and I had taken from Crenshaw's dressing room. I figured it was best to come clean sooner rather than later, in case we could be accused of withholding evidence from a murder investigation.

'Adele told you about those, I'm sure,' I said, knowing full well she hadn't. 'There was a fancy box with some letters and other papers inside the package Marjorie dropped off the day he was shot.'

'When she told us she hadn't seen him in weeks? Sounds like I need to have another chat with that little liar. This puts her at the theater in plenty of time to switch out the blanks. Yeah, I'd like to see those papers.' He said nothing about Adele neglecting to tell him, no doubt because he couldn't bring himself to criticize her. Ah, the power of love.

Strong gusts of damp, frigid air funneling down the Hudson River whipped through the narrow canyons of New York City streets, slicing through my thin coat. Along the crowded sidewalks, men hung on to their hats as they leaned into the wind and women gripped their handbags tight to their chests. I shivered. I'd been a southern California girl for more than two years, blissfully soaking up the year-round sunshine, forgetting how October up north could turn vicious without warning. I'd not brought any gloves or scarves to New York simply because I hadn't thought of it. Fortunately the Algonquin was less than two blocks away. Two long blocks.

'Let me bring the box down here,' I told Quinn when we reached the lobby. 'You can snag a quiet corner in the lounge and order something warm to drink. I'd like tea, if you please.'

The detective headed for the cozy lounge, empty this morning, while I stepped into the elevator and told the boy my floor number. Which he already knew, clever lad.

Hot tea and tiny pastries were waiting for me when I returned with the box of papers. Quinn set his coffee cup down and reached for the pile, which I had already sorted into related groups, one for old letters, another for the recent ones that had come in the past six months, the newspaper clippings mentioning his name, theater programs that documented his career, and various official documents. 'Here's a notice that their safe deposit box has been closed,' I said. 'I'll bet Marjorie emptied it and was letting him know. And here's his birth certificate.'

'Is his birth date correct?'

'I can't really tell if he shaved off a couple of years, but men don't usually change their birth dates. It's only women who have to hide their age to keep their jobs.' Thirty-four-year-old Mary Pickford was listed as twenty-eight on her publicity pages. 'Look, here's his high school diploma.'

'I'm more interested in the letters,' said Quinn as he unfolded and read each one. Adele and I had looked them over earlier, but we hadn't had time to read through them carefully. Some were from women, but I discerned none of the flowery language a lover would use. One was from a man named Wesley Crenshaw, the man that Adele's mother had mentioned, the nephew not favored by the rich, furniture-factory uncle. I took that one out of its envelope and read it.

'Listen to this. Wesley Crenshaw writes that he is unable to find the time to see Allen's play. It isn't dated but the postmark says last month. It sounds rather terse. Here, read it yourself.'

'Hmm. Unfriendly, I'll say that much. Let me keep it. I'll see what I can find out about him.'

'He's a cousin of Allen Crenshaw. Allen was the favorite of this uncle, whose name was also Allen Crenshaw and who owns a furniture manufactory. He had no children, and he wanted young Allen to take over his business. Obviously young Allen was drawn to the theater instead, but I wonder if he was in the will to inherit. Or if there was a will. Wesley was ignored by the uncle, who thought he was homosexual.'

His jaw dropped. 'You really are a remarkable sleuth!'

'Not so remarkable. I learned all that from Adele's mother,

who said she knew them. Or knew of them, I should say. She told me the other day when I visited her in her room at the Astor.'

'So with Allen dead, who will inherit the furniture business?'

'That's what I'm wondering. Would Wesley arrange his cousin's death to get him out of the way? Is Wesley now the only surviving relative? Even if he is, the uncle might not want to include him in the will.'

'There's only one way to find out. I'll talk with the uncle. You said his name is Allen Crenshaw too?'

I nodded. 'And he's across the river in Jersey City. I saw the address on an envelope that Adele's mother wrote.' I recited the address from memory. Not such an amazing feat for someone trained since childhood to memorize dialogue lines or instructions after hearing them once. 'You could ask him if he had planned to leave the company to his nephew of the same name, and what, if anything, he plans to do about that now that he's dead.'

'It certainly gives Wesley Crenshaw a motive to get rid of his cousin. And in a way that throws no suspicion on him, when he was miles away at the time and was never seen at the theater.'

I agreed and dug back into the pile of letters.

'Here's one from a woman named Ivy Devine. That's a stage name if ever I've heard one – a burlesque performer, most likely. She writes a thank you for including her in a dinner party. Doesn't sound lover-like but it could be. I can ask around vaudeville to see if anyone knows her.'

Quinn took a clean handkerchief from his pocket, pulled off his spectacles, and rubbed them thoroughly as he considered what I'd said. Nodding his consent, he then set aside the official documents and concentrated on the newspaper clippings. 'What are you looking for in those?' I asked, having found nothing of interest there myself.

'Not sure. Anything beyond the ordinary reviews. Any mention of conflict, or of a lawsuit, or a professional disagreement.'

'Here's a letter from several months ago. Sarah Landry writes that she wishes him luck in the future but she can't see him on Thursday. Kind of abrupt. I wonder who she is. An actress, probably a girlfriend.'

'Give it here. I can look her up too.'

In the end, the detective took all the papers with him – evidence, he said, to be catalogued down at the station. He promised to get in touch after he'd had the chance to track down some of the names.

I went to work on Ivy Devine. At a Broadway newsstand I picked up a copy of *Variety*, the weekly that lists all vaudeville acts playing throughout the United States and even parts of Canada. Well, not really *all* acts – it was limited to those appearing on Big Time circuits like Orpheum, Keith-Albee and Pantages. Small Time acts and the TOBA circuit for Negro players weren't included, but some acts in the burlesque wheels were. Burlesque showcased raunchy comedy routines, half-naked dancers, song spoofs, and crude gags. Vaudeville players and legit stage actors looked down on burlesquers, sniffing that only a washed-up act would stoop so low as to cross the street to burlesque. Never mind that many a vaude player – including me – has done more than dip in a toe. Some years back, I'd spent a few weeks as a magician's assistant where my job was to distract the audience with peeks at my scantily covered attributes. I quit when the magician started to insist on my cooperation off stage as well as on. Anyway, the point is, I'm not too high-and-mighty when it comes to burlesque.

Much of New York's burlesque scene, the country's largest, was listed in *Variety*. I ran my eyes down the columns, hoping to see the name Ivy Devine. No such luck. But I did see the name of a friend from years ago, Millie Mansard, a snake charmer who'd shared a room in a boarding house with me for a few weeks back in 1915 or 1916 when we were both looking for gigs. Millie was working at the Little Apollo on 125th Street, the whites-only burlesque theater that the Minsky brothers owned.

A taxi took me there in no time.

Millie greeted me with a shout of recognition and a bear hug, and we sat for half an hour in the communal dressing room catching up.

'And how is Cleopatra?' I asked, with a furtive glance toward the large basket in the corner.

'Same as always. You know what? She's seventeen now and hasn't lost a bit of her enthusiasm. Why, I do believe I'll need to retire before Cleo!' She slapped her thigh and cackled. 'Would you like to see her?'

'Sure. We were always good friends. Wonder if she'll remember me?'

Millie pulled the python out of the basket and sat beside me so I could stroke her silky scales. Her tongue flicked in and out a few times, and she curled herself around Millie's arm affectionately, ignoring me, which was just as well. As snakes go, Cleopatra took top honors, but I didn't need to hold her to appreciate her finer qualities.

'Fess up, honey, you didn't come all this way to visit me and Cleopatra. You mentioned needing my help with something. What can I do for you?'

'Information, I hope. I'm trying to find someone named Ivy Devine. With a name like that, I'm guessing she works in burlesque.'

'You guess right, but not burlesque; she's vaude. She's new to the business, attractive gal. I don't know her personally but I've heard about her routine. You don't see her name in lights because she's one of a three-girl comedy act. They bill as sisters – Holly Devine, Ivy, and Misty for Mistletoe – but of course they're not sisters. The Devine Comediennes. You can find them at the Republic Theater on 42nd.'

TWELVE

Evening at 8.00
Matinee daily at 2.00

So read the sign on the front of the Republic, labeling it as a 'two-a-day' or Big Time vaude theater. I'd arrived right at two, making it impossible to slip backstage to search for Ivy Devine until after the show was over. On an impulse, I stepped up to the ticket booth and pushed a quarter across the windowsill. Hell, if I had to kill time for a couple of hours, why not do what I loved best? I hadn't been to a bona fide vaudeville performance in months.

I was almost giddy as I walked through the lobby, greeted by the sound of the orchestra sawing away at 'Blue Skies' and some other songs that comprised the overture. Small Time venues made do with an ensemble of three musicians or a single pianist in the pit, but we were in New York City, where no respectable vaude theater would present anything less than a decent orchestra of twelve. I took a deep breath of that unmistakable aroma we used to call 'eau d'audience', a pungent mixture of flowery perfume, leather and sweat. A young usher exchanged my ticket for a printed program and guided me to my sixth-row seat. It felt like I'd stepped out of Jules Verne's time machine into the past. It felt like coming home.

The show had already begun, but as always, the first act was a dumb act, one without dialogue, so that late-comers like me could settle into their seats without missing anything important. Today's program featured a juggler who interspersed his feats of dexterity with a bit of rudimentary magic. Quite entertaining, all in all. I suspected his act was in transition from juggling to magic, which would give him a shot at higher wages. Jugglers were a dime a dozen. Magicians – good ones, anyway – were in greater demand.

I studied the program, your typical vaudeville line-up of nine acts, broken after the fifth by an intermission. Management usually slotted the headliner into the fifth position, right before intermission, or the eighth, with the expectation that the top act would run longer than the usual ten to twelve minutes. This week's headliner was 'A Modern Revue: in a Cycle of Songs, Comedy and Dances', featuring two couples whose names I didn't recognize. Nothing surprising about that – after all, I'd been out of the business for more than two years and hadn't played the East Coast in about four. The Devine Comediennes were in seventh, a respectable spot.

The requisite animal act followed, with Ferraro's Dog Musicians taking full stage in front of one of the theater's standard drops showing a forest scene. The animals not only played instruments but barked out answers to arithmetic problems and even walked a tightrope. Vaudeville managers were loath to play lions, elephants, tigers and other wild animals for fear of frightening the women and children, so most animal acts featured dogs, ponies, monkeys, cats or birds. Many of those came to vaudeville via the circus, which went dormant about this time every year, allowing trainers who worked with small animals or birds to move indoors during the colder months. Some people claimed the animals were mistreated; my experience was the opposite. In all my years on the stage, every animal I ever saw was treated like royalty – not surprising when you realize that they were the bread and butter of the act. A human trainer could be replaced far more easily than one of the animals. They were the stars.

The Dog Musicians made me think of my friend Angie, who had worked with me in The Little Darlings, a family song-and-dance act, for a couple of years. She left the act to marry her sweetheart, Walter, and join his Cat Circus. My mind wandered back to the hard times when we'd shared a lumpy pallet on the boarding-house floor or split a frankfurter when our pockets were empty, only to splurge on a restaurant meal and fancy cocktails when we were flush. Angie was the closest thing I had to a sister in those days and I missed her. I vowed to track down the location of Walter's Cat Circus and send Angie a letter as soon as I returned home to Los Angeles.

Mabel Ashford was up next 'in one', at the front edge of the stage, dressed in a glittering gown and singing a series of popular numbers while the backstage crew re-set for the next act. I didn't have to peek behind the backdrop to know what was going on. Working in utter silence so as not to disturb Miss Ashford's act, grips and flymen were changing the scenery and props for the upcoming act 'in four', the Nelson Family Acrobats. The likelihood of them being members of the same family was slim to none, but audiences loved the idea of family acts.

The emcee introduced them with a fanfare of superlatives, and three men, two women and five kids bounded on stage to perform astonishing feats of daring and dexterity. They were good – and I should know! Before my mother died, she made sure I was taken care of by hooking me up with the Kid Circus, an act with a dozen or so youngsters who did tumbling tricks, made human pyramids, flew on the trapeze and somersaulted through flaming hoops. I was twelve, but small for my age, so I stayed with the troupe for a couple of years before I grew too large. The Kid Circus is still going strong – with a regularly updated cast of kids, of course. I wondered where they were playing today.

The Modern Revue lived up to its top billing. Not a second was wasted between sketches as the four seasoned performers segued effortlessly from one song to another, then from a dance to a sixty-second comedy skit. Versatility like that is rare. Any one of the four could have succeeded on his own; as a foursome, they were unbeatable. The Modern Revue would be playing the Palace soon, if they hadn't already.

Intermission gave the audience a chance to stretch and to make their way to the lobby for juice or a snack. A dollar slipped to the bartender would get you a jigger of vodka or rum in your cocktail, no one the wiser. I settled for orange juice.

Theater managers like to open the second half of the show with something lively to pump up the audience's expectations. Today it was a colored dance team, two men who tapped their way through a medley of old Southern minstrel numbers like 'Carry Me Back to Ole Virginny' and 'Oh, Dem Golden Slippers'. Big Time vaudeville often included colored acts in their line-ups, especially in the big cities, but never more than one. The TOBA circuit was the usual place for Negro performers. This afternoon's dance duo wore sharp formal suits with tails and top hats, without the usual blackface. When they started to sing, 'Way Down Yonder in New Orleans', it put me in mind of a Negro I once knew,

Henry 'Hank' Creamer, the musician who wrote that number just a few years ago. Hank and I had overlapped on the same circuit maybe ten years back, when he would dance and sing some of his own songs. That man could knock out a new song in one sitting, like it was effortless. An amazing talent. Last I'd heard of him, he was in New York directing the Cotton Club revue. It was good to know he'd made it big.

Finally, the emcee announced the Devine Comediennes. Ivy, Misty and Holly – it took me a while to tell which one was Ivy – strutted on stage, dressed in short green flapper frocks that bordered on the burlesque, with leafy vines trailing from their backs and arms. And they were funny from the first moment, when one of them tripped over the other's vines and made a parody of stumbling over the other. Their patter was fresh and zany, with one gal providing the straight lines and the others replying with confusion and wacky misunderstandings.

'Hey Misty, Mother wants to know if you're still gambling.'

'What did you tell her, Holly?'

'I said you'd given it up.'

'That's right.'

'OK, then, you won't want to take this bet, will you?'

'What bet?'

'I'll bet you twenty dollars you can't answer three questions with the word "sausage".'

'Three questions? And all I have to answer is "sausage"?'

'That's it. Twenty dollars riding on it.'

'I'll take that bet, sister.'

'OK, first question: You're walking down the sidewalk and there's a poor little old lady with a basket of sausages, and a car knocks her down in the street. Who do you pick up, the old lady or the sausage?'

'The sausage.'

'Question two: There's a fire in a five-story building and up on the top floor is a little boy by the window eating a sausage. You put up a ladder and climb it. Who do you rescue, the little boy or the sausage?'

'The sausage.'

'Question three: In case you should win this bet, which would you rather have, the money or the sausage?'

Yeah . . . and more of that followed, interspersed with a little
song and dance. The three gals were young and cute, but their
secret was that they really seemed to be having the time of
their lives up there. The audience did not sit on their hands, and
I made sure to let go with my unholy whistle when they bowed
off the stage.

The curtain rose next on a playlet, *Aesop's Fables: Topics of
the Day*, with three shorts based on the old allegories but set in
modern times with modern names and newsworthy topics like
the Scopes Monkey Trial and the discovery of King Tut's tomb.
It was a clever enough idea but, I thought, strained to reach its
morals. Better writing might have helped.

For the last few years, it had become common to end a vaudeville program with a newsreel or a one-reel picture. Nothing
fancy like the feature-length pieces that Mary Pickford and
Douglas Fairbanks produced, just fifteen-minute shorts with
no-name actors. The ninth spot was vaudeville's least popular
spot, as many in the audience took that opportunity to make their
way to the exit, leaving the hapless performer to carry on in spite
of the demoralizing scene before him as folks walked out. A
moving picture, once purchased, didn't need to be paid in cash
each week, didn't get sick, and required nothing but a musician
(who was already employed) to provide the accompanying music.
All in all, an economical choice for the theater owner, although
one that was not appreciated by vaudevillians and their agents,
who saw their opportunities and profits cut by as much as 10 per
cent. Some vaudeville theaters had abandoned vaudeville altogether to become movie theaters – a bad omen for the trade.
I was not one of those doomsayers who believed pictures or radio
would drive out vaudeville. The pictures were only visual and
the radio was only sound. Vaudeville alone provided the entire
spectrum of the entertainment world. Vaudeville was forever.

Today's short was a Western about a cowboy who rescues the
fair maiden from the rustlers. Before it had ended, half the audience began filtering out. I waited until the asbestos curtain fell
with a soft thump before going backstage to find Ivy Devine.

THIRTEEN

The very next morning, Detective Quinn telephoned Adele to arrange to meet her at the Astor as soon as she finished her rehearsal with Fred, to tell her about his success in tracking down the names in Crenshaw's letters. Since I had usually completed my own duties by noon, Adele invited me to join them for lunch. 'I need you here with me, Jessie. You're the one with all the good ideas.'

She didn't have to twist my arm. I wanted to share what I'd learned yesterday from Ivy Devine.

Instead of dining in their suite, Adele had arranged for a private nook on the mezzanine, overlooking the sumptuous Palm Garden with its ceiling painted to look like a Mediterranean sky. Detective Quinn was late but he apologized with a winning grin. 'A thousand regrets, ladies, but I assure you, my delay was worth your wait. I have made a discovery!'

'Naughty boy, don't tease,' said Adele. 'What have you learned?'

'Wesley Crenshaw is living in Brooklyn! He works in the garment industry,' he announced with a flourish that made me think he'd turned up some great evidence.

I knew that much from Mrs Astaire. 'And?'

'And what? That's what I learned.'

'Have you spoken to him?'

'Uh, no. Not yet.'

'Did you get that from the city directory?' In answer to Adele's puzzled look, I explained, 'A city directory has the names, occupations and addresses of all the city's residents. There's one in every library. And in the police headquarters too, right?'

'Yes, I've got the address.'

'Do you have the address of the factory where he works?'

'No, I didn't, I mean, that wasn't specified.'

'Then we should wait until this evening before trying to speak to him at his home in Brooklyn. What did you find about the other name? Sarah Landry.'

'A dead end. There was absolutely nothing about her in police records, and women aren't listed in the city directory.'

'Why ever not?' asked Adele.

Quinn shrugged. He'd never thought about that before.

'Widows are listed,' I said. 'Sometimes single women if they have an occupation.'

'I see . . .' said Adele, although clearly she didn't.

'And she may not even live in New York,' said Quinn.

'But the postmark was New York, wasn't it?'

He nodded. 'I guess so. I'll continue to pursue that lead.'

And so would I.

'What did you find out, Jessie?' Adele asked.

I told them about hunting down the snake dancer and learning about the Devine Comediennes. 'After I left Millie, I went to the Republic Theater on Forty-Second Street where the act was booked. Ivy Devine and her so-called sisters were working their first performance of the day, so I bought a ticket and waited until the end of the cycle to go backstage and meet her. To meet them all.

'There was just the one big dressing room – you know how it is in most theaters, Adele – and I found Ivy pretty easily. She had four hours before their next performance, so she agreed to step out with me for a private chat. There was a speakeasy right on the corner, down in the basement, so we had a nice drink and good conversation. She was very forthcoming about her short affair with Allen Crenshaw. She wasn't the least dismayed to learn of his death; in fact, she seemed quite happy about it. He was a bastard, she said, leading her on about getting her a part in his play and then throwing her out like the trash – her words – when he got bored. In short, I think she would have liked to kill him but couldn't have done it.'

'Why not?'

'For one, she wasn't in town that week. The Devine Comediennes had a gig in Trenton that took her out of the picture all of last week.'

'And for another?'

'She just wasn't the type. Trust me.'

We arranged to meet again at twilight, after Detective Quinn had corralled a police motorcar and a uniformed cop to drive it.

Off we went, across the Brooklyn Bridge and into the maze of factories and houses that would have tortured Adele and me, helpless as babes in any part of New York City beyond the Theater District. Especially at night. By the time we arrived at Wesley Crenshaw's house, a murky haze had wrapped the neighborhood like a damp blanket.

Wesley Crenshaw lived in a small but neat building in a row house next to a pungent cigar manufactory and down the street from a large sugar refinery belching smoke, even at night. Adele and I coughed.

A tall, gangly middle-aged man answered the doorbell.

'Excuse me, sir,' said Detective Quinn, flashing his badge. 'We are looking for Wesley Crenshaw.'

'You found him,' he replied, looking from the detective to Adele and me with understandable confusion.

We must have looked confused too. A man less like Allen Crenshaw would be hard to imagine. It would appear that Wesley Crenshaw had inherited none of his handsome cousin's face or figure. Bald as a tonsured monk, he wore wire-rimmed spectacles that kept slipping down to the tip of his Roman nose. Pulling out a handkerchief, he wiped his watery eyes and blotted his splotchy red face as he squinted at the badge Quinn proffered.

'How can I help you, detective?'

'I am investigating the death of Allen Crenshaw. You are a cousin, I believe?'

'Yes, I am. And I was sorry to read of his death in the newspapers. How can I help you?'

'May we come in?'

For an answer, he moved aside and indicated the way to a first-floor parlor lit by one weak lightbulb. 'I'm afraid I wasn't expecting company. Certainly not ladies.' An overfed tabby cat sprang up off the sofa and lumbered out the door.

Since the detective seemed to have left his manners in the car, I stepped up. 'I am Jessie Beckett,' I began, 'and this is Adele Astaire.' I paused for his reaction to the Astaire name, but none was forthcoming. We were not in the Theater District any longer, I reminded myself. Adele was no one special in this neighborhood of hard-working men and women who had neither money nor time for frivolities like the theater. 'We are helping the detective with his investigation.'

If Wesley Crenshaw found this odd, he didn't show it. 'Please have a seat. How can I be of service?'

A cloud of dust rose from the sofa when Adele and I sat down. I sneezed. Detective Quinn remained standing. They probably taught you that in detective class: standing enhances your authority.

'Were you and your cousin on good terms?' he asked, pulling out a small pad of paper and a pencil.

'We were on no terms at all, good or bad,' Wesley Crenshaw replied.

'When did you see him last?'

He cast his eyes upward, as if the answer was written on the ceiling. After a moment of thought he said, 'About two years ago, at the funeral of our aunt.'

'And you had not seen him since?'

He shook his head.

'Yet, we have a letter from you postmarked just last month.'

'You asked if I had seen him since the funeral. I have not. He wrote to boast of his new play and invite me to see it. Without sending a ticket, I might add. I declined politely. That would be the letter you have in your possession. I'm surprised he saved it.'

'Where were you on the night of his death?'

'Here.'

'Can anyone confirm that?'

'My cat.'

'I'm afraid . . .'

'I was at work that day until six o'clock, as usual, a fact that the factory foreman will confirm, and there would not be time to have come home, changed clothes, and traveled into Manhattan to the theater to shoot him, if that is your thinking.'

'So you know nothing of his romantic affairs, any enemies he may have had?'

'I expect my cousin had a goodly number of enemies. He was a thoroughly disagreeable fellow who never hesitated to step on others when it furthered his own interests. But about his life I know nothing and care less.'

'Have you seen his wife Marjorie lately?'

'I've never met his wife. I did hear that he married some years ago, but I wasn't invited to the wedding, if there was one. As you can see, I'm in no position to help with your investigation, so if there are no other questions . . .?'

'Still,' I said as Adele and I climbed into Quinn's motorcar, 'don't you wonder who will inherit the uncle's furniture fortune now that the favorite nephew is gone?'

FOURTEEN

'Why are *you* going to Crenshaw's funeral?' asked Adele later that night. We were in her suite at the Astor, scarfing down a delicious room-service meal of lobster Newburg and creamed Bermuda potatoes. 'You didn't even know him.'

'Funerals are great for research. You find out all kinds of things, especially after the service at the gravesite when people are milling around. After that, if there's a reception, that's an even better opportunity. People are drinking, talking carelessly about the deceased, saying nice things . . . sometimes not so nice. I wouldn't miss it.'

'Well, I'll come too then. At least I can say I knew Allen and Marjorie.'

'It's tomorrow morning, Adele. You have rehearsal.'

'I'll just have to break the news to Fred that I'm taking the morning off. He's getting too big for his britches anyway. Did you get a half-day off?'

'Ever since I helped Douglas solve the murder of a director friend of his, he's insisted on giving me any time off I need to investigate crimes like this. As long as I get my important work done, of course. So if I wake up early, I can polish off their correspondence and a few other chores and take the rest of the day. And speaking of Marjorie, if you're going to the funeral, you can help the investigation by asking her if she has any idea what a thief might have been looking for in Allen's apartment.'

'Valuables, I suppose?'

I shook my head. 'Not valuables in the sense of money or jewelry. Crenshaw was a successful actor, sure, but he wasn't wealthy and we've heard hints of debts. My hunch is there was something else, something they didn't find, which means they're still looking. It wouldn't hurt to let Marjorie know about the break-in, just in case her apartment's next up on the thief's list. Lucky she has a doorman – that should discourage burglars.'

'Shall we go to the funeral together, or is it cleverer to pretend we don't know each other and work independently?'

In the end, we went together, taking a taxi to Trinity Church where Wall Street dead-ends at Broadway, alighting in an October drizzle that chilled the air and provided an appropriately gloomy setting – 'Kinda like Nature herself has staged the funeral,' Adele remarked. I hadn't brought my black mourning dress or my hat with the half-veil, so Adele lent me a simple navy-blue dress from her wardrobe. It was too long – she towers over me – so I raised the hem with basting stitches, like anyone would do . . . that is, anyone who'd grown up in vaudeville altering costumes on a daily basis. No one would be looking at me anyway.

'Take this shawl too. It's cold out.'

'Geez Louise, Adele! Where did you get this? It's gorgeous!' The garnet-and-black Indian paisley had been woven from the silkiest wool my fingers had ever caressed, and I stroked it reverently as I threw it over my shoulders. Instant warmth!

'It ought to be. It was a present from Princess Mary.'

'No fooling?'

'No fooling. She's a real music lover, a patroness of music festivals and whatnot. When we were on tour in London, she enjoyed *Stop Flirting* – especially the music – and Fred and I were invited to several receptions. I'd never say we were friends, but we were friendly, and she gave me this lovely shawl. You'll need it today, especially at the gravesite.'

We arrived at Trinity Church early so as to get a good seat, which in this case meant a seat in the back so we could watch people coming and going and figure out who was who. Trinity was the most beautiful church I'd ever seen – not that I'd seen that many, but it looked like it came right out of one of those European travel books. The stained-glass windows pulsed with jewel-box colors in spite of the overcast sky. The stone carvings and statues were so life-like, I had to keep reminding myself I was there to watch the people, not the architecture.

If popularity can be measured by the number of mourners at your funeral, Allen Crenshaw wasn't much of a success. Naturally, all the actors and stage crew from the Morosco were there, but Adele recognized not a single theater critic – 'They admired his talent, not his character,' she surmised – and there were no family

members other than his estranged wife Marjorie and his furniture-
fortune uncle, who sat in the front pew with just enough distance
between them to make me think they were not on cordial terms.
I had hoped to see cousin Wesley Crenshaw, but he skipped the
funeral, just as he had skipped his cousin's wedding and his
Broadway play. No love lost there.

My attention was drawn to three burly men in black raincoats
who strode down the main aisle together, one in front, two
behind; the front man had his eyes firmly fixed on the open
casket before the altar, while the two behind him twisted their
heads right and left, suspicious of the mourners in the pews.
They looked like gangsters, and I oughta know what gangsters
look like. I saw gangsters galore back when my vaudeville act
was playing Chicago or Detroit or Baltimore or Philadelphia,
wherever they controlled the illegal liquor markets. And I knew
gangsters from Los Angeles, when David got involved with
drug smugglers, before he was sentenced to prison. There's a
look about them that words can't describe. A shiver ran up the
back of my neck.

When the three thugs reached the casket, they stood motionless
for about half a minute, staring at the body. The guy in front,
who was now in the middle, reached into the casket. To put
something in it? To take something out? To poke the stiff? I was
too far back in the church to see what he was doing. He turned
abruptly and headed back down the aisle, trailed by the other
two. But rather than slide into an empty pew, they kept walking,
right out of the church. Adele and I exchanged glances.

'They're gangsters,' I whispered. 'I'm sure of it. I think they
were coming to check that Allen really is dead.'

'Why would they do that?'

'He probably owed them money – remember Marjorie
mentioned something about not wanting to pay Allen's debts? If
that's true, Allen wouldn't be the first person to try faking his
own death to throw the gangsters off his trail.'

'I thought they broke your legs when you didn't pay, to
encourage you to get the money.'

'That's a bit theatrical, but sure, they might rough you up at
first. But when threats don't work, they kill you. Sets an example
to others.'

Her eyes widened. 'How do you know this?'

There was no chance to respond. And I'd rather not have told her about my experience with David's criminal organization in Oregon or the subsequent tangles I'd had with 'Iron Man' Ardizzone and his thugs in Los Angeles. I knew way too much about gangsters.

A priest materialized out of a dimly lit corner behind the altar and glided to the center of the stage, I mean, altar. 'I am the resurrection and the life, saith the Lord; he that believeth in me, though he were dead, yet shall he live; and whosoever liveth and believeth in me shall never die.'

'No one does ceremonies better than the Episcopal church,' sighed Adele when the Bible readings, psalms, prayers and short eulogy were complete. 'It used to be part of the Church of England, you know, Jessie. That's why this choral music is so very English, so inspiring, just like the churches in England we went to when we were in London. And I love the pageantry and the bells and the priests in their beautiful vestments.' She was spot on. It was like a masterfully staged pageant, complete with actors, costumes, music, dialogue, and an appreciative audience that managed to hold its applause. On cue, a bell rang, and a phalanx of pallbearers stepped from the wings and hoisted the casket onto their shoulders. Down the aisle and out the front door they marched, into the churchyard where Allen Crenshaw would be laid to rest for eternity. We mourners followed in a solemn stream, leaving the gentle organ music inside.

Thankfully the rain had let up, so, although the air was heavy with mist, few people opened umbrellas. I pulled Adele's shawl snug around my shoulders and surveyed the graveyard, its tombstones arranged in disorderly rows like crooked teeth. With some surprise I nudged her. 'Look,' I whispered, nodding toward a familiar figure standing at the edge of the empty grave, as if waiting for the procession to come to him. It was Wesley Crenshaw, who had, indeed, shown up, if not to his cousin's church service, at least to the burial. He could have stood near Marjorie and Uncle Crenshaw as a member of the family, but obviously chose not to. Or was he warned away? Near him, but not close enough to suggest they were together, stood a pretty girl of about my own age, crying softly. The only one I could see shedding real tears.

'Look,' Adele nudged me back. 'Alexander Hamilton's grave, right over there with the pyramid on top. I wonder if anyone else important is buried here.'

The priest led us in a prayer, then intoned, 'Into thy hands, O merciful Savior, we commend thy servant, Allen. Acknowledge, we humbly beseech thee, a sheep of thine own fold, a lamb of thine own flock, a sinner of thine own redeeming. Receive him into the arms of thy mercy, into the blessed rest of everlasting peace, and into the glorious company of the saints in light. Amen.' After a long pause with bowed head, he straightened up and let his gaze wander over the small crowd before making his final pronouncement. 'The family will welcome friends of Allen Crenshaw at a reception in the parish hall.'

The service was over. My work had begun.

Inside the parish hall, I positioned myself a few feet behind Marjorie Crenshaw who was standing beside Uncle Crenshaw to receive condolences. 'He's a strange one, isn't he?' murmured Adele as we focused on the elderly gent. His out-of-style whiskers and rumpled black suit made him look more like a hobo than a wealthy factory owner. 'Do you suppose he's as rich as they say?' She pulled an old theater program out of her handbag. 'Here. Pretend to be absorbed in this while you eavesdrop. I'll go speak to him and see what I can learn.'

'Mr Crenshaw,' Adele began as she planted herself before him and introduced herself with her irresistible smile. 'I knew Allen from the theater world, and my mother, Johanna Astaire, was a friend of your late wife.'

'Yes, my dear. Yes, Johanna was a good friend to us both. I received an expression of condolence from her just this morning. I'm so sorry she's not well.'

'She understood how much you cared for your nephew. Your namesake. She told me he was more than a nephew to you, more like a son.'

'That's very true, my dear. A dear boy.'

'She told me you and your wife had hoped he would take over your furniture business.'

'We did indeed. Of course, he was enjoying great success in

the theater, but we always understood that it was a young man's passing fancy, and that he'd come home to the furniture business in due course, when the novelty wore off.'

'No doubt he would have. Such a shame you won't be able to keep the business in the family now.'

'Well, yes, or . . . perhaps . . . that remains to be seen . . .'

Marjorie, who was listening in at this point, inserted herself into the conversation. She must have been vastly annoyed that Allen had died before he'd inherited the furniture fortune, but she was too good an actress to show it. 'It's good to see you again so soon, Adele. So kind of you to come. I hope that detective has made some progress in tracking down Allen's killer?'

Uncle Crenshaw looked surprised. 'I thought . . .'

'The police believe that someone other than Norah Rose could have switched real ammunition for the blanks in her gun,' Adele explained. 'The investigation is ongoing.'

'I didn't know . . .'

'You wouldn't,' Marjorie muttered.

'Marjorie,' Adele began, her voice lowered so I heard only a word or two. I knew what she was saying, telling Marjorie that Allen's apartment had been ransacked and warning her that they might be coming her way. I saw Marjorie shake her head and surmised that she was answering Adele's question about whether or not she knew what the thieves were looking for.

At that moment, Wesley Crenshaw approached them. He recognized Adele from our visit to his home and nodded to her politely, then turned to face Marjorie and introduced himself. 'So sorry for your loss, Marjorie. I'm sorry, too, that we've never had the chance to meet except under such unhappy circumstances. I hadn't seen Allen in a long time, but I have fond memories of playing with him in our grandfather's barn when we were children. His death is New York's loss. And Uncle, good to see you again. It's been a long time.'

'You missed the service,' the uncle growled.

'The indoor part, yes. People like me have been rejected by organized religion, so you can't expect me to go where I'm considered a pariah. I came to the burial to show my respect for my family. That will have to suffice.'

Uncle Crenshaw looked away. Several uncomfortable moments

passed until Adele, adept at smoothing ruffled feelings, spoke. 'My mother sends her condolences, Marjorie. She's been doing poorly, or she would have been here today too.'

'I understand. Give her my regards.'

'I remember your mother, Miss Astaire,' said Wesley. 'I'd forgotten until you mentioned it just now, but she and my Aunt Cyrene were fast friends from the old days. Aunt Cyrene loved to talk about her time in vaudeville. She and I were quite close. I miss her dearly,' he said, looking pointedly at his uncle.

Whatever reconciliation might have occurred at that point was interrupted by the next group of mourners who inched over to pay their respects, politely pushing Adele and Wesley aside. It was a short parade.

'I'm so sorry for your loss, Mrs Crenshaw,' said one stout older woman. 'Your husband was a rare talent.'

'Thank you for coming,' said Marjorie.

'I've known Allen for years, sir,' said her companion, 'and he'll be greatly missed, I assure you.'

'Thank you.'

A young couple holding hands like newlyweds expressed their sorrow in halting terms. A bent, white-haired gentleman in a loud striped suit who appeared to be a friend of the uncle's clapped him on the shoulder and shook his hand vigorously. A pregnant woman who seemed nervous – the uncharitable thought that Allen might be the father flitted through my head – spoke hastily to Marjorie without meeting her eye. Several skinny, pimply-faced ushers from the Morosco, unsure of proper etiquette, shook hands and said nothing just to be safe. Perhaps it was their first funeral. They were followed by the makeup artist from the theater who made a few perfunctory remarks before heading to the punch bowl. And then who should approach but Ted Youngerman, the understudy, overacting his part with swollen red eyes and a mournful face. I stretched my ears to hear their exchange, but he spoke nothing but platitudes.

'You think those are crocodile tears?' Adele was back at my side behind the Crenshaws.

'He's probably using the slice-of-onion-in-the-pocket trick.' Everyone on stage knows that one.

'I'm surprised Norah Rose isn't here,' whispered Adele. 'Looks bad, don't you think? Like she was feeling guilty. I mean, she did kill him, whether or not it was an accident, but staying away makes her look even more guilty, like the woman scorned, don't you think?'

'Maybe. I was hoping to see her today. We need to talk with her, and soon.'

Adele kept busy supplying me with the names of some of the other actors and actresses while I kept my eye on the pretty girl who had been crying real tears, hoping it would be . . .

FIFTEEN

. . . and it was. Finally, the girl I'd been wondering about sidled up to Uncle Crenshaw and shook his hand.

'I'm Sarah Landry, Mr Crenshaw. I counted Allen as a friend for only a short while, but a kinder, more compassionate gentleman never existed. I am so very sorry for your loss.'

So this was the shadowy Sarah Landry, the one who had written the short note, the girl Detective Quinn couldn't find. There was an edginess about her, the way her eyes darted around without settling for any length of time on any one person. She was a pretty brunette with hair cut in a blunt bob, and had a low, scratchy voice that sounded like she'd recently recovered from a sore throat.

Moving along to Marjorie, who was methodically working the short line, Sarah Landry sniffed into the handkerchief and managed a wan smile. 'Mrs Crenshaw, I'm Sarah Landry, a friend of your husband's. His death was such a shock. A terrible loss, not only to his family but to the theater world.' Marjorie was facing away from me so I couldn't hear her reply very well, nor watch her reaction. I don't think she recognized the name, but she may well have deduced that this attractive young miss was another of her husband's conquests. Sarah Landry said a few unintelligible words, then moved along to the table where the church women were ladling punch.

'I'm going to follow her and see who she is,' I whispered to Adele. 'You stay here and pick up whatever you can.' Punch glass in hand, I trailed Sarah Landry to a table spread with plates of tiny cucumber sandwiches, sugared almonds and pimento cheese crackers.

'Sad day,' I remarked when we came close enough for conversation. Not one of my better opening lines, but it served.

'Sure is,' she said with a sniffle. 'How did you know Allen?'

'Just a theater connection.' It was kind of true. 'I'm Jessie Beckett, by the way.'

'Sarah Landry. Pleased to meet you.'

'Marjorie seems to be holding up pretty well. Losing Allen must've been a shock for her, all things considered, even though they hadn't spoken in a good while.'

'They hadn't?'

'Not since they were separated after all that unpleasantness.'

'They were separated? I had no idea. What unpleasantness? Since when?'

'They've been living apart for a couple of years, I think.'

'Really?' She ate a cucumber sandwich in one bite as she contemplated this information. 'That makes me feel a little better,' she said softly, almost to herself.

A conquest. I'd guessed right. 'How did you know Allen?'

She blushed. 'Oh, we were seeing a bit of each other until a few months ago. I really fell for him, I gotta admit. He was so kind and gallant. I thought . . . well, I thought maybe he was The One. Then someone mentioned a wife, and I cut it off at once. Of course. I'm not that sort of girl.'

She didn't look like that sort of girl.

'But if he was separated from his wife and planning to divorce her, it puts a different slant on everything, doesn't it?'

'I guess so. At least I can understand how he must have rationalized the situation, thinking he wasn't really cheating on her, even though he was.'

'If it makes you feel any better, Sarah, he had quite a reputation for the ladies. You weren't the only one.'

She shook her head. 'That's so hard to believe. He wasn't the masher type.'

This was the first time I'd heard anyone say a kind word about Allen Crenshaw, certainly the only time anyone had described the quintessential masher as 'not the masher type'.

'I didn't even know he was in the play until I saw the newspaper article about his death. I mean, I knew he was an actor but he said he had small parts. Never mentioned he was a leading man on Broadway. So modest . . . I never saw him on stage. He didn't talk about that side of his life much.' This was getting weirder and weirder. According to others who knew him, all Allen did was talk about himself. A real braggart. I wondered if he had a secret twin. Sarah went on, 'I would have liked to see him play a part on the stage. My mother liked him too.'

'Is she here?' Instinctively I looked around, even though I was pretty sure Sarah had come alone.

'She died a few months ago, shortly before I broke things off with Allen.'

'I'm sorry to hear that.'

'Do you know what he did after she died? I had to clean out her apartment, and Allen spent two days helping me get rid of stuff and lugging lots of boxes and furniture to my place.'

'That was a kindness, for sure. Do you live far?'

'Manhattanville area. Near Columbia University. My mother was a secretary for one of the professors and my brother once studied there.'

'Is that where you work too?' I asked her.

'No, I'm a musician. I play violin.' That made sense. She had the hands of a musician, strong and capable, with short fingernails she had painted the same coral color as her lipstick.

'For the symphony?'

She gave a rueful laugh. 'The Philharmonic doesn't hire women musicians, Jessie, except for Stephanie Goldner, the harpist. The violin is a man's instrument, or so they tell me. And the New York Symphony Orchestra doesn't have a single female in it either. No, I play with a small neighborhood orchestra. It's more of a hobby than a job, but sometimes we get work at one of the off-Broadway productions when they can't pay what the professionals are asking.' I wondered how she supported herself, but maybe she had family money.

'I was there the night Allen was shot.'

'Oh, my goodness. How awful that must have been!'

I nodded. Our conversation was interrupted when several people came up to the table to sample the meager fare, and at that point, Adele sauntered over. 'Gosh, it's getting warm in here,' she remarked. 'Too many people in this small room.' She helped herself to a cheesy cracker.

'Sarah, can I introduce my friend Adele Astaire? Adele, this is Sarah Landry, a friend of Allen's. Sarah, Adele is the headliner – with her brother Fred – of the musical *Lady Be Good*. She and Allen and Marjorie were good friends.' An exaggeration, to be sure, but I needed to cement this relationship if I were ever to learn what Allen had been up to, pursuing this naïve young musician who had minimal theatrical connections.

Sarah's eyes widened. She hadn't seen *Lady Be Good* but, as a musician, she certainly knew the Gershwin brothers' latest work and had heard of the Astaires. Adele explained that they would be taking the play to London's West End shortly. 'And Jessie here will be back in Hollywood soon. She did tell you what she does, didn't she?'

Sarah shook her head slowly and raised eyebrows in a question.

'I'm an assistant for Douglas Fairbanks. He and Mary Pickford are in New York for a few weeks and I came with them, along with several others, to help with their busy schedules.'

'Oh my goodness, really?' she squeaked. 'What an exciting job!'

'It sounds more glamorous than it is, I assure you. They are two very down-to-earth people.'

We chatted a bit about Hollywood – everyone likes to hear about their favorite film actors – before Adele excused herself to step outside for some cooler air. I had learned what I needed to know, so I eased away from Sarah Landry and drifted back to Adele's side when she came back indoors. Clearly this picture-of-innocence had nothing to contribute to our investigation. She hadn't seen Allen in a few months, and it didn't sound like she knew him well at all. Or maybe she did. Maybe Allen had a decent side to him that wasn't apparent to the rest of the world. Maybe the ingenuous Miss Landry brought out the best in him. We'd never know.

'Look, that's Ira Belkowitz, *Rules of Engagement*'s director.' Adele drew my attention to a spry man in his forties with his left arm in a sling. 'We've never met, but I can introduce myself.'

'Let's go.'

For the first time I could recall, Adele's winsome ways were not enough to charm a man. She started, as always, with that coquettish smile and a come-hither tilt of her head, and then introduced me, mentioning in passing that I was in New York with Douglas Fairbanks and Mary Pickford. That warranted a rise of his bushy eyebrows and a quick perusal of my person, but no comment. So she continued, explaining that we were helping Detective Quinn with his investigation into Allen Crenshaw's unfortunate demise. 'The detective asked us to come to the funeral,' she said, in an outrageous falsehood, 'and see what we might learn from the mourners. I don't believe you've spoken with the detective yet. Might you give us an idea of your relationship with the deceased?'

'I have not spoken to Detective Quinn, Miss Astaire, and you may relay the message that I will be happy to speak with him at his convenience in my office at the theater. I will not, however, be speaking to any unofficial surrogates. Good meeting you, ladies.' And with a slight nod of his head that could have passed for a bow if he'd been friendlier, he walked off.

'Well, that couldn't have been plainer,' I said when he was out of range. Then, in my best gangster voice, I snarled, 'Whaddya say we blow this joint, kid?' She giggled. 'Seriously, Adele, I think we've gotten everything we could out of this. Let's hot-foot it to the subway and head home.'

'I'd rather hail a cab. My treat. We'll have lunch at my place. I'm starved.'

'Your wish is my command, milady.' And within minutes we were tucked in the back seat of a black sedan speeding toward the Astor.

'So did we really learn anything significant, Jessie?'

'Well, yes. We learned that Allen must have been in debt to some gangsters, probably gambling debts. We learned that no one has anything nice to say about Allen except Miss Landry, who thought he hung the moon until she learned that he . . . Oh my god! Adele!' I gasped and I looked around the back seat frantically. 'I've lost your shawl! I left it in the church hall. It was getting warm and I laid it down – geez, I'm so sorry, Adele! How could I have . . .? Driver! Driver! Turn around, please, right away. I've got to go back to the church. I'm so sorry!'

Adele's soothing words did nothing to calm me. Her precious shawl, the gift from Princess Somebody! I remember laying it down on the chair beside the food table when I was talking to Sarah Landry, and walking away from it without a second thought moments later. It would still be there. It had to be there! No one would have taken it. Who steals from a church, right? I wanted to urge the driver to greater speeds but managed to hold my tongue as I twisted my fingers together nervously. It had to be there.

The church hall was empty, save for two stout ladies dragging the chairs back into a large closet. 'Have either of you seen a red and black wool shawl?' I asked them. Surely one of them had found it and set it aside.

'I'm sorry, miss. Did you lose it here?'

'Yes, I left it on that chair,' I pointed. 'Is there any place someone might have taken it? A Lost-and-Found?'

The ladies shook their heads. One pointed to the hallway behind me. 'You might check the sexton's office, right around the corner.'

I ran down the hall and around the corner to the door marked SEXTON, but it was locked. I raced back into the church itself, now silent as a morgue, thinking perhaps I had left it there before we all moved into the hall, but our pew was empty. So were all the rest of them. I stumbled across the sexton who assured me he had not seen it. I checked the Ladies' Lounge in case anyone had set it there for safe-keeping. I looked in the closet where the chairs were stored. Nothing. Every part of the church was clean and empty, and there was no place a shawl could hide. I had to face the unpleasant truth: someone had taken it.

Adele, bless her, insisted over and over that the shawl meant nothing to her and I shouldn't give it another thought, but I knew darn well it was one of her most cherished possessions. Even if I could find another as beautiful, which I couldn't, and even if I could afford to buy it, which I couldn't, it wouldn't have been a gift from a royal princess for some memorable performance. I was devastated.

SIXTEEN

After a lunch of hot barley soup and cold tomato aspic, we took advantage of our free afternoon to walk to the Morosco to see if we could waylay Ted Youngerman or Norah Rose. Detective Quinn had, presumably, questioned them, but Adele and I had not, and there were some things I wanted to ask them. The guard told us Norah had not come in, but we could find Mr Youngerman in his dressing room. With unseemly speed, he had moved his kit from the communal dressing room to the private one that was formerly Allen Crenshaw's. We found him there, stretched out on a shabby lounge chair, his legs crossed at the ankles, looking over a sheaf of papers. His door was ajar, so Adele knocked as she pushed it open.

'Well, well, well,' she said in her teasing voice. 'Aren't you the picture of a carefree leading man?' Youngerman bolted upright. He must have come directly from the funeral; his black suit was hanging on a hook. He had changed into casual clothes with bright argyle socks. 'Lose your shoes?' Adele kidded.

He grinned the sly grin of a ladies' man who believes himself devastating. With a practiced movement, he ran his fingers through his curly brown hair, allowing one lock to fall on to his forehead, creating what he no doubt considered a charming picture.

'Miss Astaire! What a treat to see you lovely ladies twice in one day! Do come in.' With a fluid motion, he swept the papers off the wooden chair at the dressing table and indicated that I should sit. With another, he steered Adele toward his lounge chair while pulling up a stool for himself. 'To what do I owe the honor?'

'First, I don't believe you've been introduced to my friend from my vaudeville days, Jessie Beckett.'

'Pleased to meet you, Miss Beckett. I saw you with Miss Astaire at the funeral. How did you know our dearly departed friend Allen?'

'I didn't know him at all,' I replied. 'But that's what we wanted to talk with you about – Allen Crenshaw's death.'

His expression hardened, and the playboy turned into someone you would not want to meet in a dark alley. 'I've talked myself blue in the face to that officious detective. I have nothing more to say to anyone – and even if I did, why would I say it to you?'

'Because we're not interviewing you as a suspect,' said Adele. 'The police consider you a possible murderer because you benefit from his death. Jessie and I don't agree.'

'Well thank you very much,' he said, his voice heavy with sarcasm.

'We just want some information about that day and think you can supply it.'

'And what information would that be?'

Adele gave me a take-it-from-here look, and I caught it. 'What do you think happened that night?'

He looked thoughtful for a long moment, not because he was searching for an opinion, but because he was deciding whether or not to talk to us. At last, the decision went our way and he spoke. 'Do I think Norah did the deed, you mean? I certainly hope not, since she's pointing the same gun at me every night and twice on Saturdays. But no, my answer is no, I believe Norah thought she was shooting blanks, as always. She may have wanted to kill Allen – he was a real bounder, I might add, never picked up the tab. But she doesn't have the fortitude to do anything as bold as that, no matter the provocation.'

'Who would be your chief suspect?'

'Marjorie makes a good one. She was in the theater that day and could have made the switch. Bill Levine comes a close second. They had a grudge going way back, and it flared up again just last week when Levine showed up to work late and sozzled. Crenshaw hated drunks – I heard him say once that his father was a worthless drunk – and he threatened to have Levine fired if he dared touch another drop. He meant it too, and he had enough pull with Ira Belkowitz and Ed Ricks to make it happen. Still, I don't see either of them handling the killing in such a public manner, in front of a theater packed with witnesses. It would have done tremendous damage to the play they cared so much about. Seems to me there are easier, quieter ways of going about killing someone that are far less risky.'

'Were you and Allen on good terms?' Adele asked.

'No one was on good terms with Allen. He was a monumental ass. But I didn't kill him.'

'You benefited from his death.'

'So what? Every understudy benefits from an unfortunate occurrence. An illness, an accident, a sick mother in Peoria . . . a death, natural or un-. It's the nature of the role. Sure, I got my big break. But I would've had it soon anyway. Allen let drop that he'd tried out for the lead in another play, one that started rehearsal in a month. He was sure he'd gotten it.'

'Which play?' asked Adele.

'He didn't say. But he wouldn't have left *Rules of Engagement* for something off-Broadway. So I was pretty certain my star was rising regardless.'

'Where were you when he was shot?' I asked.

'For shame, Miss Beckett. That doesn't sound very friendly. However, I'll take it in the spirit in which it was *not* intended and answer that I was in the communal dressing room, awaiting my scene.'

A commotion in the hallway turned our heads. A noisy gang trooped into the theater, laughing and calling friendly insults to one another. One voice stood out in the commotion – Norah Rose. Adele and I had the same thought.

'We'll let you go back to whatever you were studying,' she said, edging toward the door.

'Thanks for the information,' I said, 'and break a leg tonight.'

Without another word, we followed the noise through the halls, downstairs to the basement dressing room shared by the cast, male and female. It wasn't very large – they never are – but it had two sinks and a toilet closet off to one side, plus several folding screens that offered a modicum of privacy to anyone changing costumes, although, in my experience, only the greenest, shyest performers ever made use of them. Norah Rose's role in the play was significant, but she was not the female lead and therefore didn't rate a private dressing room. We found her with half a dozen others gathering for the daily pre-show meeting with the director. A meeting the author, Edward Ricks, usually attended so that he could, according to Adele, tweak the script or critique the actors. A playwright with that much authority was unheard-of, but the producers had insisted.

'Hello, Norah,' Adele began, motioning her to one corner of the large room. The young woman blinked in surprise. 'Can I speak with you for a moment?'

Norah was a natural red-head with the lovely complexion those women usually have. Although the clear preference in hairstyles in those days was for a sleek bob like Louise Brooks of Hollywood fame, Norah set her own style, bucking the trend. She left her wavy tresses long, falling loose down over her shoulders or tied back with a ribbon. Occasionally she plaited the hair in two side braids which she wrapped across the top of her head, German-maiden style. She knew how to get noticed.

'Um, sure,' she said. Ignoring the curious glances, she separated from the cast and moved toward the corner. Adele introduced me as a friend from vaudeville and then asked if there was somewhere a little more private where we could talk.

'Um, not really. Is this about Allen?'

'It is.'

'Well, maybe come this way.' She led us into the hallway down to one end where there was an overflowing storage room with no door. 'It's not like everyone here doesn't know everything about everything, so I can't see it matters if they overhear us, but here's about as private as we can get.'

It would have to do. I nodded to Adele to continue. 'Sorry we didn't see you at the funeral this morning.'

'Yeah, I thought about going. For about two seconds. I didn't want everyone watching me walk up to Marjorie and tell her how devastated I was, when neither of us cared that much. Hell, both of us were delighted he was gone. Everyone would have been watching us, hoping for a catfight, or at least some throwing of punch glasses.'

'You spoke to Detective Quinn, though, didn't you?'

'The day after.'

'Unfortunately, we couldn't be with him during that interview, but Jessie and I have been helping his investigation. We wanted to hear your story, not from some police report but directly from you.'

'I can only tell you what I told the detective and his sidekick.'

'Sidekick?'

'Some policeman. In uniform.'

'Please know that we don't consider you a suspect. You're a pawn in this deadly game, Norah. We know that. Someone used you to kill Allen. We just want to ask whether you know anything about Allen's debts. Gambling debts, we believe.'

She gave the question some thought before shaking her head. 'Debts? No. I know he liked going to the races – we went several times. And a coupla times he left me after dinner and went to an all-night poker game. Men only, he said. I don't play poker anyway, so no skin off my nose.'

'He never mentioned winning or losing big bucks?'

'Losing? He told me he always won because he was a really sharp poker player and all the rest were idiots. And he had contacts who gave him tips on the ponies. There's a lot of cheating going on in the races, that I know for sure from the comments that creepy-looking men would make when they would bump into him "accidentally", if you get my meaning. Drugs for some horses to make them faster or slower. Whatever the case, he always had a wad of cash in his wallet.'

'What broke up your relationship?' I asked her.

'I broke it off. Everyone thinks I was dumped, but I was the one who dumped that jerk. He was just getting too mean, too bossy. Telling me what we were doing, never asking what I wanted to do. You can ask Ray if you don't believe me. Ray Marshall – he plays a soldier in the first act. I told Ray last month I was going to split up with Allen. I know people think I killed him out of jealousy that he was seeing another woman, but it's not true.'

'Did you notice anything different when you pulled the trigger that night?' Ever since the night Crenshaw was shot, I'd been confused about the gun and the number of gunshots I'd heard. There was certainly one – it went into Crenshaw's chest. Had there been two, like Norah claimed she shot every night? The police found two casings in the revolver. I thought I'd heard three or even four shots, which was impossible, so I must have been mixing up drumbeats with gunshots.

'Different?'

'Did the gun feel different? Did the recoil feel different?'

She shook her head. 'Recoil?'

'The recoil, the kickback – it felt the same as always?'

'I guess so.'

'You fired twice?'

'Like every night.'

'Have you had much experience with guns, Norah?'

'What do you mean?'

'That was a remarkably accurate shot you fired off, striking Allen squarely in the chest. You must have had some practice shooting when you were growing up, right?'

'Not a bit. I never even held a gun until I got this part.'

'Just a lucky shot then? Or unlucky, rather.'

'I guess. I didn't really aim at Allen. I never do. I just kinda point it straight out there and pull the trigger.'

'Who do you think switched out the blanks?'

She looked over her shoulder. A few of the cast members were in the hall, too far away to overhear us.

'Allen and Teddy Youngerman had a big fight the day before.'

'What about?'

'No idea. Well, maybe an idea. Maybe about money. Ted liked to play the ponies too. And I always thought it was pretty amazing that he had been so well prepared to step into Allen's role. Understudies should be prepared, of course, but he was picture perfect from the second Allen hit the floor. We didn't even do a complete run-through the following day; it was so obvious that he was ready. Like he *knew*. Gave me the willies.'

'Anything else give you the willies?' I asked.

'Edward Ricks. But he gives everyone the willies. I mean, big egos aren't exactly rare in this town, but he takes first prize. I can't stand the man. And if I don't get upstairs quick, I'm gonna miss his daily rant, which will get me in trouble I can't afford.'

'Just one more question, Norah. Did you see Allen's wife Marjorie in the theater that day?'

'No, but someone else did. Can't remember who, but one of the cast mentioned she was here, backstage. I wondered why. It could've been her who switched the bullets, but there's never gonna be proof. I'm always gonna get the blame.'

I wasn't so sure.

We ran into Detective Quinn on the sidewalk out front of the Morosco.

'Miss Astaire,' he said, doffing his hat. His face lit up with a boyish smile. And then he noticed me. 'And Miss Beckett. What have you ladies been up to today?'

It sounded a bit condescending, but I let it pass. Without his support, we'd not be able to do half what we were doing. He was really just talking to Adele, so I let her respond.

'We went to the funeral this morning.'

'Oh, that's right. I'd forgotten about that. Was it a moving service? At Trinity, right? How was the crowd?'

'Trinity, yes, and the crowd . . . well, let's just say Crenshaw didn't have a lot of friends or family. We came here this afternoon to chat with Ted Youngerman and Norah Rose – luckily both were in.'

'I was hoping to catch Norah Rose, too, for a few more questions.'

'I'm afraid your timing is off. She's in a cast meeting for the next hour or so.'

'Well then, maybe you ladies would like to join me for a cup of coffee across the street while I wait? You can fill me in about the funeral.'

Buddy's Diner had a checkerboard floor and a long Formica counter where, although well beyond lunch hour, every stool was taken. Fortunately, Quinn spotted an older couple leaving one of the corner tables and seized it.

'Coffee, please, for three,' he said to the waitress, a stocky woman who waddled up to our table like her hip was hurting.

'Tables are for folks who are eating,' she snapped. 'Coffee drinkers take the stools.'

'Oh, sorry, ma'am. There were no stools, so we . . . never mind. What are you serving today for dessert?'

'Apple pie, cherry pie, rhubarb pie, pineapple upside-down cake, angel food cake and rice pudding.'

We ordered a cake, a pie and the pudding and settled in for a long chat. Adele started off, telling Quinn about the funeral. I filled him in on our recent conversations with Ted Youngerman and Norah Rose. He didn't seem much interested and, I have to admit, our revelations weren't exactly ground-breaking.

'I just got back from Jersey City,' he announced as our waitress delivered our order. 'I drove over to talk with Allen Crenshaw, Senior. I wanted to look into this business about the will.' He paused to stir cream into his coffee. I reflected that he could have met with the old man if he'd come to the funeral, but never mind.

'What did you learn?' prompted Adele.

'I asked if he had a will and he said yes. He made it out years ago and, even though circumstances have changed, he hasn't revised it. He wanted his furniture business to stay in the family, so he left it to his four nephews.'

'Four? I thought there were just two.'

'There were four originally. Two died some time ago, and now Allen is dead, so the business goes to the remaining nephew, Wesley. That gives him a big motive, doesn't it?'

The news set my thoughts racing. 'When did the other two die?'

'I don't know, why?'

I bit back a sharp retort. Did New York not train their detectives before sending them out on assignment? Benjamin Quinn wasn't stupid and he was certainly earnest, but he couldn't seem to see the Big Picture. He wasn't suspicious enough to ask the right questions. Was this a skill someone could learn, or was it innate?

'Four men are named to inherit,' I explained. 'Three are dead. One we know was murdered. What happened to the other two? When did they die? Were their deaths suspicious?'

'What are you thinking?'

'Could this be Wesley's plan, knocking off his cousins so he could inherit the whole kit and caboodle? We need to find out how and when the other two nephews died.'

'I'll get right on it.'

'Is the furniture company worth a lot?'

'Crenshaw didn't say and it seemed rude to talk dollars, but he owns two factories, one in Jersey City and another in Baltimore, plus hundreds of acres of forest in Pennsylvania and New Jersey where he gets the wood. He employs over two hundred men in the factories and a dozen or so women in the office. Makes a lot of money, I don't doubt.'

'Four nephews . . . were there any nieces?'

'Two nieces, but no man is going to leave a business to a woman. The will gives them a little money.'

'What did old Mr Crenshaw think about the business going to the nephew he didn't like?'

'He didn't say much about that. Still seemed shocked that Allen was gone. Maybe he's thinking his late wife might have been right about Wesley. The guy seemed to be the hard-working sort, and he has experience in factory work. He's sure better suited for the job than an actor! They'll probably work out some sort of mutually satisfactory arrangement.'

As long as Wesley doesn't get arrested for murder, that is.

The more I balanced what we knew against what we didn't, the more uneasy I became. Allen's death removed the last person who stood between Wesley and a fortune. It would have been a simple thing for him to have paid someone in the cast or crew to switch bullets. I had no way to find out about the two dead nephews, so I'd have to rely on Detective Quinn's investigative skills. Not a reassuring thought.

SEVENTEEN

Douglas Fairbanks didn't just walk into a room. He strode into the room. He bounded into the room. He burst into the room. All eyes turned to him, a force of nature, this compelling actor who had invented a new sort of male film star: the man of daring and action. Robin Hood. Zorro. Don Juan. D'Artagnan. Swashbuckling heroes all, handsome athletic men who swung from chandeliers, leaped from rooftops, and saved the girl from a fate worse than death. With Douglas, it wasn't an act. He really was those men, the same whether he was out in public, in front of a camera, or alone with friends or employees. A bit of the overgrown boy with his pranks, but always the gentleman with the ladies. Auditioning actresses never had to endure the casting couch with Douglas Fairbanks.

That evening, my boss marched into the living room of the suite his four female employees were sharing. He plopped his lithe frame into a cushioned chair with a great sigh. Jeanne, Miss Pickford's French maid, was reading in the adjoining room; Susan, the makeup girl, was out with Miss Pickford at an interview with *Screenland* magazine; Natalie, the wardrobe girl, was sitting on the sofa behind me, nearest the lamp, as she repaired one of Miss Pickford's puffy sleeves.

'A long day?' I asked, and before he could answer, 'Can I get you something to drink? The boy just brought up some fresh-squeezed orange juice for the icebox.'

He waved his hand to signal 'no thanks' and propped his feet up on the coffee table. 'Mary and I are dining in our rooms tonight. No guests. She's exhausted.'

'Is there anything I can do?'

'Not at the moment,' he said, running his fingers through his hair, which, I noticed, not for the first time, was looking a bit thin in front. He glanced at Natalie and seemed to make a decision. 'I just stopped by to get an update from you about the case you're working on. What's the latest with the murder? Who do you suspect?'

'That's the million-dollar question, isn't it? There are a lot of suspects, and I'm having trouble eliminating most of them.'

'Give me the current run-down. What's happened since dinner with Queen Marie?'

'In no particular order, then, we have the dead man's wife, Marjorie, who clearly hated her husband. She's been claiming they had reconciled, a story that saves her pride and bolsters her reputation. All too convenient as there's no one to refute it. She lied when she said she hadn't seen him in weeks. She was at the theater with a package for him the day he was shot.'

'Maybe she didn't see him. Maybe it wasn't a lie.'

'Possibly. But she was there and could easily have put the two live rounds in Norah's gun.'

'What was in the package?'

'Papers. Letters. Newspaper clippings. His high school diploma. Looked like miscellaneous stuff from a desk drawer. At least the names on the envelopes provided some leads. Which ultimately went nowhere, I'm afraid.'

'Like where?'

'Like to some of his conquests: a vaudeville dancer and a young musician, neither of whom had the motive or ability to switch the ammunition. There was nothing in the clippings that seemed relevant to his death, mostly just reviews. Which leads us to the next suspect, Wesley Crenshaw. A mild-mannered sort who has never gotten along with his handsomer cousin. He would seem to have no motive at all, until you realize they have a rich uncle with a couple of furniture factories and no sons of his own.'

'Ahh, I'm seeing the light. Wesley bumps off his cousin and inherits the fortune, eh?'

'That sums it up. But again, he wasn't in the theater that evening and sure, he could have paid someone to switch bullets, but why on earth do it that way?'

'I'm told that hiring a torpedo from Murder Inc. costs very little and the results are guaranteed.'

'Murder Inc.?'

'That's what these New Yorkers call their hometown gangster syndicate.'

'Ah, I see. While we're on the topic of gangsters, it seems our Allen had a penchant for poker and ponies, and evidently ran up some serious gambling debts. His wife feared they'd come after her to pay them off. At the funeral, Adele and I saw three thugs walk down the aisle to check out how dead the corpse was. They left satisfied. Didn't bother to stay for the service or the burial.'

'You think some gangsters did him in?'

I winced. 'Not really. If the Murder Inc. syndicate wanted to make an example of Crenshaw, they'd have done it in a way that made it obvious why he was killed. Gangsters don't switch bullets in a stage gun, they mow you down on the street in full view of the public so everyone gets the message. I don't know much about the New York crime world, but I can't think it's that different from ours in Los Angeles.'

'Sadly, you're right. If it's not gangsters, who else?'

'The stage manager has a liquor problem and it seems our Allen had a particular dislike for drunks, his father being one. Their quarrel goes back some years, but it flared up again recently when Bill Levine – that's the manager – came to work reeking of booze, or so said Crenshaw. Someone overheard Crenshaw threatening to get Levine fired if he didn't quit. Sounds serious, and Levine is the person who most easily could have swapped bullets.'

'So he's your lead suspect?'

'One of them. There's also Ted Youngerman, the understudy, who claims he didn't have any motive because he would have gotten the role in a few months anyway. Crenshaw was trying out for the lead in a new play, or so he says. But again, we can't check his story because Crenshaw is no longer speaking.'

'Is he, indeed, a "younger man" than Crenshaw?'

'Ha! No, actually he's about the same age as Crenshaw. Forty-ish.'

'Young indeed!' said the forty-three-year-old actor, slapping his knee.

'Then who can forget the undisputed actual killer, the dead man's former girlfriend, Norah, who pulled the trigger that sent the live rounds in his direction. She claims she didn't know they were live, and frankly, I believe her.'

'Well, Jessie, you've proven to be a pretty good judge of character in the past.'

'Thanks. I believe her, largely because her motive is so weak. Yes, he dumped her – she claims she broke it off with him, and I don't think that's true, but Norah's not some fragile ingénue. She's around my own age and must have had some experience with love's ups and downs. I don't think being dropped by a cad like Crenshaw would devastate her to the extent that she would kill him. And even if it did, there are, as you've noted, easier ways to go about it, ways that wouldn't implicate her. I think she's a pawn in the murder game, and so does Detective Quinn.'

'Sounds like it. What do you think of the detective?'

'An honest man. Head over heels for Adele, which is why he's allowed us to trail along behind him as he goes about questioning suspects. But he's pretty new at the job. A bit inept.' He was no Carl Delaney, I said to myself.

'Who else have you considered?'

'The rest of the cast. The stage crew. Ira Belkowitz, the director, and Ed Ricks, the playwright. Trouble is, none of them have any known animosity toward Crenshaw. Quite the opposite. He was pivotal to the success of their play. Every one of those people had a strong reason to keep him alive and working.'

'Don't tell me the master sleuth has reached a dead end!'

'Certainly not. But I admit, there are some puzzling aspects of the case that need answers. What bothers me most right now is the gunshots fired that night. First, Adele and I were in the second row and we clearly heard the gunshots. Unfortunately, the orchestra plays a drum crescendo that builds up to the gun firing, and that made it hard to tell exactly how many shots there were. I thought I heard three. Adele thought maybe four. Norah says she fired two, like always, and the cops found two shell casings in the revolver, so that must be right. One bullet struck Allen. Where's the other? Detective Quinn and I searched the stage but couldn't find a slug in any of the walls where it should have been.'

'Maybe it went out toward the audience, over their heads. It could be anywhere.'

'Maybe . . . but for that to happen, Norah would have had to point the gun toward the audience and she says she didn't.

Someone in the audience would have noticed. She said she just aims in the general direction of Crenshaw, who is standing in front of a wall, as you will remember. The police interviewed the members of the audience who were sitting in the first two rows and no one saw the gun pointed anywhere but at Crenshaw.'

'OK. You said "First." What's second?'

'Norah's aim. For someone who has never handled a gun, never done any target practice, never even loaded one herself, she certainly turned into Annie Oakley that night, hitting Crenshaw in the heart with one shot. Doesn't that seem miraculous to you?'

'Very.'

'And I asked her if she noticed anything different that night when she fired the gun. Did it feel different? She said no.'

'I see where you're going. Does firing blanks feel different from live ammunition?'

'Does it?'

'Most certainly. Have you never used a firearm?'

'I'm afraid not.'

'I've fired all sorts of firearms: pistols, rifles, shotguns, automatics, most everything. And I've fired blanks when filming. The recoil is noticeably less.'

'Would a novice like Norah, used to firing blanks, have noticed the increase in recoil if she was using live ammunition?'

'I can't believe she *wouldn't* notice that.'

'All I can figure is that Norah really *was* firing blanks, just as she always did. And if that's true, and if it's true that Adele and I heard more than two shots, then there was another gun firing the third shot.'

Douglas clasped his hands behind his head and stretched back, giving a long, low whistle.

Natalie, who had been silently sewing, could remain quiet no longer. She raised her head. Her eyes sparkled. 'That means Norah didn't kill Crenshaw after all, doesn't it? She was firing blanks like always, poor girl. So who fired the real bullet that killed him?'

Who indeed?

EIGHTEEN

When Douglas Fairbanks eased himself from the chair, I assumed he was going to leave. Instead he said quietly, 'Jessie, we need to talk about something else. Some business. Would you step out in the hall for a moment?'

Natalie caught his meaning. 'Excuse me, Mr Fairbanks, you don't need to do that. I was just getting ready to go downstairs, so I'll leave you to your work.'

As soon as she had slid out the door, Douglas sat back down. He fiddled with his tie, retied one of his shoes, ran his fingers through his hair, and cleared his throat. This display of nerves was not at all like Douglas. It was making me anxious.

Finally, I could wait no longer. 'What is it?'

'I have news, Jessie. Bad news, I'm afraid. I heard it just a couple hours ago . . . your friend David Carr is out of prison.'

My heart soared! David was free! Bad news? This was terrific news! 'What happened? Did the governor commute—'

'No, no. Nothing like that. I mean, I should have said, he's escaped from prison.'

'What!'

'I'm not sure of the details, but he and another prisoner were being transferred somewhere for some reason and they seized the opportunity to escape.'

'Oh no! How could he do that? He had only another year on his sentence. Now if they pick him up, he'll be put away for life.'

'It's worse than that. They killed two guards.'

My heart started pounding like a timpani drum. 'No! David couldn't do that! He wouldn't do that! He only killed in self-defense that time. He told me . . .'

Douglas spread his hands apart in a helpless gesture. My thoughts raced. What on earth had happened? There had to be more to the story than this. The other prisoner must have been the one to kill the guards. The other prisoner must have planned to escape and forced David to join him. David wouldn't do anything so foolish as to escape when he had already served nearly half his sentence. He would be out a little more than a year from now, scot-free. He would be able to return to Los Angeles and take up his life – our life together, an honest life with no ties to the criminal world, like he promised.

'I'm sorry, Jessie. I know you care for him.'

'When did this happen?'

'Four days ago, I think. I only just had word. My office manager read it in the newspaper and sent me a telegram after he'd made the connection.'

'Where is David now?'

'I have no idea. I expect he's in Mexico by now. If he's smart, he'll keep going to South America. If they catch him again . . .'

He didn't have to finish the sentence. I knew exactly what would happen to an escaped convict who had killed two guards. He'd be executed post-haste. Hanged by the neck until dead, if he wasn't gunned down for 'resisting arrest' first.

One thing I knew for sure: he wasn't in Mexico. I knew David. I knew how he thought. He was cleverer than that. The first place he'd go would be to my house in Hollywood. The house he put in my name before he went to prison. He'd go there to retrieve the suitcase full of cash from that drug deal that went sideways last year. He'd left it under my bed for safekeeping. I'd spent hardly any of it. He'd wouldn't expect to find me at home. My last letter told him that I was going to New York for a couple of weeks with Miss Pickford and Douglas. He'd find Myrna at home. Myrna Loy, an actress who lived with me along with Kit, a young girl who was deaf. Myrna had struggled for the last few years, getting insignificant parts in various film productions, but lately directors had been taking notice of her pretty face and exceptional acting abilities, and the parts were growing in import-ance. She had always liked David. I knew she'd invite him in. Maybe he'd clean up at the house. Get a shower and retrieve some of his clothes. Get the suitcase and get out quick before the police could trace him there.

But he wouldn't head to Mexico. It was too obvious. Everyone expected him to go south, so he'd head north instead, to Canada where he had underworld contacts from his days of smuggling Canadian liquor into the Northwest.

What then? Would he go back to his old ways, to what he knew best? He would certainly change his name – again – and change his appearance. What would happen then? Would he contact me? Would he tell me he couldn't live without me and urge me to come at once? Would I leave the job I loved and the friends I'd made and the city I'd come to think of as home for the man who meant the world to me? The man I loved. The man who'd promised me again and again that he was going straight.

A shot glass of whiskey materialized in front of my eyes. Douglas – I'd forgotten he was there. 'Oh, I'm sorry . . . I just . . .'

'Drink this.'

'I'm . . . I don't know what to do.'

'There is nothing for you to do. You can't help him and, anyway, he doesn't need your help. Your friend had some good qualities, Jessie, but this, well, this is beyond the pale. I will pass along any information I get in the future, but all you have to do now is continue with your job and solve your murder case here.'

I could only nod. The whiskey burned my throat. My hands trembled. My life had just spun upside down.

'Is there anything I can do for you at the moment? Maybe call your friend Adele to come over?'

'No, thank you. I'll be fine. This has just been a shock. It was so unexpected. But I'll be fine. I think I'll lie down.'

'I'll send up some food for you.'

'No, I'll throw up if I eat anything. I just want to lie down. When Natalie gets back, I'll ask her for some of her Veronal to help me sleep. Don't worry about me, Douglas. I'll be fine.'

He patted my head like I was a little girl. 'I know you will be. You're a strong one, Jessie Beckett.'

Minutes after he left, the telephone bell jangled loud and long. At first, I let it ring, then jumped up from the bed at the thought that it might be more news of David. The operator's nasal voice at the switchboard said, 'A call for Miss Beckett.'

'Put it through.'

A minute later, I was speaking to Adele. 'Jessie, I've got news! Fabulous news! Direct from Benjam— I mean, Detective Quinn. He's arrested Wesley Crenshaw for the murder of his cousin!'

'What? When?'

'An hour ago. It'll be in all the papers tomorrow. Isn't that fun, knowing something in advance, before anyone else knows? Sleuthing is so exciting!'

'It's not a game, Adele.'

'Sure, Jessie, I know that. I didn't mean . . .'

'Never mind. I understand. Did your detective say what evidence he'd found?'

'There was an anonymous tip telephoned into the police station saying that a police search of Wesley's house would turn up some incriminating evidence. Someone had seen a box of ammunition there. They relayed the message to Detective Quinn and he went right over with another cop and, sure enough! They found a red and white box of real bullets hidden in a cupboard, probably the cupboard in his living room, remember? And here's the kicker: it matched the brand that the theater uses – STANE – and, best of all, it was missing two shells! And when he learned that there had been four nephews mentioned in the uncle's will, and Wesley was the only one left alive, that made him think Wesley had maybe bumped off the others.'

I was momentarily at a loss for words. Just when I'd decided some unknown shooter had fired the shot that killed Allen Crenshaw, here came hard evidence to the contrary.

'Did he say who switched the bullets? Wesley couldn't have done it – he was at the factory that afternoon.'

'Quinn is going to check with his supervisor about that. If it's true, he must've gotten someone else to make the switch.'

'Well . . . that's good news, Adele.' And good timing. I couldn't work up any more enthusiasm for this case after what I'd just learned about David. 'I guess Detective Quinn won't be needing any further help from us.'

'I'm so pleased! We solved the case, didn't we, Jessie? Or maybe not exactly by ourselves, but we helped in important ways, right?'

'Right.' She must have heard the lack of enthusiasm in my voice, for she rang off a moment later. I lay back down on the bed and let my thoughts travel wherever they wanted to go.

I hated to admit it, but this solution left too many questions unanswered. Had I heard three or four shots that night? Where was the missing second slug? How did Norah get to be such a crack shot? Why didn't she notice a stronger kick when she fired the live rounds? Yes, Wesley had a motive, and now the police had evidence to back it up. But couldn't someone have planted that evidence – someone who had fired the deadly shot – in order to take the spotlight off himself? Or herself? Or themselves?

But I didn't care who had done it. If the detective wasn't very thorough, it wasn't my problem. I'd done what I could. If they had the wrong person, I didn't care any more.

In spite of the double dose of Veronal, I had a restless night. Vivid dreams woke me again and again. David standing in the wings, shooting at Allen Crenshaw and telling me he hadn't done it; Detective Quinn counting the number of bullets fired and complaining that there wasn't enough ammunition for another test because Douglas Fairbanks had stolen the box and put it in Wesley's cupboard.

I awoke, panting hard, my heart pounding. Thankfully, I hadn't disturbed Natalie, who was sleeping like the dead in the bed beside mine. At least someone could sleep! I didn't suppose Wesley Crenshaw was having a restful night in his miserable prison cell or that David Carr was snoring peacefully in his Canadian hideout. But someone out there was sleeping very soundly indeed. If I could only figure out who.

NINETEEN

'Jessie!' Jeanne's voice came through the bathroom door where I was just stepping out of the tub. 'Jessie, telephone! What shall I say?'

'Hold on, I'll be right there.' And, wrapping the towel around my dripping body, I tiptoed into the living room and put the receiver to my ear, hoping it was news about David.

'Is this Jessie Beckett?' a small female voice asked.

'It is. Who's calling please?'

'I'm Sarah Landry. We met at the Crenshaw funeral, remember?'

'Yes, of course. I remember you, Sarah. What can I do for you?'

'I rather hope I can do something for you. Did you lose a shawl at the church?'

'Yes!' I shouted so loudly that Jeanne and Natalie turned to stare. 'Yes! Yes! Yes! Did you find it?'

'I picked it up after you left, hoping I could locate you. I'm sorry it took me so long, but all I could recall was that you worked for Douglas Fairbanks and Mary Pickford, so I had to track down what hotel they are staying at, hoping they could tell me where you were. And you're at the same hotel!'

'You have no idea how grateful I am. You see, it isn't my shawl. It's a very special one that Adele Astaire lent me, her favorite, and losing it made me feel like a heel. She will be so relieved to have it back. Where can I come to fetch it?'

'If you don't mind, today would be good. I live near Columbia University.' She gave me an address on West 120th and before you could say Jack Robinson, I had dressed and flagged down a taxi.

Sarah Landry lived three floors up in a tidy red-brick apartment building. Large pots of white geraniums flanked the entrance and more geraniums overflowed the flower boxes that hung outside every first-floor window. She welcomed me at the door and invited me in for coffee.

'And here it is – your shawl. It's the most beautiful weave I've ever seen.'

I snatched it up and gave it a fierce hug. 'I'm *soooo* happy to have it back. I could never have replaced it. You see, it was a gift to Adele from Princess Mary of England. Adele pretended its loss didn't matter to her, but I know it did.'

'It was just luck that I saw it. Frankly, it was just luck that I was even there at the funeral. I nearly didn't go . . . you know, worried at how it would look to his wife, if she knew her husband had been courting me. I was so ashamed.'

'I don't believe she knew who you were. She may have been suspicious – after all, Allen had a lot of pretty, young girlfriends, but I don't think she knew you were among them. And you have nothing to be ashamed of. He's the cad. You didn't know he was married.'

The doorbell chimed. Sarah excused herself. There was a brief exchange of voices, after which she reappeared with a tall man dressed in an ill-fitting tan suit.

'Jessie, let me introduce you to a dear friend of mine, Peter VanHorn. Peter, this is Jessie Beckett, in town for just a few weeks with Douglas Fairbanks and Mary Pickford. Jessie is their assistant.'

'Wow!' he exclaimed, running his fingers through his dark hair so it stood up like a little boy's. And a little boy was exactly what he reminded me of, with a big smile that dug dimples into his cheeks and wide, round eyes that looked out at the world with wonder. He must have been at least thirty, but his energetic manner made him seem like a teenage boy. 'A pleasure, Miss Beckett, that's for sure. It's not every day I get to meet someone who rubs shoulders with film stars!'

'Good to meet you too, and please call me Jessie.'

'I've known Peter for years,' said Sarah. 'He was my brother's best friend.'

Was? The way she said it made me realize her brother was no longer with us. I didn't know what to say. Peter must have picked up on the awkward pause, because he hurried to fill in the blank. 'That's right. Simon and I met at Columbia when we were studying English lit, and we hit it off like we'd shared the same womb. He passed away seven years ago. Sarah and I miss him every day.'

'I'm so sorry,' I said uselessly, wondering at the cause of death for a young man. Considering his probable age, it could have been the Great War, but Peter had said 'passed away' not 'killed in action'. It was probably the Spanish flu or yellow fever or the measles – there were a lot of ways to die young. They didn't offer any further explanation and I couldn't ask.

Sarah shrugged. 'It was a long time ago. Although it seems like last week sometimes. He was a terrific big brother. So now Peter has taken over his job and big-brothers me all the time,' she teased. It crossed my mind that Peter might have been hoping for something more than big-brother status.

'I take it you've finished your studies, Peter?'

'Yes siree bob. Loved Columbia but glad to get out into the real world. Finished my master's degree in English literature and now I teach at Xavier. That's a boy's high school not too far from here. Our claim to fame these days is that Mayor Walker was one of our students!'

It seemed a bit much to mention that I had just dined with the mayor and his wife, so I let that slide. 'What do you teach?'

'English lit, natch. And I coach the baseball team and direct the theatricals too. It's a great life. Great boys, great colleagues.'

'My brother Simon was studying English literature too,' added Sarah. 'He lived and breathed literature.'

'And he was the smartest one in the program,' said Peter. 'Smartest by far. We took a lot of the same classes, so I know whereof I speak. His death took us all for a loop. Way too young, and so unexpected. But hey, how long are you in New York, Jessie?'

'I'm not really sure. It all depends on when Mr Fairbanks and Miss Pickford finish their work. It's not a holiday, but they've been kind enough to give me – to give all of us who came with them – time to ourselves while we're here.'

'Is another Fairbanks picture coming out soon, Jessie?'

'There's always another picture in the works, but it won't be released any time soon. Mr Fairbanks is writing the screenplay now. He calls it *The Gaucho*. He thinks it's going to be his best

yet, but he always says that. And he's usually right! We'll probably start filming when we get back to Hollywood. Look for it
in the middle of next year.'

'You don't mean to say that Fairbanks writes the screenplays
too?'

'Not all of them, but some, yes. Although you won't see
his name in the credits. He uses a pseudonym, Elton Thomas, his
middle names, when he writes. He's a man of many talents. He
does all his own stunts and directs and knows more about the
new color technology than almost anyone.'

'Man alive, I've never tried writing a screenplay, but I'll bet
its harder than it looks. I've written a couple of stage plays.
Nothing to brag about.'

'Nonsense, you should brag, Peter. Jessie, one of his plays
was staged by the Xavier schoolboys last year. It was quite the
hit with the parents!'

'Shucks, Sarah, that was just a little romp. Nothing like Simon
used to write. So, how did you two girls meet?'

'Jessie and I met at Allen Crenshaw's funeral. She left her
shawl and I picked it up.'

At the mention of Crenshaw's name, Peter's mood darkened
noticeably. He said nothing. Words were unnecessary. Peter's
disapproval of Crenshaw and his short relationship with Sarah
telegraphed loud and clear.

'It was a stroke of luck for me, because I'd borrowed this from
Adele Astaire and it was very precious to her.'

'And a stroke of luck for me because I got to meet Adele
Astaire! And talk to her. That was a thrill. I hear so much about
them, Adele and her brother. I wish I could meet Fred too.
They're saying he's as good a dancer as Adele, maybe even better.
And he does all their choreography. One of these days, I'm going
to see them on the stage.'

It was the least I could do. 'Would you really like to meet
him?'

'Are you kidding?'

'If you could come to the Astor Hotel tomorrow, I'm meeting
them there at noon. Adele will like to see you again and thank
you for rescuing her shawl, and I'll introduce you to Fred.' I was
relieved she hadn't said she wanted to meet Mary Pickford or

Douglas Fairbanks. I would impose on my friends, but never on my employers.

Her eyes lit up. 'Geez Louise. That would be . . . copacetic!'

'It would be my pleasure. And you could come too, Peter, if you like.'

'I'd like nothing more, but Monday is a school day for me.' He snapped his fingers. 'But at eleven, the boys have their sports segment, followed by lunch hour at one, and I think I can persuade a colleague to sub for me with the baseball team. That would give me a few hours to get away. I'd be honored to join you.' He put his arm around Sarah's shoulder and gave her a gentle squeeze. Was he a protective big brother or a jealous would-be lover?

Yet another person with a grudge against Crenshaw?

TWENTY

'Jessie! Over here.'

I wouldn't have noticed the two men sitting in the shadowy corner of the cave-like lounge off the Algonquin lobby if Douglas hadn't called my name. They were relaxing in two of the buttery soft leather chairs that clustered around a bar where nothing stronger than coffee, tea and fruit beverages was served to the general public. But it also doubled as a private club, where privileged members could legally enjoy the fine imported liquors and wines that hotel owners had stashed during the one-year grace period when the law allowed people to stock up before Prohibition began at the stroke of midnight on 20 January 1920. Heck, Miss Pickford's own mother had bought out an entire liquor store, moved the contents to her basement, and carried on as if nothing had changed – and she was not alone. Private clubs could legally serve their legal liquor to members until their supply was exhausted. I'd bet my last nickel that the Algonquin had laid in enough to last decades.

Douglas and the other man rose to their feet as I approached. The other man turned, drink in hand, and gave me a familiar grin. 'Miss Beckett! Delighted to see you.'

'Prince Nicholas just stopped by to say farewell,' said Douglas.

'You're leaving New York? I hope you and your mother and sister have had a good visit.'

'A most enjoyable stay. One to remember,' he replied smoothly.

'Where will you be going next?'

'To the famed falls of Niagara for pleasure, then on to Washington for some official business at the Romanian embassy. After that, she is keen to see the wilds of Florida and ride the Over-Sea Railroad to Key West. We shall sail for home from Miami.'

'That sounds lovely. I hope you have a wonderful trip.'

'His Highness has been sharing some very interesting information with me,' said Douglas, giving the prince a go-ahead look.

'Manners first. Would you care for a drink, Miss Beckett?'

My boss disapproved of liquor, so I wasn't about to order a highball. 'Cranberry juice, if you please,' I said. The prince raised one hand to signal the bartender.

'The other night at the theater, do you remember, Miss Beckett, that Mr Ricks told us about his service in the Royal Navy?'

'I do.'

'I have to say, it sounded a bit contrived to me. A man of his age, and an American to boot, on a British cruiser?'

'Americans did volunteer with the Allies before 1917. I know of several men who served.'

'Yes, yes. I didn't mean that. My apologies. Of course they did, and very welcome they were too. But they served mostly in the French or British armies or the air service before the RAF was formed. The oddity was that it seemed, to me at least, that Edward Ricks would have been rather old to have served in such capacity at sea. In any case, my sister and I were inspired by your sleuthing and decided to dig into the man's claims, as it were. I contacted Earl Beatty, First Sea Lord, and asked if an American had served on the *Aurora* during the Battle of Dogger Bank.' The young man must have noticed my mouth twitch in a half-smile at the thought of a lowly officer in the Royal Navy sending telegrams to the First Sea Lord, for he added quickly, 'The earl is a good friend of my mother and she gave permission, or I should not have presumed.'

'And you received a response?'

'Hours ago. David Beatty contacted the former captain of the *Aurora* to ask if there had been any Americans serving under him back in the day. He was familiar with all of his crew – there would have been about four hundred fifty, including officers, and of course he didn't know all of them by name, but he was certain that there had been no Americans among them. Three Canadians, he remembered, but they were all quite young. He checked his own records to be sure. No Americans, and no one by the name of Ricks.'

'The man is an out-and-out liar,' said Douglas. 'Why would anyone do such a thing?'

'It is disgraceful,' said the prince. 'Only a cad would try to claim the honor due those who served King and Country. No doubt he thought he could get away with it because no one here in New York would know of any seamen who had served on the *Aurora* who could disprove his falsehoods. And as the years pass, memories fade.'

'He won't get away with it any longer. I've half a mind to—'

Prince Nicholas laid his hand on Douglas's arm. 'You want to expose him, naturally, my friend, but I must beg you to remain silent. News like this would inevitably bring my sister and me into the picture as the ones who uncovered the lie, and my mother would not appreciate the publicity.'

'Yes, of course. I understand.' Clearly, Douglas's strong sense of fair play chafed under this restriction, but he would do nothing against the wishes of the queen. However, I wouldn't put it past him to whisper into Mr Ricks's ear the next time they met.

'So you see, Miss Beckett. I have solved your murder for you! It is obvious that the killer of the actor was Edward Ricks!'

'It is?'

'Any man who would make false claims about his wartime service is just the sort of bounder who would kill someone who threatened to expose his lies. No doubt the actor – what was his name?'

'Crenshaw.'

'No doubt this Crenshaw fellow learned about his falsehood and threatened to expose it. Too cowardly to kill the man himself, Ricks arranged for someone else to do it for him. The pretty actress Miss Rose. He boasts of being in the theater nearly every day, so he would have found it a simple trick to exchange the ammunition.'

'But how would Crenshaw have learned about Ricks not serving on the *Aurora*? He couldn't have sent telegrams to the First Sea Lord, as you did.'

'That part I cannot answer. But I'm certain you'll find the link.'

Douglas and I exchanged glances. 'And we appreciate your help in the matter,' he said, shaking the prince's hand as he wished him and his family a delightful tour.

'A nice young man,' commented Douglas as we watched the doorman spring to attention as His Highness strode out the front door. 'What do you think?' he asked, sinking back down into the chair.

'Nothing's impossible, I suppose,' I replied, sitting down, 'but that theory has serious flaws.' The prince's chair was still warm.

'Indeed. How would Crenshaw have discovered Ricks's lie about his service?'

'Exactly. His mother isn't a queen who can ring up her friend, the First Sea Lord, to check the records.'

'And former crew members from the *Aurora*, being British or Canadian, are unlikely to have encountered a playwright in New York.'

'Even if someone stumbled on such information, all Ricks would need to do is say the fella's mistaken. Suppose some English sailor happens to come to New York, meets Ricks, and says he served on the *Aurora* and doesn't remember Ricks. You heard Prince Nicholas. There were four hundred and fifty men on that ship, and you know how fluid things were in those days. On any ship, men were frequently added, transferred, or killed throughout the war. No one could know everyone. Ricks might be irritated to be challenged on his big lie, but I can't see him killing someone over an accusation he could so easily refute.'

In spite of everything, I was being dragged back into the investigation. Was Ricks behind the killing? Or had the cops arrested the right person when they hauled in Wesley Crenshaw?

TWENTY-ONE

The following morning, Jeanne, Susan, Natalie and I were finishing up with our room-service breakfast when Mary Pickford breezed through the door wearing a diaphanous silk kimono – a gift from the Japanese ambassador. Her dark blonde hair fell almost to her waist in soft ripples; her famous complexion glowed even without a drop of makeup. Anyone seeing her at this moment would have guessed her age at about twenty – no joke. Made up and coiffed correctly, she could pass on the screen for twelve.

She had been spending much of her time in New York promoting her latest film, *Sparrows*, which had just been released on 19 September. In it she plays Molly, the oldest of ten children hidden away in a 'baby farm' deep in the Southern swamplands, where unwanted children of unwed mothers are sold illegally for slave labor. Molly rescues the youngsters from their evil captor, and in the final scenes leads them to safety through the treacherous swamp, past hungry alligators. The picture cost an astonishing half a million dollars to make. Critics are calling it her finest work yet.

Susan, the makeup girl who always traveled with Miss Pickford, looked up anxiously from her toast and eggs. 'Oh, my, am I late? Did you need me?'

'No, no, dear, I'm taking the morning off and so should you. All of you. Have another cup of coffee. I won't need you until noon, Susan. I'm spending a lovely quiet morning in my room with a book, until the one o'clock interview with *Ladies' Home Journal*. After that, there's a photo shoot for the *Photoplay* cover, followed by one for *Screen Romance*, then at four, a meeting with the Pompeian Beauty people about my new face-cream line they're introducing next month – I'll want you there too, Susan. We'll be going to their corporate headquarters. I just stopped by to let you girls know our departure plans. It looks like we can start for home Saturday on one of the early afternoon trains.

We'll go through Chicago again but won't stay overnight this time, I'm sorry to say. We'll all be pretty busy until the moment we board, so I wanted you to have this morning free to get your personal affairs wrapped up.'

I figured that last bit was aimed at me. Meaning that I had a deadline of 30 October to solve the Crenshaw murder. Curiosity and my fierce sense of justice made it hard to leave something like this unfinished, but worry about David kept pushing any thoughts of the murder out of my head. I tried to console my conscience with the thought that Detective Quinn was perfectly capable, even if he was new to the job, and would surely rise to the occasion in my absence. I rang up Adele to give her the news, but her assistant said she was in rehearsal with Fred.

I knew exactly what I could do with my free morning. I could look into the other two dead nephews of Allen and Wesley Crenshaw. How had they died, and when? Detective Quinn was supposed to follow up, but I had my doubts about his ability. His previous investigations had not been particularly thorough. I had an idea how to proceed, but I needed a famous person's help.

When I had explained what I wanted to do, Douglas was keen to join me. The doorman hailed a taxi to take us to the *New York Times* offices on Broadway. 'The newspaper has some sort of library,' I told Douglas. 'It's called "the morgue", and it's where they keep files of photos and indexed daily papers that their reporters can look up when they need to find information. I called to ask if I could have a look and was told the service was only for newspaper employees. You can help me persuade them otherwise.'

You could always count on Douglas for an adventure.

Needless to say, we turned heads as we walked through the front door of the Times Tower and approached the receptionist.

'Good morning, young lady,' Douglas began. 'My name is Douglas Fairbanks, and I'm wondering if my colleague and I might be shown to your library. I believe you call it "the morgue"? We would appreciate the opportunity to ask some questions of the librarian.'

The receptionist managed to pull herself together enough to pick up the telephone and dial a number. Within minutes, a sharply dressed young man strode out of the elevator to greet us.

'May I ask what it is we can help you with, Mr Fairbanks?'

'My colleague here, Miss Beckett, and I would like to get some information about the death of two New Yorkers. We believe they would have had obituaries in your newspaper, but we don't know when. I'm afraid we don't know the whole names either. Is there some way we can look those up?'

'There certainly is. We have an alphabetical file of all our obituaries dating back to 1896 when the Sulzbergers assumed the publishing. Right this way, sir.'

In no time an awe-struck librarian had located the two obituaries, one for Daniel Crenshaw and the other for Andrew Crenshaw. Daniel had died of the Spanish flu eight years ago at the tender age of fourteen. Andrew was drafted in 1917 and died in the Argonne Forest on 2 November 1918. Mustard gas. I winced. A hard way to go, by all accounts.

Douglas was profuse in his thanks to the librarian, happily writing a friendly note and signing his name for her before we left.

'There you go, Jessie,' he said as we climbed into another taxi. He rubbed his hands together with satisfaction. 'Was that a help?'

'Very much. Detective Quinn suspects Wesley Crenshaw of engineering Allen's death on the stage, but I have always had my doubts. I think the box of ammunition could have been planted in his house by the real killer. It's just too pat. The detective also suspects that Wesley had something to do with the deaths of his other two cousins, because now that all three are gone, he inherits the uncle's factories. I admit, I put the idea into his head, but these obituaries prove that was impossible.'

'Good work.'

'I'll pass the information along to Quinn as soon as we get back.'

'I hope he's not resentful. You seem to be showing him up at every turn.'

'I'm trying hard not to. And he's a decent sort. Too new at the job to think he knows it all. I'll just let him know what we did and let him take the credit.'

'Thatta girl. There's always plenty of credit to go around.'

No sooner had I returned to my room and made the call to Detective Quinn than the telephone rang again.

'Front desk calling for Miss Beckett.'

'This is she.'

'A gentleman wishes to meet you in the lounge, if you are not busy.'

'His name?'

'He prefers not to give a name, miss. He says he's planning to surprise you.'

That sounded like some trick Fred would pull, but he had morning rehearsal. Prince Nicholas was off to Niagara Falls by now and I'd just spoken with Detective Quinn. Who else did I know in New York? Surely not Ted Youngerman?

'What does this mystery man look like?'

'Dark hair. Chevron mustache and a goatee. Thin, thirty-five, maybe?'

That description fitted no one I knew. I meant to tell the clerk to say I was not in, but that pesky curiosity put other words in my mouth. 'I'll be right down.'

Dimly lit as usual, the Algonquin lounge was empty at this hour of the morning. Either it was too early for the bartender, or he was in the stockroom counting bottles – the place was quiet save for a lone gentleman leaning against one of the columns, his face obscured in the shadows, his ankles crossed in the casual pose of a carefree man-about-town. Something about that pose made my heart skip a beat. Then I threw myself at him with a stifled cry of joy.

'David!'

He hugged me tight with strong arms, lifting me a few inches off the ground and swinging me in a circle while he laughed with satisfaction at my reaction.

'Surprised you, huh, kid?'

I couldn't speak. I squeezed back tears and covered his face with kisses. 'It's you! It's really you!'

'I wondered if you'd recognize me.'

'Anywhere,' I laughed again, glancing about to make sure no one was within listening distance. The few guests in the lobby were paying no attention to the couple in the empty lounge. The young colored boy who operated the elevator had his eyes on us, but he was too far away to hear our conversation. 'Oh my gosh, let me look at you.' I held him at arm's length and squinted. 'What have you done with yourself, David?' I managed to ask, although I knew very well why he'd dyed his blond hair and let his mustache and beard grow. It was so good to see him, I could hardly speak.

'Jack Wilson, at your service, ma'am. New name, new clothes, new face, and a whole new life ahead of me.'

'Oh, this is wonderful! Marvelous! I've missed you so very, very much! And worried every minute since I heard the news.' The light was dim but I could still see his cheeks were hollow where they hadn't been before, and his body was noticeably thinner than it had been last year. And that mustache and beard made him look older. I touched a scar on his forehead that was still swollen. 'How did you . . .? What . . .?'

He eased me over to the darkest corner and pulled me on to his lap. 'Hang on there, kid. Give me a chance and I'll tell you everything. But first, tell me about you.'

'Me? You know all about me. I've been telling you everything in my letters. Did you get them? I wrote every week.' I couldn't prevent an accusatory tone from staining my words with resentment. I had written faithfully every single week with only one response! It hurt more than I wanted to admit.

'I got 'em. They were the only good thing that happened to me in there, I can tell you that.'

'But you never wrote back. Not after that first letter.'

'What was I going to say? Lousy food, filth everywhere, crappy company. Prison's a scary place. I went to sleep every night hoping I'd be alive in the morning. I didn't want to worry you. There was nothing I could say in a letter that you would want to hear.'

A letter now and then would have meant the world to me, but complaining would do no good now. I was too happy and, now that the shock had passed, too troubled.

'You escaped,' I said hesitantly, like I was afraid of hearing his story. Which I was.

'You heard about that?'

'Douglas Fairbanks heard from someone at his office. He told me.'

'Well then, you only know what they wrote in the papers, and you're smart enough to know that isn't the whole story.'

Sure I was. I was also smart enough to remember how he had gulled me before with a phony tale about his background. So he'd changed his name to Jack Wilson, had he? When I first met him, he was David Murray. Once upon a time, I had thought that was his real name, one that he'd changed to Carr when he fled the Oregon police to Los Angeles. Now David Carr was Jack Wilson. Was any of those his real name? Well, you've changed your name over the years too, said a niggling little voice. Yes, many times, for many reasons. But never to evade the law.

'So, tell me the whole story.'

For an answer, he stood up and walked behind the bar. With no one there and no one watching from the lobby except the elevator boy, he helped himself to a bottle of something and poured a glass. 'Want one?'

'No thanks.'

Returning to the corner, he shoehorned his body beside mine into the big chair and took a gulp. 'I've been in jail before, for a few nights. Like you, eh? But a real prison sentence is something else. Two and a half years, man, that's a lifetime when you're in hell. You don't want to know about that. I don't think I could have made it the whole two and a half years without losing my mind or my life, so when the chance came, I took it. Me and another prisoner, a guy from Oklahoma serving five years for manslaughter – we were being transferred to San Quentin. I was hearing all about that place. Like, if you think Central Number One is bad, wait 'til you get to San Quentin. Anyway, him and me were in a van going north when we got ambushed by some buddies of his, there to break him out. We overpowered the guards and got away.'

'The newspapers said they were killed.' I desperately wanted to hear him say that was wrong, that the guards were alive or merely wounded or beaten up, or that the other prisoner's gang had killed them and he hadn't been involved. He denied nothing.

'They were sadistic pigs. I knew them from the jail. They got what they deserved.'

'But now . . . now you'll be wanted for murder, not just

bootlegging. The cops hate people who kill cops. Or prison guards. They'll never let up searching. You'll never be safe.'

He shrugged. 'Anyway, I split from those guys right away. They wanted me to come with 'em, but I figured the law was going to throw everything they had into chasing after the gang, and they wouldn't realize I wasn't with them until they caught up to them, which happened two days ago.'

'Did the cops capture them?'

'Capture? Hell, no. Shot 'em all dead for "resisting arrest", said the papers.'

'Oh.' Exactly what I had feared. No one would bother taking escaped cop-killers alive.

'The minute I split from the gang, I headed back to LA quick as I could. I went to our house.'

'I knew you would go there first. When I heard about your escape, I knew you would go there. For the valise.'

He took another swig of his drink. 'Myrna let me in. Great gal, Myrna. Didn't know anything about the valise. You didn't tell her, did you?'

'Are you kidding? I didn't breathe a word to anyone. Least of all your shyster lawyer.'

'Good girl. Yeah, I didn't trust him either. Anyway, I left you some money, under your pillow, to tide you over in an emergency. Myrna gave me some hair color she had left over from one of her movie roles, and in less than an hour, I'd gotten into my clean clothes, packed my suitcase, and split with the cash. The cops would expect someone like me to head south, so Mexico was out of the question. I considered Canada, but they'd think of that too, eventually: a fella like me who used to run booze across the Canadian border would have friends up there. Anyway, I told Myrna to tell the cops, when they tracked me to the house, that I had said something about Mexico and Canada, figuring that would keep them busy looking both ways. And I made sure to go east.'

I counted the days in my head. It had been almost a week since he'd escaped. It takes four days to cross the country, five if you're not in a hurry or can't make good connections. He would have been in a hurry, and he had plenty of cash to buy speed. He must have arrived in New York a day or two ago.

'You knew I was here. You knew from my letters. I told you I was going with Miss Pickford and Douglas.' He'd come to find me! He'd come to get me. He was going to take me with him wherever he was going. We would disappear together into the wilds of Australia or Rhodesia or the Argentine. A thrill of excitement surged through my body like an electric current. 'Did it take you long to find me? I thought I told you in my letter that we were staying at the Algonquin.'

'Yeah, I knew that. I had some business to take care of first.'

'Oh,' I said, rather deflated. I wasn't the first thing he did when he arrived. 'What business was that?'

He returned to the bar and refilled his glass. Then he stood, leaning up against the bar, looking at me with ice blue eyes that had turned gray like cold steel. His voice was harder than I remembered too. 'Bought a new wardrobe to start. Had a barber fix up my mustache and beard. Whaddya think?'

'Makes you look older. Certainly different. No one will link you to any photos of David Carr that might be circulating. What business did you have here?'

'I needed to meet with some businessmen about setting me up again.'

'Businessmen?'

'You heard of Arnold Rothstein, the guy they call "the Brain"?'

'Rings a bell. Isn't he the fella who fixed the 1919 World Series?'

'Never been proven. The Brain was the first to get it that there was big money in bootleg booze. He started importing from Europe, Canada, everywhere, even before Prohibition had gone into effect. He saw the writing on the wall, as they say, and he set up distribution systems in New York and Philadelphia, and other guys – me included – all over the country followed his example. He's the biggest operator in the city, probably in the country, and he'd heard of me and my little game in Oregon. I was flattered, I can tell you.'

My heart fell into my stomach. 'You're going to work for Murder Inc.?'

'You gotta understand, Jessie, bootlegging is what I do best. The Brain asked me to meet him again this afternoon at his place over on Forty-Ninth so he can introduce me to his main man,

Lucky Luciano. They're planning to expand into Cuba. He says
he can use a slick operator like me, one with leadership experience and a proven record. He wants me to go to Havana and
set up the networks, buying and selling, with Havana as the
hub of the wheel.'

A wave of nausea swept over me, I swallowed hard to keep
from throwing up. This was what he had come to New York for:
not to find me, but to hook up with the gangsters in the Murder
Inc. syndicate and help them spread their tentacles overseas. He
would leave the States for Cuba and never return. He'd become
like them, ruthless killers. Hell, who was I kidding? He already
was one of them. I had been fooling myself ever since he'd come
to Hollywood, convincing myself that he'd gone straight and
we'd have a regular life together. What a sucker.

'What do you think, kid?'

I blinked. It was worth one more try. 'I think we could do
something better, David. Together, just the two of us. We could
take the valise with all that cash and go to Australia and set
up there, buy a ranch or a general store. No one would look
for us there. We could go straight. You used to work in your
mother's store, you know how to do that. You used to work on
a ranch too, or you told me you did.'

He just smiled that clever smile of his. And I saw something
in that smile, something that told me he hadn't come to New
York to take me with him at all. He had come to cement this job
with Rothstein.

'Going straight! That's exactly what I'm doing. Don't you see,
kid? I won't be breaking any laws in Cuba. Buying and selling
liquor isn't illegal there. Neither are casinos. Gambling at race-
tracks is legal. It's perfect. I'm Jack Wilson, respectable
businessman. I'm doing what you always wanted – going straight.'

Straight to the grave, more like it. I used to think David could
sell ice to the Eskimos, but he'd taken me in once too often. I
wouldn't fall for it again. He had no intention of taking me with
him to Havana – not today anyway; maybe not ever. I was already
in the past. Just another one of his former lovers that he was
'crazy about' but had never loved.

'When do you leave?' I asked dully.

'Right after the meeting with Rothstein and Luciano. Rothstein has booked passage on a ship to Havana tonight for me with another of his agents, a Jew name of Meyer Lansky, so we'll have plenty of time to get acquainted. But don't worry, you're coming too. Just not right now. Give me some time to get set up in a nice house – two houses: one in the city and another one in the mountains where the cool breezes blow. I'll hire some servants – you'll be a queen. I'll get the job squared away and send for you. I can't write to you at your house address. The detectives will be watching your mail to learn where I am. I'll get a message to you at the studio.'

'They'll be watching that mail too.'

'Yeah, you're probably right. Well, I'll figure out something, never fear.'

'You always do.'

To be fair, I think David truly believed what he was saying. But I had turned to fortune-telling, and I could see deep into the future as he arrived in Havana, strode down the gangplank straight onto the bustling docks and arranged for rooms at a fancy hotel. Within two or three days, he'd have bought himself a cozy cottage near the water, hired servants – they come cheap in other countries, I'm told – and opened an office for an import/export company with a pretty Cuban secretary to answer the telephone. He'd contact suppliers in Ireland, France and Italy, and put out feelers to buyers in New Orleans, Tampa, Miami, Galveston and Corpus Christi. It wouldn't be hard. He was, as he had said, good at bootlegging. He meant to notify me when everything was set up. But he'd put it off, again and again, waiting for the right time, until finally, he'd let it go, like he did the letters from jail. A pretty señorita would come along – maybe that secretary – and move into his cottage, just temporarily, at first, and then, little by little, he'd forget about me. Oh, he'd not really forget; we had made too many memories together. But he'd remember me fondly and the great times we had, and he'd move forward without me.

'Take care of yourself,' I said, pretending it was all still possible. 'I'll be counting the days.'

'Sure thing. Well, kid,' he said with a glance at his watch. 'I gotta run if I'm going to make it to Lindy's on time. The Brain hates to be kept waiting.' He stood up, pulled me against him, and we gave the elevator boy an eyeful, that's for sure. I wanted to say 'I love you' one more time, but the words stuck in my throat. His words flowed easily, as always. 'I'm crazy about you, kid. Always have been.'

And he was. But it just wasn't enough. I blinked back the tears as he walked across the lobby, out the door, and out of my life.

TWENTY-TWO

Tuesday noon found me at the Astor with Sarah Landry and Peter VanHorn at my side, both dressed to the nines, watching for Fred and Adele to come down to the lobby. When they stepped off the elevator, Sarah gave a tiny shriek of excitement. I introduced everyone, and Fred invited us all to go into the Palm Garden for champagne. 'We have time for a chat and a glass of bubbly before Adele and I run off to meet our director for lunch.'

'And I have news,' whispered Adele in her most mysterious voice.

Fred had reserved a corner table between two enormous palm trees that spread their fronds over our heads. 'If it rains, we'll be protected by the foliage,' he joked, holding a chair for Sarah. Her eyes widened as they took in the bright floral arrangements, the tables set with elegant porcelain china and gleaming sterling silver, and the hanging ferns. Her head tilted up at the gargantuan chandelier that hung from the top of the Italianate dome far above. 'It's like a little slice of Italy,' sighed Adele, which was amusing since none of us had ever been to Italy. Two ice buckets with two bottles of Veuve Clicquot awaited. Fred waved away the waiter and did the honors personally, popping the cork with a flourish and filling each crystal goblet with the sparkling liquid. I suspected Sarah had never tasted champagne.

'Is it legal?' she whispered to me.

'No one is going to raid the Astor,' I assured her.

Fred led the conversation in his witty way, flitting from one subject to another like he was tap dancing on stage. Sarah was enchanted, and even Peter fell under the spell of this charming sister-and-brother team. I was the literal fifth wheel, but it was a nice feeling to see them getting along so famously.

'I cannot begin to thank you for rescuing my shawl,' said Adele as we settled into our seats.

'It was my good luck to have noticed it,' Sarah replied. 'You and Jessie were distracted by your investigation. Imagine, you two, helping the detective – that is so fascinating! Tell me, what's the latest news?'

'Detective Quinn has his culprit locked securely in jail.'

'And who has done the murder?'

'Wesley Crenshaw, Allen's cousin. An anonymous tip sent the detective to his home where they found the box of real bullets, minus two, hidden in a cupboard. That and his motive – an inheritance – was enough evidence to arrest him. Jessie thinks he might have been set up, don't you, Jessie?'

'It's a possibility.'

'No matter, I have news that throws a monkey wrench into the machinery.' Adele looked about dramatically, as if to make sure no one nearby could hear her, and in a lowered voice said, 'Norah Rose has disappeared.'

I was shocked. 'Where did you get that?'

'Direct from Benjamin Quinn. He told me this morning when we met for coffee. She's vanished into thin air.'

'What's his opinion? Does he think she's dead?' I asked.

'Ira Belkowitz – he's the director – telephoned Quinn when Norah didn't show up at the theater yesterday. Quinn took another cop with him to her address, a boarding house in the theater district that's popular with actors and actresses, and found her room clean as a whistle. She'd done a flit.'

'No one cleans out their closets while they're being abducted,' I said, 'so we can cross that out. Why on earth would Norah have run away? She had a job any actress would kill for. Uh, sorry . . . poor choice of words.'

'Maybe she was traumatized by her part in Allen's death,' said Fred. 'Having killed someone, even accidentally, would weigh heavily on anyone's conscience. Even if she wasn't to blame, she still pulled the trigger.'

'But that was nearly two weeks ago. Surely she'd have had a nervous breakdown the day or two after his death, not two weeks later. If she ran off without telling anyone, she was afraid of someone. She's hiding. Did she see something, overhear something? Something that made her think her life was in danger? Has Detective Quinn tried to trace her? Has he spoken to her close friends at the theater about where she might be? Norah might have told a friend where she was going.'

'He did question the cast,' said Adele, 'but no one had anything to contribute.'

'A scared girl might run home to her parents. Has Quinn checked the city directory for Roses? A shame it's such a common name; there must be pages of them. But I'll bet Norah Rose is her stage name. It sounds like one, doesn't it, Adele? If we can find someone who knew her well, we might learn her real name, which would let us locate her family.'

'I'll nose around at the theater and see if she had any particular friends.'

'No guarantees, but it's a lead worth following.'

'You can't leave it alone, can you?' teased Adele. 'A shame you're leaving us on Saturday.'

'Oh, I didn't tell you? Douglas said I should stay as long as it takes to settle this case. They're still leaving Saturday, but he's paying for my room at the Algonquin for as long as I need to stay.'

'He's a brick!'

I nodded my agreement. 'He's always been interested in solving crimes. He encourages me. Often he helps with his opinions, which are usually insightful, or his contacts, which are legion.'

'This play has certainly brought good luck to understudies,' mused Fred. 'First Crenshaw dies, now Norah vanishes. I hope her understudy was prepared to step into the role. What did you think of the play, Sarah?'

'Oh, well . . . I haven't seen it. I didn't know Allen was in it until I read about his death in the paper. He never talked about his career, other than to say he had the occasional small part on Broadway. I didn't know he was a leading man.'

Once again, I marveled at Sarah's estimation of Allen Crenshaw and how it differed from the Allen Crenshaw everyone else seemed to dislike. Could he have been genuinely in love with the girl? So much in love that his personality softened? Stranger things have happened.

'And you, Peter? Have you seen it?'

He gave a rueful smile. 'A teacher's salary doesn't stretch to many Broadway plays, I'm afraid. I would like to see it, though; in fact, now I'm determined to go, the hell with the cost. I have an interesting connection to the playwright, Edward Ricks. Back before he was a famous Pulitzer Prize winner, he was a professor at Columbia. I had a class with him.'

'No kidding!' I said.

'No kidding. It was seven years ago.'

'What sort of class was he teaching?'

'As I recall, he taught several classes in the English department. The one I took – with Sarah's brother, by the way – was playwriting.'

'Was he a good teacher?' I wondered aloud.

'Pretty good, I guess. Tough. Critical. But that's all for the best. After all, you don't learn from compliments! They only make you complacent. I have to admit, I learned a lot in Professor Ricks's class. He doesn't teach any longer, of course, now that he's hit big time.'

'My brother and Peter were getting their master's degrees in literature,' Sarah explained for the benefit of Adele and Fred. 'My brother died shortly before graduation.'

The two expressed their sympathy. This time, I was bold enough – or crass enough – to ask, 'Was it an illness? He was so young.' She took a sip of champagne before answering, and I regretted my indiscretion. 'I'm sorry, Sarah, forgive me. I shouldn't have asked such a personal question.'

'No apologies necessary. I'm happy to talk about Simon. It keeps him alive in my heart when I can share him with others. I was just thinking about my answer to your question, because it's not an easy one. He just went to sleep and died. The doctors couldn't say why for sure. He was only twenty-seven, my age right now.' Peter reached across the table to pat her hand.

'When he didn't show up for evening class,' Peter said, 'someone went to his boarding house and the landlady let him in. They found him in bed. He died very peacefully. There was an autopsy but it revealed nothing. The doctor said sometimes a heart just stops or a blood vessel in the brain just bursts. It was a great loss to his family and friends.'

'Well,' said Fred, in an attempt to lighten the tone, 'I think you should both see the play. I'm going to call up for tickets to be held for you at the box office. Would tonight suit you? Tomorrow night?'

'Oh, we couldn't put you to the trouble . . .' protested Sarah, but Fred brushed aside her objections.

'Nonsense, it's no trouble at all. Adele and I can get complimentary tickets for any play on Broadway, whenever we like. It's the least we can do to thank you for rescuing Adele's shawl. And what about you, Jessie? You've seen it already, but would you care to go another round?'

'I've seen it twice, or one and a half, if you count the first time when the play was cut short. But truthfully, I wouldn't mind watching Norah Rose's understudy tackle her role, if tickets are available.'

'Probably won't be front row or box, but we'll get what's there.'

We settled on the following night and made arrangements to meet at the Morosco Theater box office ten minutes before the play. Fred and Adele made their apologies and left for their lunch meeting with their director. Sarah and Peter and I stayed long enough to polish off the last of the Veuve Clicquot. It's a sin to waste good champagne.

TWENTY-THREE

Turns out Norah Rose was her stage name. Adele made some inquiries after she called for tickets that afternoon and learned the identity of one of Norah's friends – another actress who lived in the same rooming house. The friend was as shocked as everyone else when she found out that Norah had done a flit. Unfortunately, she had no idea where she might have gone; however, she did know a bit about her background.

'She told me Norah once mentioned growing up in Ohio, but she couldn't recall a town or city or anything more specific than that. And her given name really is Norah, but your hunch was right about Rose being a stage name. Her real last name is Smith.'

I groaned aloud. The most common name in America! Highly undesirable for anyone hoping to make a splash on the stage. A more memorable moniker would look better in lights. I wasn't surprised Norah Smith plumped for Norah Rose, but it made tracing her nigh on impossible.

I passed this along to Sarah Landry while we waited for Peter VanHorn that night at the Morosco box office.

'Gosh,' she said. 'I had no idea actresses changed their names that often.'

'All the time. Mary Pickford's original name was Smith too. Gladys Smith. It was judged too ordinary by the great Belasco, who chose her new name.'

'Who?

'David Belasco, the legendary impresario, director and playwright?'

'Oh, right. I've heard of him. He's pretty old now.'

'He managed her early career on Broadway. Truth be told, there are precious few actors or actresses in vaudeville who haven't changed their names, including Adele and me, and virtually all burlesque performers use pseudonyms. In legit and films, it's a bit less common, but it still happens, especially with foreign actors who have names that are hard for Americans to pronounce or remember. Rodolfo Guglielmi thought Rudolph Valentino would be easier for Americans to remember.'

'Yeah,' she giggled, 'I guess it is easier. Valentine, Valentino. Makes you think of hearts and love.'

'Exactly. And Apolonia Chalupiec? Who do you think that is?'

'Um . . . I give up.'

'Pola Negri. Shorter, simpler. What about Marion Douras?'

'Marian Davies?' she guessed.

'Right! Sounds more English than Douras. And you know Fred and Adele were born Austerlitz, not Astaire.'

'You don't say!'

'Their mother thought Austerlitz sounded too German.'

Just then, Peter VanHorn walked up, gave Sarah a peck on the cheek, and shook my hand. We ambled into the theater lobby and handed our complimentary tickets to the usher, who showed us to three very respectable seats at the edge of the center of the tenth row. Peter sat between us. Several times, I stretched my neck to see if Edward Ricks was in his usual seat in the front row far right, thinking Peter would probably like to pay his respects to his old professor. But Ricks wasn't in attendance tonight.

The lights dimmed. The audience hushed. With a rise of his baton, the conductor launched into the peppy overture. Behind the ruby-red curtain, the actors were taking their places. As the music slowed to its more somber finish, the curtain rose on the opening scene, a French battlefield smothered with smoke. The drum section provided explosions and the rat-a-tat of machine guns. I'd seen it all twice, so everything felt comfortably familiar, which meant I could devote my attention to the lead actress, Pauline Hill, a talented young woman. Neither pretty nor slender enough to make it in the pictures, where every successful actress had to be rail thin and drop-dead gorgeous, Pauline was perfect for her role in this play. I wondered briefly how she was reacting to the loss of her two main colleagues, but could find nothing to indicate that the understudies had thrown her off her game. I studied the way she used the tempo and tone of her voice, her body language and her facial expressions to portray a character with two personalities, one that was hidden from the outside world, and to draw the audience into the story.

I was so absorbed in the play that I was late to notice Peter's reaction. Sitting beside me, he had gone still as a stone except for his fingers, which twitched rhythmically in time to the drumbeats, squeezing his thighs in what I assumed was a nervous tic. I paid little attention at first, but then I heard his breathing become labored, and I became concerned.

'Are you feeling all right, Peter?' I whispered. 'Do you need to leave?' He seemed not to hear me, so I asked again, 'Are you ill? Do you need to take a break outside?'

'Is intermission almost here?'

'About ten or fifteen minutes more. Are you all right?'

'Fine. Yes . . . Fine, I can wait. I dare not miss a minute of this.'

The story had reached a tense moment, but it didn't seem to affect anyone else in the audience as seriously as it did Peter. There was the usual coughing, squirming and whispering that one expects at a play, not frozen concentration. I looked past him to Sarah, but her attention was on the stage, not on her friend. Out of the corner of my eye, I kept close tabs on him for the remainder of Act One. Thankfully, his condition didn't seem to worsen. Did this story hit too close to home? Had he served in the Great War? He was of the age to have been drafted, so perhaps he had fought in France and this brought back horrible memories or rekindled some of the shell shock that was so widespread among soldiers in the trenches.

Finally the curtain dropped; the lights came up. The audience breathed as one and came to life. I put my hand on Peter's shoulder. 'Peter, are you feeling unwell? Let's stand up and go to the lobby for a stretch and something to drink. Maybe you would like to leave?'

That alerted Sarah to his odd reaction. 'What's wrong, Peter? You look like you've seen a ghost.'

His eyes had glazed over, as if they were peering inward, seeing nothing of the world in front of them. His hands twisted nervously.

'I think I know this play,' he said hoarsely. 'But how can that be?'

Sarah took his arm and guided him out of row ten up the aisle to the lobby, where I stood in a short line to purchase some juice for all of us. Peter gulped his gratefully. The cold liquid seemed to loosen his tongue.

'I couldn't figure it out at first, and then it seemed too incredible, but this play is very familiar. I swear I knew what was going to happen before it happened. I knew who was going to say what before they said it. But I'm sure I've never seen it before.'

'Could you have read a review?' I asked. 'A detailed discussion of the plot? Maybe overheard people talking about the story?'

'I don't think so. I didn't know anything about the play before we arrived, only that it was Professor Ricks's and that it had won the Pulitzer. Now that I've had time to think, I realize this is very similar to one Simon wrote. That was seven years ago and my memory may be at fault, but how can I know all this unless I've read it before?'

'How did you come to read one of Simon's plays?'

'I read it in our critique group. Not all of it, perhaps, but parts.'

'What's a critique group?' I asked.

He shook his head as if ridding his brain of cobwebs. 'We had a group. Back in graduate school. Simon, me and Bob Holdrup. All three of us taking Ricks's class in play-writing. We read each other's work and tried to make it stronger. Simon's play was like *Rules of Engagement* but with a different title.'

'Exactly like *Rules of Engagement*?'

'I can't remember it that clearly. I don't know what to think.'

I knew what to think. I just didn't want to say it.

TWENTY-FOUR

My heart was beating hard with anticipation as we returned to our seats for Act Two. My interest in observing Norah's understudy had evaporated in light of these new thoughts that wrestled in my head for supremacy. I glanced repeatedly toward the front row to see if Edward Ricks had joined the audience for Act Two. Tonight the meddlesome playwright was nowhere to be seen.

Ever since the murder of Allen Crenshaw in Act Two Scene One, audiences had grown eerily silent as that moment approached, as if waiting – even hoping – for a similar catastrophe to befall the lead actor. Each time the gun went off and Ted Youngerman fell to the ground clutching his leg rather than his heart, the audience exhaled in relief. Which is what happened tonight. Norah's understudy did a fine job in the role; not as good as Norah, perhaps, but I noted little difference in her delivery or her actions. What I did notice in that scene was the drum roll.

Or absence thereof.

Someone had deleted the drum crescendo that Adele and I remembered, the noise that had obscured the number of gunshots when Norah fired. Tonight, without the drums, it was easy to hear two distinct shots. No one tonight would mistake two for three or four, as we had. As we were meant to. Who altered the orchestra's score? There were only three possibilities: the conductor, the director or the playwright.

The 'why' was easy – to cover up the sound of an extra gunshot or two. Once that had been accomplished, the drum crescendo could be deleted.

If I had been suspicious before, I was now utterly convinced that Norah's gun had not been tampered with that night at all. We had been running around like headless chickens, trying to figure out who had switched blanks for live rounds, when no one had done any such thing. Norah had fired two blanks just as she always did. Someone else had shot Allen Crenshaw. Someone in the wings below the spot where Norah was standing on the platform eight feet above the stage, waiting for her entrance. Suddenly, the likely reason for Norah's flit became clear. She had put together two unrelated details: the fact that she hadn't felt a stronger recoil when she pulled the trigger, and her observation of a person lurking in the wings moments before she fired. She must have concluded that the lurker had shot Crenshaw and would likely do the same to her if he realized what she had seen. So she packed up and fled.

Adele and I had been up on that platform a few days ago with the stage manager, when he was showing us where he placed the pistol. As I recalled that view from on high, I realized that a person could see down into the wings from that vantage point. Edward Ricks was often in the wings. He had been at the theater that night – we'd seen him in the front row. And when Adele had gone to introduce me during intermission, he was not in his seat. Had he gone into the wings then to prepare to shoot the actor? Had Norah seen him from her platform? And if she had seen him, and if he had been holding a gun, why hadn't she told anyone? It would have been in her own self-interest to throw the blame on to someone else.

But why on earth would a playwright want to kill the lead in the play that was making him famous? If Peter VanHorn was correct, it was because Professor Ricks had stolen the play from one of his conveniently deceased students, a man named Simon Landry, and somehow, Crenshaw had discovered that when he was romancing Sarah Landry. There were a lot of blank pages in this story, but I thought I was reading the right book.

Sarah, Peter and I huddled on the sidewalk outside the Morosco after the play had finished. A damp wind was blowing and there were a lot of people waiting for taxis. We decided to walk the two blocks to my hotel where we could get a hot drink and talk freely. The doorman at the Algonquin could hail them a taxi home afterwards.

A bewildered Sarah was at a loss for words.

Peter was not. As soon as we were out of the crowd, he exploded. 'That bastard! He stole Simon's play!'

'Wait a minute, Peter. How can we be sure Ricks stole Simon's work?' Leveling an accusation like that against a Pulitzer Prize-winning playwright was not something to undertake casually.

'I know his play. We critiqued one another's work.'

'It was seven years ago.'

'I am absolutely certain that I read something very like this play when I was in that critique group with Simon and Bob Holdrup. I even recognized some of the phrases, some of the dialogue. They were Simon's words. He had a distinctive voice.'

'It could be explained another way, though. It could be that Simon and Professor Ricks discussed the play in great depth. It could even have been a joint effort, with Simon working on it under Ricks's guidance. Then he died, and Ricks finished it. In which case he could justifiably claim it was his work, although it would be more gentlemanly to give joint credit. Is that scenario possible?'

'Well . . . I guess so. I never read the whole play. Only the first act seemed familiar. The second was new to me. Either Simon didn't share that part with Bob and me, or he hadn't finished it before he died.'

'If that's what happened, Ricks would have no reason to fear Crenshaw's accusation of plagiarism. Or, more likely, his attempt to blackmail him. But I think he did fear Crenshaw and he did kill him, and I think Norah Rose figured that out. Sarah, did Simon serve in the Great War?'

'He was drafted and sent to France in 1918. He never talked much about it. Mother and I gathered that it was too gruesome, so we didn't press. I do know that he served as a medic, dragging wounded soldiers from the trenches or no-man's-land and taking them to the hospital tents, and one time he said that dealing with the screaming and the crying and the pain that he couldn't relieve gave him nightmares.'

It made sense that the play was written by someone who had experienced the worst of combat, someone who grasped the anguish of the common doughboy and who understood the fluidity of honor on the battlefield, where doctors on both sides treated enemy soldiers and prisoners could be guarded by monsters or by decent men. Edward Ricks hadn't seen combat. I doubted that he'd ever left the States.

'Did Allen Crenshaw ever say anything to you about Ricks or the play?' I asked Sarah.

'No, I told you, I never even knew he was in the play.'

Now Crenshaw's odd reluctance to talk about his theatrical success made sense. So did his chaste courtship of Miss Sarah Landry. He wasn't on the prowl for sex, not with this girl. He needed to keep her sweet until he had control of the original play. I saw the betrayal in Sarah's eyes as she came to the same conclusion.

'He wasn't interested in me, was he?' she said in a small voice.

'Perhaps not,' I said. 'How did you meet?'

'At a little concert. I was playing in a string quartet at the YWCA on Lexington. He was there with a friend and they paid their compliments to us at the reception after the concert. He said he had taken violin lessons as a boy and asked if I'd like to get a coffee with him some time. I gave him my mother's telephone number – I didn't have one at that time – and he called the next week.'

'Was he, indeed, familiar with the violin, or was that a line?'

'No, he was quite musical. We had that in common. Among other things. Or so I thought.'

'Did he ask you about your brother right off?'

'He never asked about Simon. He never brought up his name or showed any interest in the fact that I had a brother, beyond saying he was sorry he'd died.'

Had he known about Simon and his play before he met Sarah? I couldn't be sure.

I turned to Peter. 'What about that third man in your critique group? What did you say his name was?'

'Bob Holdrup.'

'What happened to him?'

'I've no idea. We were in several classes together, but we weren't fast friends like Simon and me. Bob was a decent writer, a serious scholar. The work he submitted to us was very philo-sophical, as I recall, something about a crisis of faith. Frankly, I found it a bit tedious and didn't think a subject that cerebral would make for a good stage play. People want entertainment, laughter, music, and a happy ending. But I remember him pushing

Simon and me both to inject more philosophy into our work, which, as you noticed tonight, Simon did.'

'It might be a good idea to talk with Bob Holdrup, if we can find him.'

'I know,' piped up Sarah. 'Bob was a student at Columbia. He'll be in their records. My mother got a job as a secretary in the history department when my father died, and she knew everyone in Records. I'm sure I can get one of her friends there to give me an address for Bob Holdrup. Of course, it depends on whether he's maintained contact with the school since he graduated, but it's our best bet. I'll get right on that first thing tomorrow, the minute Records opens up.'

TWENTY-FIVE

The Staten Island ferry runs every thirty minutes, come rain or come shine. As soon as I got the call from Sarah Landry with what we hoped was Bob Holdrup's current address, I hopped the next ferry, armed with a map and a bite of bread and cheese for lunch. There's no subway system over there, but the driver of a bus that traveled the northeast coastal road let me off at the stop nearest St John's, an average-size stone church nestled amidst several large residences. Bob Holdrup was now Father Robert Holdrup, Episcopal priest, with a wife, a child and a parish.

The priest was short and stout, like the little teapot in the children's song, and like a little tea kettle, he whistled as he walked. The black suit he wore had seen better days, but his white collar was stiff and clean. His face lit up when he saw me, before he had any idea what I was doing there. Perhaps he thought I was a new resident of Staten Island looking for a church home. The day was a fine one, so he beckoned toward a bench on the steeple side of the church where the sun shone warmly. His smile faded when he learned of my mission.

'Yes, of course I remember Simon Landry. What a tragedy his death was!' He clucked his tongue like a farmer calling his geese. 'What can I tell you about him?'

'Do you get to the theater very often, Father?'

'I'm afraid not, my dear. I often think I'll have the chance to indulge in such pleasures once my duties lighten and my child grows up, but then,' he sighed, 'something comes along to prevent it. Why just last week, my wife and I learned we are expecting another blessing from heaven.'

'Congratulations!' He nodded his thanks and I went on. 'Simon Landry's death prevented him from finishing the Columbia program. Did you finish?'

'I did, yes. Shortly thereafter, I realized I could no longer ignore the calling from God that had pursued me for years, and I embarked on another educational journey to earn a master's in divinity. Within a few short years, I married, completed that degree, welcomed our son into the world, and came here to St John's.'

'Do you remember any of the classes you and Simon Landry took together?'

'We were in the English literature graduate program, a two-year degree program that required certain classes of all its students. There were perhaps fifteen of us, all men save one. Everyone took classes in Shakespeare, the Middle Ages, poetry and drama.'

'Didn't you also take the play-writing class taught by Professor Ricks?'

'Ah, yes. That one, I'd forgotten. It wasn't required, but Landry and I were in that class together as well as the others.'

'Did you know that Professor Ricks had left Columbia and written a play that is currently on Broadway?'

'No, I'm not aware of that. Congratulations to him.'

'What did you think of him as a professor?'

He pursed his lips. 'Average.'

'Would it surprise you to learn that his play won the Pulitzer Prize?'

'I don't suppose it would. There's no accounting for the tastes of the public. Whether it is worthy of awards or not, I cannot say, not having seen it. And who am I to judge?'

'You were in a critique group with Simon Landry and another man. Do you remember that?'

'Of course. The other student was Peter VanHorn, a teacher now, I believe.'

'As I understand it, each of you critiqued the others' work before turning it in to Professor Ricks. Do you remember much about Simon's writing?'

He folded his hands as if in prayer and touched his fingertips to his lips as he traveled back in time. 'Something about the Great War. A soldier whose encounters with a German doctor and a French prisoner of war . . . or a French doctor and a German prison guard, or something like that . . . his encounters alter his views on man's inhumanity to man. I found it a bit superficial on the first go-round and urged him to push deeper into the philosophical themes.'

'Tell me about his sad death.'

'Sad, it surely was. If I remember correctly, his father had passed away some years before, so it was his mother and younger sister who grieved most profoundly. I attended the funeral. He and I lived in the same building.'

'Really? Where was that?'

'It was a dormitory-like place, five stories, built specifically for students, male students, although it wasn't part of the university proper. Each student had one small room. Showers and water closets were located on each hall and also a common room. A widow with a young son lived on the ground floor. She managed the building and cleaned the common areas. It was still there, the last time I passed through the area.'

I took note of the address. 'When did you see Simon last?'

'The night he died. As I told the police at the time, he and I and about four or five other students – I remembered their names back then for the police report, but no longer – we had dinner at Tom's, a homey restaurant across the street where students could eat cheap food and plenty of it.'

'Was there any drinking?'

'This was before Prohibition started, my dear, so yes, there was always some drinking, but our pocketbooks did not stretch to whiskey or fancy cocktails. We had beer.'

'And afterwards?'

'After dinner, I returned to my room in the dormitory. I lived on the second floor; Landry was on first. I gathered the others stayed a bit longer, but no one remembered Landry leaving, so perhaps he was the last to go. The next evening, when he didn't show up for class, his professor called the dormitory manager, Mrs Ivanovitch. She found him in his room, dead in his bed, and called the police. He'd died in his sleep. Sad for one so young, but a peaceful death is a blessing denied to many.'

'What was the cause of death?'

Father Holdrup shook his head sadly. 'The coroner couldn't say for sure. The man had no bruises or broken bones that would indicate a fight. He was in bed, under the covers, wearing his underclothes, meaning he had undressed and set his shoes carefully under the bed, then climbed into bed without undue difficulty. He must have felt ill, for he had placed two pails beside the head of his bed.'

'Pails? What sort of pails?'

'Galvanized tin pails. The sort sold for a dollar in every hardware store in America. If he had lived on the top floor, I'd have said the pails were placed to catch dripping water from the ceiling, but his was a ground-floor room and, even so, there was no trace of leaks and no rain that night. Anyway, they were empty. No vomit, so no reason to think he had been seriously ill. Probably just felt nauseous from something he ate or drank, or so said the doctor.'

'And the room, were there any signs of a search?'

'No indication of an intruder, if that's what you mean. His room was neat, not ransacked as if a thief had come in. All orderly and normal.'

'Did you read any of this in the newspapers, or did you see it all with your own eyes?'

'I was there in his room when his body was still in bed. My room was above his. Not directly, but on the floor above. Nothing I've told you is second-hand.'

'How do you think he died?'

'I am singularly unequipped to give an answer to that question, Miss Beckett. It was the coroner's conclusion – the only logical conclusion – that Landry had suffered a sudden heart attack or a stroke. It's always sad, but it happens, even with young, outwardly healthy young people.'

TWENTY-SIX

Some lucky people find solutions to their problems in their dreams. I am not one of them. I did, however, have a revelation that very night while tossing about in my bed, trying not to waken Natalie as I mulled over the troubling details of the Crenshaw murder that wouldn't leave me alone.

Poor Wesley Crenshaw was still in jail for the murder of his cousin. I hoped the wheels of justice would grind to a sensible conclusion once Detective Quinn realized that there was simply no evidence to hold him other than that box of bullets, which were surely planted in his house by someone. Who? I had to suspect Edward Ricks. It was looking more and more like he was the one who had shot Allen Crenshaw from the wings, camouflaging the sound of the extra gunshots with a robust drum crescendo. He had the opportunity (he was always in the theater), and the means – a pistol with real bullets identical to the one used as a prop. What he had always lacked was a decent motive. Until now.

Through luck or simple chance, Allen Crenshaw had come across information that led him to believe Ricks was not the author of *Rules of Engagement.* Someone else had written it – maybe not all of it, maybe just half; that was hard to say at this point. But there was a cloud hanging over Ricks's credibility as its author and Crenshaw had put it there. I would bet good money he was blackmailing Ricks, and either Ricks couldn't pay his price or he got tired of forking over the cash to his greedy lead actor. Maybe he was concerned that Crenshaw would leave the play for another role, and that his chance to eliminate the man would be lost. The solution: get rid of the actor before he could blow the whistle, before he could leave.

What came to me in the wee hours was how Crenshaw must have heard about Ricks's cheat. At first, I thought he had to have learned of the existence of Simon Landry's play and cozied up to his sister to discover what she knew about it, but that put the

cart before the horse. To be sure, the connection was Sarah
Landry, but when I remembered something she'd said about Mr
Gentlemanly Crenshaw helping her move her mother's belongings
to her apartment, I understood that he had most likely come
across the play accidentally, when his romance with Sarah, if it
could be called that, was in its early stages. It was happenstance
– or fabulous luck, Crenshaw must have thought. Not so fabulous
in the end, since it brought about his own murder. The key had
to lie in those boxes. There must be something in there that
Crenshaw stumbled upon – a copy of Simon's play, most likely
– and I was going to find out what as soon as daylight dawned.
If it was still there.

Daylight brought Friday, and Douglas Fairbanks and Mary
Pickford were leaving the following afternoon, so I was engulfed
in a whirlwind of final meetings, errands, letters, trip plans,
purchases and goodbyes. Douglas had insisted that I keep a room
in the Algonquin – although Mary's frugality moved me out of
the suite and into a smaller, single room – until I was satisfied
that the police had arrested the right man. Still, I managed to
squeeze in a telephone call to Sarah Landry, asking if I could
come to her apartment again and have a look through the boxes
that had been brought over from her mother's apartment. She
followed my thoughts at once.

'You think there's some of Simon's writings in there, don't
you? Yes, come right away. There are quite a few boxes. I've
been meaning to go through them ever since Mother passed away
a few months ago, but couldn't bring myself to do it. Now there's
a reason. Come any time. I'm home all day.'

'Don't you go to work somewhere?'

She gave a little laugh. 'I work at home. I give piano lessons.'

'Not violin?'

'Not many mothers want their children to learn violin, but
everyone wants a pianist in the family. I do have a couple of
violin students, older ones, but the piano is my bread and butter.'

The sky was darkening when I extricated myself from Douglas
and Mary's errands and arrived at Sarah's door. Strains of
Beethoven's 'Für Elise' stopped mid-measure as I rang the bell.

'Continue!' Sarah called to her pupil as she opened the door.
She showed me into the spare room where cardboard boxes

were stacked high against the wall, perhaps three dozen of them. 'I'm so sorry they're not labeled. My fault, but it didn't seem important at the time, we were in such a hurry. And I'm sorry there are so many. I've been meaning to unpack them and go through everything, but just couldn't face all the memories that seeing Mother's and Simon's things would trigger. I'll be in to help you as soon as I've finished lessons. Just two more after Elizabeth, half an hour each.'

I set to work, pulling down the top box and cutting off its string. It quickly became obvious that Sarah and Allen Crenshaw had packed up her mother's belongings haphazardly, without any effort to sort like with like, working their way from one shelf to the next, from one side of the room to the other, without any organizing scheme. The first box held some books, several porcelain figurines wrapped in newspaper, a few magazines, a dozen silver spoons and knives, four small framed prints of *The Canterbury Tales*, a chenille bedspread and a stack of embroidered pillowcases. One down, I thought, dragging it to the opposite side of the room. I was searching for papers, maybe in a binder or notebook, probably typed, which meant a quick glance into a box wasn't good enough. Everything had to come out. Papers could be lying at the bottom.

The job went faster once Sarah joined me, and after an hour, she cried, 'Eureka! Look,' she said, handing me a stack of folders. 'Here are some of Simon's university papers.'

We flipped through pages of notes, essays, short stories, even a few plays, before she said, 'What's this? Is this it, Jessie? Does this sound like *Rules of Engagement*? It looks like a play but there's no title page.'

She handed me a stack of papers a full inch thick, with typed pages numbered in the upper right corner, starting with page 2. They were carbon copies of an original, which was nowhere to be found.

Seeing the play three times had practically burned the lines into my brain. I skimmed page 2 and then page 3. 'Yes, yes, this sounds like it. But hang on, we need to be sure. Let me keep reading . . .'

And I kept turning page after page, muttering, 'Yes . . . yes, this is the same. Yes . . . yes . . . this is what I remember, almost word for word.' Until I reached the end and sat back on the floor with my legs straight out in front of me, flabbergasted. 'That son of a bitch Ricks. He stole Simon's play.'

'Are you sure?'

'There's no question. Oh, there may be some little word changes here or there, but this is virtually the same as the one playing on Broadway right now, from beginning to end. Look here – there's no title page. What do you want to bet that Allen Crenshaw filched it? He must have come across this when he was helping you pack up your mother's things. She had all of Simon's belongings, didn't she?'

'When he died, we moved everything of his to her house. We never went through Simon's belongings. We didn't have the heart.'

'I understand. But Crenshaw realized what he was holding. He would have recognized the dialogue right away, because it's his own dialogue. Did he ask you about Simon?'

'No, I don't think he ever mentioned him.'

'The title page probably had Professor Ricks's name on it. And a date. It wouldn't take a genius to come to the correct conclusion. He must have torn off the title page to take to Ricks, to prove that he had a carbon copy of the original play. And . . . oh my gosh, that explains why Crenshaw's apartment was ransacked. The thief wasn't looking for valuables, he was looking for the carbon copy of the play. Which means he didn't already have it!'

'And the thief was Edward Ricks.'

'Bingo. He didn't find it at Crenshaw's apartment because it's right here. And there's no way he could know that because he didn't know the link between Crenshaw and you. That must be driving him mad with worry, knowing that the carbon copy is still out there somewhere.'

'What do we do now, Jessie?'

TWENTY-SEVEN

Mary Pickford is the smartest woman in the film industry and the most famous woman in the world. She founded a film studio, United Artists, to produce and distribute her own pictures, which typically gross more than a million dollars each. Although she had no formal schooling, she is a ruthless businesswoman who thrives in the cutthroat filmmaking industry, and she knows more about money than a bank president. Who else would I turn to for help?

'Let me see it,' she said, holding out her hand for Simon Landry's carbon copy. Adept at evaluating stage plays, she paged through the script quickly, nodding a bit now and then, pursing her lips a few times, scowling once. Finally, she handed back the pages.

'You're right, Jessie. Edward Ricks is a fraud.'

'What do we do?'

'Plagiarism is a tricky thing. It's cheating and it's theft. Cheating in school will get you expelled. Cheating like this would be a copyright issue, meaning the real author, or in this case his heirs, could sue Ricks in court for monetary damages. It could also be a criminal issue involving jail time, but that depends on state laws, and while I know the relevant California laws, I don't know New York's.'

'So Miss Landry needs to hire a lawyer?'

'First let me ask my lawyers back in LA about this. If they can't answer my questions, they can recommend a New York lawyer who can.'

'That would be swell, Miss Pickford! I can't thank you enough.'

'It's no trouble, Jessie. Frankly, I'm happy to help. I find this whole business disgusting. Douglas will be horrified. It's a terrible blot on our entire profession. At the very least, Edward Ricks will be ruined . . . humiliated, and deservedly so. I can only hope there aren't wider repercussions for the industry. Plagiarism is serious, mind you, but not nearly as serious as murder. Does this prove Ricks shot Allen Crenshaw?'

'Is it iron-clad proof? I'm afraid not, but it certainly gives him a motive more immediate than the one attributed to Wesley Crenshaw. I'm confident that he's the murderer. The trick now is to prove it.'

'If anyone can do it, Jessie, you can,' she said fondly. 'You have a real knack for this sort of investigation.' Which made me feel great until I realized how ashamed I was going to be if I disappointed her.

It was too late to reach Detective Quinn at the police station, but I did telephone Adele at her hotel. Luckily she was in when I called.

'We need to meet, Adele,' I told her. 'You, me and Detective Quinn. As soon as possible.'

'You sound like you've dug up something.'

'I know the detective thinks the Crenshaw case is closed—'

'He does. Wesley Crenshaw did it. They've assigned Benjamin another case. Something about a man who killed his wife and her lover.'

'I'm sure he won't be pleased to learn that the Crenshaw case is open again. At least, I'm trying to reopen it.'

'What have you discovered?'

'I'll show you tomorrow. Can we meet at your hotel?'

'Sure. Rehearsals have finished, so I'm free in the morning. I'll get word to Benjamin.'

'No more rehearsals?'

'I've been meaning to tell you . . . Fred booked us on the *Aquitania* bound for England next week. *Lady Be Good* opens at the Empire Theatre in London a week after we arrive.'

'I wish I could see you and Fred in that. I know you'll be spectacular. I'll be heading home soon too. Miss Pickford and Douglas leave tomorrow.'

'Our coincidental little interlude is nearly done. What a treat it has been to overlap in New York with you! And to solve a murder!'

'We haven't solved it yet, Adele.'

'All right, we still have a week before I leave. Let's get on it!'

She was far too playful about such a serious subject, but without Adele, I had no link to Detective Quinn and no way to pursue the case. We arranged to meet in the morning in the breakfast room.

A girl couldn't keep her flapper figure by eating from the Astor breakfast menu with its lamb chops, calf's liver, pork tenderloin, and other gargantuan entrées. I ordered fresh straw-berries – where on earth did they get them this time of year? – and toast with cream cheese and guava jelly. Adele had a grapefruit and puffed rice cereal. Detective Quinn, who knew darn well that Adele's backers were footing the bill, ordered broiled sea bass, hashed brown potatoes, Boston brown bread and a bottle of champagne. Before our food could be served, the detective began quizzing me.

'What's all the fuss about, Jessie? Come clean. What have you turned up?'

'Have you seen *Rules of Engagement*?' I asked him.

'I'm not much of a theater-goer. Why?'

Silently I handed Adele the carbon copy of Simon's play. As she looked through it, her forehead creased, then deepened into a full frown.

'What is it, Adele?' the impatient detective asked.

I waited until she looked up from her reading. 'It's the script from Ricks's play,' she said. 'What does this mean?'

'It means it's not Ricks's play. This play was written seven years ago by a student at Columbia University, Simon Landry, a graduate student who was in Professor Ricks's class. He died, although only in his late twenties. Five years later, Edward Ricks, who had quit his teaching position at Columbia, produces a play he claims to have written. It's a hit. It wins the Pulitzer. He's rich. He's famous. But it's not his play. Here's the proof that he stole it from his deceased student.'

'That's awful!'

'Pair that with the disappearance of Norah Rose, who I believe realized that she was being falsely accused of shooting the fatal bullet when she became convinced that her gun did not contain live ammunition and when she remembered seeing Ricks in the wings at the time of the gunshots. Pair that with the drum crescendo that obscured the number of gunshots, a drum crescendo that was part of the orchestra's score for only a few days, mind you. And pair all that with the ransacking of Crenshaw's apartment – it was Ricks looking for the rest of the carbon copy you are holding. Edward Ricks killed Crenshaw.'

Detective Quinn protested, 'But Wesley had the box of—'

'When you started getting too close, Ricks needed to give you a suspect, so he played to his own script by taking a box of live rounds, removing one – remember, he'd already used one – and stashing it at Wesley's house before calling in an anonymous tip. But there were never two live rounds fired. Only one, the one that hit Crenshaw. You and I searched long and hard for the other and never found it, because it was never fired.'

'Let me see that.' He reached his hand out for the carbon copy.

'No one suspected Ricks because he had no motive and his regular appearances at the Morosco were routine. Here's his motive: Crenshaw was blackmailing him, threatening to expose the fraud.'

Detective Quinn flipped through the pages. 'Where's the first page?'

'That's probably what Crenshaw took from Sarah Landry's house when they were moving all the boxes with her mother's and brother's effects. He didn't need to take the whole thing. It was safer left with her where it had been all along. He needed just the title page to prove to Ricks that he had the carbon copy.'

'OK, I see what you're saying. And I'm not saying you're wrong. The title page would have had Simon Landry's name, a date probably, and maybe the professor's name and class number. Missing that, all we have is a carbon copy that could have belonged to anyone. Ricks could say it was a carbon of his own play that he gave Simon Landry to look over all those years ago.'

'Which is why we need to find the title page.'

'He probably destroyed it,' remarked Adele. 'In his shoes, I would have. He would have destroyed this copy if he had found it at Crenshaw's apartment.'

'No doubt. Which is why we need more evidence. The police have got to re-open the search for Norah Rose, or Norah Smith, so we can find out exactly what she witnessed that night. You don't think she's dead, do you?'

'I very much hope not. But one thing I've learned in my short career on the force is that killing gets easier the second time around.'

'And meanwhile, shouldn't you release Wesley Crenshaw?' asked Adele.

'I guess we could now, except news of that will tip off Ricks that we no longer believe in Wesley's guilt. He'll know something's up.'

I hated to say it, but I did. 'Perhaps you could keep him a few more days. Poor man. You might at least ease his mind by telling him he's no longer a suspect.'

'Maybe there's a way to release him without any news getting out,' said Quinn, 'as long as he doesn't go back to his house.'

TWENTY-EIGHT

When I got back to the Algonquin, there was a telegram waiting for me at the front desk. David had contacted me, already! I'd been mistaken about his sincerity. He did want me to join him after all. My pulse raced as I ripped it open.

It was not from David.

Transporting prisoner to Philadelphia STOP *Arriving Sunday* STOP *1 hour from NY* STOP *Shall I come say hello?* STOP *Carl Delaney.*

I gave a disappointed sigh and blinked back the sting in my eyes. Well, why not? Why shouldn't Carl take a detour and come to New York? I'd liked the fella ever since we'd met, when he and his partner responded to a call at the home of an elderly friend of mine who had been murdered, and I was the initial suspect. Carl was one of those rare birds: an honest cop in a thicket of corruption, where everyone from the police to the politicians, lawyers, judges and juries were on the take from the bootleggers, except for those who were actually in the bootlegging business themselves. Not that Carl didn't enjoy a drink now and then, but he had a healthy way of looking at a situation and judging when exceptions were prudent. I'd worked with Carl to solve several murders, and once he got over trying to protect me, we got on just fine.

Policemen weren't high on my list of trustworthy people. Uniforms made me nervous. Growing up, I'd learned to steer clear of the law, which was prone to blaming transient vaudeville players for whatever crimes occurred as they passed through town. Admittedly, it didn't help that I *was* occasionally to blame for some of those crimes, but it wasn't right for vaudeville to take the blame for everything that went south. I came to trust Carl, especially when he wasn't wearing his uniform, which was every day now that he'd been promoted to detective. I hadn't seen him for a month or more, and now he was a short train ride away from New York City. It would lift my spirits to 'say hello'.

I scribbled my reply at the front desk. The boy sent it back to the telegraph office along with sixty cents, the minimum for under ten words. *Welcome to NY* STOP *Algonquin Hotel.* And I went upstairs to see what I could do to help the Pickford/Fairbanks entourage get aboard the train west.

Douglas had been offered a luxurious private coach for the trip back home, something on loan from Clara and Henry Ford. He and Mary had met the Fords two years ago when they did a publicity shoot riding in the ten millionth Ford motorcar that came off the assembly line – think of it: *ten million!* – and I suspected that Mr and Mrs Ford were admirers of both actors. We'd come east on a Pullman Palace Car, long and fancy and very private, but even that would pale beside the amazing work of art the Fords had commissioned for their own use. Accompanying everyone to Grand Central Terminal offered me the chance to have a look at the sort of luxury few people in this world ever see.

'Geez Louise!' exclaimed Natalie as we gals climbed aboard to inspect the quarters. 'It even has a name: Fair Lane. Have you ever seen the like?'

We tried to pop our eyes back into our heads as we gawped at the stainless-steel kitchen with a dining room beside it. 'Look at that, Jessie,' said Natalie, pointing to the chandelier, anchored with fasteners to keep it from rocking back and forth as the train rolled down the track. She and the rest of the staff would sleep in the tiny bedchambers next to the kitchen, plainer than the large bedroom at the opposite end, but more than serviceable. A walnut-paneled lounge stretched the width of the car, with large windows on each side to allow for frequent head-turning, and another smaller lounge nearby. I don't know how many bathrooms there were, but the one I saw boasted hot and cold running water as well as a shower! There was even a porch at the back, and since the Fair Lane would always be the last car in the train, one could sit outside in fine weather and enjoy the breeze as the countryside vanished into the horizon. My own journey back to Los Angeles would be nothing like this.

Miss Pickford motioned to speak to me privately.

'I heard from my lawyers this morning,' she began. 'They recommend a New York lawyer by the name of Henry Mattingly, a man who specializes in copyright laws and who naturally knows the New York legal system better than our own California men. They did, however, think your friend has an excellent case.' She handed me a piece of paper with the address and telephone information.

I thanked her profusely and disembarked. Trunks were still being loaded in the baggage car in front of Fair Lane, and it would be an hour or more before they pulled out of the station. I did not wait to wave goodbye. I returned to the Algonquin and watched as a maid moved my things to a single room.

TWENTY-NINE

'It was grindingly boring,' said Carl with a rueful grimace. 'Four days on trains shackled to a cold-blooded murderer – you can imagine the interesting conversations.'

'How awful! What about going to the water closet? Or sleeping?'

'I stood outside the open door of the toilet cabinet for him, and when it was my turn, I'd fasten him to the arm of the seat and leave one of the conductors to stand over him. At dark, we slept sitting up. You know what that's like, I'm sure, what with all your years in vaudeville.'

'I sure do. Most vaudeville players schedule their jump to the next town on an overnight train, saving the dollar for the hotel room. I can sleep as well sitting up as lying down.'

'Well, I can't. I was never so glad to get rid of a prisoner in my life as I was yesterday in Philly. I turned him over to the guards at the Eastern State Pen and checked in to the nearest hotel for a bath and a shave and a very long sleep.'

We were sitting in the Bamboo Forrest, a Chinese restaurant on MacDougal Street that served genuine Chinese food, even though it was located outside Chinatown. On advice from Fred and Adele, we'd ordered their special, a fried shrimp with pineapple, and the owners kindly supplemented the food offerings with illegal beverages of our choice. I knew Carl often ate in LA's Chinatown and figured this would hit him in the right spot. And Adele swore we'd enjoy the décor. She was right – it was garishly, gorgeously, magnificently Oriental.

'What did your prisoner do?' I asked, spearing another shrimp.

'Killed two shopkeepers in Philly during a robbery, then ran as far as he could go. He'd have gotten clean away if it weren't for Fate and the eagle eye of one of our office secretaries, Elsa Rayne, who moved to LA from Philadelphia a year ago and still gets the *Inquirer* sent to her every week. She read all about these murders when they happened back in September and she remembered the name of the killer. When he showed up in our jail accused of robbing a jewelry store, she went straight to the chief and let him know what sort of fish he'd landed. Chief gave her a medal.'

'And what did you do to get saddled with the transfer job?'

He grinned. 'Most of our transfers are pretty routine, like to San Francisco or San Diego or Sacramento. Almost never do we have to send someone out of state, mostly because we haven't got a lot of secretaries reading newspapers from other parts of the country to clue us in to the crooks who are running around LA. Anyway, it was my turn. I could have pled my workload and pushed it off on someone less senior, but I thought it would be a good chance to see more of the country, even if it was only through the window. And I have an aunt – my mother's younger sister who was more sister to me than aunt – who lives in Newark, across the river. I promised to spend a day with her and her kids. And the chief guaranteed that this would be the last transfer I'd have to take for a whole year.'

'That's worth something.'

'Your turn. Tell me what's been going on with you. First off, I gotta warn you, I've heard about the murder on the Morosco stage. Something like that makes the papers throughout the country. And I know you were there that night.'

'How did you hear that?'

'A little bird.'

'Myrna?'

He nodded. Myrna Loy and I had sent a couple of letters back and forth, so she knew about my goings-on in New York. 'Well, that's fine, it's no secret. Here's what happened that night.' I told him about the play that had been interrupted by the shooting. It was interesting to note how fast he focused on the bullets, grilling me as to whether Norah had noticed a stronger recoil, whether we'd found the second slug, and the reasons for Norah's disappearance. I had no sooner mentioned the anonymous tip about the box of live rounds at Wesley's house than he shook his head and muttered, 'A plant.' I couldn't keep the smile off my face.

'What's so funny?' he asked.

'Where were you when I needed you?' I asked playfully.

'Seriously, though, after working with Detective Quinn and Adele, it's a relief to have a professional to discuss the case with.'

'Quinn not worth much?'

'It's not that. He's just green. He means well. He confessed to Adele that this was his first assignment. They assigned it to him because it was supposedly so easy. Give him a few years, maybe just a few months, and he'll grow into the job. Right now, he's so ga-ga over Adele, he can hardly see the case.'

He gave me an odd look, so I resumed my tale. I told him about the discovery of the carbon copy in Sarah's brother's boxes, the futile search someone had made of Crenshaw's apartment, and my conversation with Mary Pickford and her lawyers' advice about plagiarism. I explained the significance of a Pulitzer Prize, something Carl hadn't heard of, and reviewed the details of Professor Ricks and his Columbia University students. I told him about Sarah Landry and her brother, Simon, the brilliant graduate student whose promising future was cut short by early death. My account of meeting the Queen of Romania and Prince Nicholas, and his inquiry into Ricks's bogus claims of service with the Royal Navy, was met with an expression of disgust.

'I've known a few men like that. Men who inflate their role in the war or who create a heroic tale from whole cloth. When I think of the brave soldiers who served honorably or died trying, it makes me sick.'

All this he absorbed with little more than an occasional nod or grunt, but as I finished painting the clearest possible picture of the case, something Detective Quinn had said days ago exploded in my head like a land mine. *Murder is easier the second time around.*

What if Professor Ricks hadn't merely taken advantage of Simon Landry's unexpected death? What if he had murdered his student as part of a larger plan to steal the play and present it later as his own? What if Simon was his first murder and Crenshaw was his second?

Carl brought me back to the present. 'Where did you go, Jessie?'

I blinked rapidly and struggled for words. 'I need to think about this.'

'What?'

'Simon Landry's death. Everyone thinks it was natural. The coroner, the doctor, his family, his friends. No one has voiced any suspicion that there was any foul play involved. But . . . but what if . . . what if it was murder? The first murder, the one that allowed Ricks to steal what he thought was a brilliant play that he could hold on to for a few years, until he was sure no other copies would turn up, and then publish as his own work.'

'What evidence is there that it could have been murder?'

'None that I know of right now. But no one has investigated that, not since they found Simon's body. He could have been poisoned.'

'Did the autopsy check for poison?'

'I don't know. I've not seen any of the reports.'

'Maybe it's time you talked to Detective Quinn about this. It's never wise to go off on your own. He can dig up the reports from years ago. You can't.'

'The report should tell us who was at the dinner that night Simon died. Which students ate together, and when they left the restaurant. Someone might have seen something that seemed insignificant at the time.' I snapped my fingers. 'I'll get the date of Simon's death from Sarah, then call Detective Quinn and suggest he pull the file.'

'If it still exists.'

'What do you mean?'

'If the death wasn't deemed suspicious, the file may not have been considered important enough to keep. Come on, we're done here. Let's go dig up some facts.'

THIRTY

T he subway took us back to the Algonquin where I used the lobby telephone to place a call to Sarah Landry. She had a telephone in her apartment, a necessity with her piano-teaching business. When she answered, I could hear wobbly music in the background.

'I don't mean to interrupt your work, Sarah. I just need to know the date of Simon's death.'

'Gracious, why?'

'Just so Detective Quinn can get hold of the reports that were written back then.'

'OK, sure, I see. He died the night of the eleventh of December, a Thursday, 1919, or maybe in the early morning hours of the twelfth. The doctors couldn't say.'

'But the police were called on the twelfth?'

'Yes. And so were Mother and I.'

'That must have been a dreadful day for you, Sarah, and your mother. I'm so sorry. Thank you for the information. Now go on back to your lessons. I'll fill you in later, if there's anything to fill you in about.'

My next call went to the police station where I left a message for Detective Quinn to return the call to the Algonquin Hotel. I told the switchboard gal I'd be waiting for it in the lounge. Carl and I made our way through the lobby just as a group of witches dressed in black rags and pointy black hats scurried through the lobby, giggling self-consciously.

'I forgot it was Halloween!' I exclaimed.

'On their way to a party, I guess,' said Carl.

'Probably to the nearest speakeasy.'

'I hear they got plenty of 'em in New York.'

'Where are you staying? And for how long?'

'They tell me I can bunk down cheap at a YMCA. The chief said I could take some time off after I delivered the package, so I thought I'd play tourist for a couple of days, maybe see the

Statue of Liberty, ride to the top of the Woolworth Building, see a show. What do you recommend?'

'Since all I've seen is *Rules of Engagement*, I can't be much help with theater recommendations. But you'd like Coney Island and Central Park, as long as the weather holds.' I thought he was going to propose we go to some of these places together, but maybe he needed to be alone after that tough trip. I didn't have the time anyway, I told myself. As soon as I was confident Detective Quinn had this case well in hand, I would be heading home on the next train west.

'Telephone for Miss Beckett,' called a bellhop.

I slipped into the booth and found Detective Quinn on the other end of the line. 'I've been thinking,' I began.

'Always trouble,' he teased. 'But before you share your thoughts, let me tell you something. I tracked down five of the patrons who had been sitting in the front row the night Crenshaw was shot, and I asked each one what they remembered about the number of gunshots. They all said they couldn't tell how many shots had been fired because the drum roll was so loud. That tells me you are right about the drums covering up the gunshots. We're going to release Wesley Crenshaw.'

'I'm glad to hear it!'

'Not only that. I talked to the drummer. Asked him about that drum roll you said was missing. He was pretty annoyed with Ricks. Said he was sick of this playwright messing with the music. Seems a couple of weeks ago, Ricks insisted on adding the drum roll for heightened effect. The drummer protested that it was excessive. The conductor backed Ricks and the drum roll was in. Then, a few days ago, the conductor pulled it out, saying Ricks had changed his mind.'

'That's interesting. I'm not at all surprised. Ricks was covering up the gunshots.'

'OK, your turn. What's your news?'

'Well, now that we know the reason that Ricks shot Allen Crenshaw was to prevent the world from learning about his plagiarized play, and we know the plan to steal the play started with Simon Landry's death, I'm wondering if that death really was from natural causes, as the doctors ruled.'

'You think Ricks killed him too?'

'I think it's possible. The timing is awfully convenient, wouldn't you say? Coming as it did right after Simon turned in his written assignment at the end of the semester. Don't you have some way to look back in the records and see exactly what the police found that day when they were called to the dormitory? And see the doctors' notes and the coroner's finding?'

'Theoretically, although it's been a while.'

'Simon died sometime during the night of December eleventh or the early morning of the twelfth. The police came on the twelfth, so reports should start on that date. Could you check the files? Anything you find would help prove or disprove my theory. Adele and I could meet with you afterwards and look over whatever you turned up.' If that didn't do it, nothing would.

It did. Quinn promised to get back in touch as soon as he had checked into the paperwork. I exited the telephone booth beaming with satisfaction. Carl, who had heard everything, just shook his head and smiled.

'This is Sunday. He won't get back to you before tomorrow. What if we walk off that big lunch? How far is it to Central Park?'

'If we walk, about fifteen or twenty minutes, depending on the sidewalk crowds. Have you never been?'

'Nope. And I've heard a lot about it. I know it's too big to see in one fell swoop, but I wouldn't mind having a look.'

So we hoofed it down Fifth Avenue, threading through the crowds of office workers and shopkeepers, grinning every time we saw an adult dressed up in a funny costume. Skeletons outnumbered devils that year, but the number of pointy-hat witches outstripped them all. We entered the south end of the park, across from the Plaza, where, I told Carl, the Queen and her children had stayed. Dodging carriages on the lanes and horseback riders on the trails, we cut through open ground to the zoo to see the hippos and elephants, then made our way to the carousel, where nannies and mothers were riding their little ones on the painted ponies. At one of the larger fountains, toddlers sailed their toy boats as their minders held on to their waistbands to keep them from falling in. At a larger lake, men fished off a bridge. 'Catching dinner, I suspect,' said Carl. Judging from the scruffy look of their clothes, he was probably right.

We were nearly run down by a gang of boys stampeding toward the open field to join the pick-up baseball games; others were yelling and pushing and chasing one another over bridges and around trees. 'I was here once in the winter,' I told Carl. 'It was years ago, when Mother was at the height of her career, singing at the Palace, and she took me ice-skating on that pond one pretty Sunday afternoon, like this one. I was about ten but I remember it like it was last week. We sat on that iron bench, right there, and she strapped the skates on to my shoes. Then she strapped on her own and away we went!' I closed my eyes, I could see her, in her cherished mink coat, slipping clumsily around the edge of the pond, holding my hand as we shrieked with laughter, trying not to fall, but launching nonetheless into the snow bank along the edges.

'She must've been something,' was all Carl said.

'She was.'

As the shadows lengthened, we left the park and warmed up inside the Plaza Hotel where we admired the sumptuous décor. It was dark by the time we started back to the Algonquin.

'How 'bout you show me one of those famous New York speakeasies before we get a bite to eat for dinner?'

There were plenty of speaks closer to the Algonquin than the Bar Centrale on 46th Street, but it was a class joint located in the basement of a brownstone a short walk from my hotel. No signs, no welcoming door, you just had to know it was there. And you did know, as soon as you opened the door, when the music from the jazz trio reached your ears and the smoke from a hundred cigarettes and cigars reached your eyes and nose. There was no peephole, no secret password, no 'Joe sent me', just open the door and welcome. Carl was entranced.

'Mayor Walker is a big patron of the speakeasies, so naturally the police don't bother much with enforcement. As long as you're minding your own business, they avoid raids and arrests.'

'Sounds sensible.'

'You can still get arrested, though. There are prohis in the city who try to justify their pay by rounding folks up. You heard of Izzy and Moe?'

He shook his head.

'They call themselves "champion hooch hunters". They get

up to all sorts of tricks to arrest people serving booze. They dress up like someone you would never suspect, like a football player or a streetcar driver or an ice delivery man, and they order a drink. As soon as the bartender delivers it – bang! They slap the cuffs on him and everyone else in the joint.'

'How does it work at the police station?'

'I've not had the pleasure, but Fred Astaire tells me that one of New York's US attorneys came up with a foolproof plan he calls 'Bargain Day'. He asks his clients to plead guilty in exchange for a guarantee that the judge will give them a small fine. That way, he handles hundreds of cases every night and there are no trials to clog the courts. It seems to work well enough. The judge gets a cut, the lawyer gets a cut, and the offenders go home to their own beds.'

'Good to know. I'll take my chances.'

And we took our chances for about an hour, listening to the seductive strains of the Negro musicians and sipping our gin rickeys and whiskey, neat, and watching the other guests, many of whom wore funny costumes with pointy black hats. Carl, always the gentleman, walked me back to the Algonquin where we ate a light supper, then took off to find a room at the YMCA.

THIRTY-ONE

'I tracked down those reports pretty easy,' said Detective Quinn when he telephoned the following morning. 'Shall I read 'em out to you?'

Didn't he want to meet with Adele? 'I thought we'd get together for lunch . . .'

'Too busy. But there's a restaurant across the street from headquarters. I can meet you there for a few minutes at, say, eleven? You know where police headquarters is, right? Centre Street in Little Italy?'

Adele snagged a taxi and picked me up at the Algonquin. Despite the hour, the restaurant was packed with enough uniforms to make the hairs on the back of my neck prickle. It felt like all the cops were looking at me, wondering what I'd just pinched. Nonsense, of course – they were looking at Adele, not me. We threaded through the tables to an empty booth in the back, where Adele ordered a plate of pastries and coffee for three. The coffee was cold by the time Quinn arrived.

I had been keeping a sharp eye on the front door, watching for him so I could wave him over, but he materialized behind me as if he had come from the kitchen in back.

'Sorry, ladies. I have two new murders on my desk and no more hours in the day,' he said, hanging his hat on the hook beside our booth and sliding in beside Adele.

'How did you get here? I didn't see you come through the door.'

He grinned sheepishly, like a little boy caught with a slingshot and a broken window. 'I came through the tunnel under the street. It lets us avoid the winter weather and, ahem, has the added attraction of letting us slip over for a quick eye-opener without anyone noticing.'

No wonder the place was so full! It was a veritable speakeasy for cops.

'I did what you asked,' he continued. 'I looked back into the files from 1919. The files on murders are kept here at headquarters, but any reports involving natural deaths are stored in the basement of an annex over in one of the medical buildings. The man in charge found the file you wanted easy as pie, but he said I was lucky. Not all those files get kept that long.' He slapped the envelope on the table and ordered hot coffee. 'You can look these over and take notes, but I gotta return them pronto. And, by the way, we released Wesley Crenshaw yesterday and told him to keep his head down until this thing is settled.'

The few simple pages chronicled the end of Simon Landry's life. The police report stated that there were no signs of violence about the small room, no disturbances or evidence suggesting a break-in or theft, no indication of foul play. The doctor who answered the call on 12 December wrote that there were no cuts or bruises on the body and that the deceased had evidently undressed carefully, folded his clothes, lain down in bed, and died peacefully. He also noted that there were two tin pails beside the bed, indicating that the deceased had been feeling sick, but that there was no vomit in the pails. Although vomiting is a symptom of arsenic poisoning, the autopsy found no indication of that in his organs or any other poisonous material in his stomach. The unanimous conclusion was death from natural causes.

The police report included some information I was eager to have – the names of the students who had eaten dinner with Simon the night he died. The police had interviewed every one of them and none had experienced symptoms of food poisoning. None had noticed anything unusual about Simon that night. All agreed that he drank only a beer or two. I jotted down their names: Earl Spaulding, Roy St John, Beverley Carter, Arthur MacDermott, and the one I'd already met, Bob (now Father) Holdrup. I was surprised that one of the people at dinner that night was a woman. Father Holdrup hadn't mentioned that.

Tracking down those former students would prove challenging, and Detective Quinn had no time for a challenge. He was, however, willing for us to undertake the chore for him. I contacted Sarah Landry to ask her to use her influence once again at the Records room of Columbia University, checking for any updated information about the four new names. She came back within a couple of hours with the results.

'I wasn't as successful as I was with Holdrup,' she began apologetically. 'The only significant thing I learned is that Roy St John is dead. He died last year.'

I was immediately suspicious. 'Did the file say how?'

'Cancer. There was an obituary attached. And before you ask, student files don't normally keep track of deaths, but in this case, Mr St John's will provided for a one-hundred-dollar donation to Columbia's scholarship fund. Evidently he'd been a scholarship boy and was kind enough to try to help someone else.'

I drew a line through his name. 'What about the others?'

'No address or other information since graduation. I'm sorry.'

'Don't be. That's a big help, eliminating one of the names. We'll try to track the other three. If we could find just one here in town, that would be a huge deal.'

There were six million people living in New York City, and finding three of them – assuming they were still in New York City – would be like searching through the proverbial haystack. Six million names cannot fit into a city directory, no matter how small you make the print, so New York divided its city directories into boroughs, with one book for Manhattan and the Bronx together, another for Brooklyn, another for Queens, and so forth. These listed every man in the city and some of the women, along with their street addresses and their occupations, like barber, foreman, doorman, varnisher, lawyer, magician, or piano tuner. The telephone company put out its own directories three times a year, listing those citizens and businesses that owned telephones. For our purposes, city directories were more useful, at least at first, so Adele and I set out for the immense New York Public Library on Fifth Avenue where you could find city directories galore, along with anything and everything ever published.

The library looked like a Greek temple on the outside and a royal palace on the inside. Neither of us had been there before, which was probably obvious to the clerks when they saw us craning our necks to gape at the gold-leaf carvings and the painted clouds on the ceiling. No doubt they were used to that sort of reaction from the tourists who flocked to the city each year. New York wasn't the premiere city in the world for nothing!

The clerks directed us to the books we needed and set us up at one of the polished tables in the great reading room.

'You take Earl Spaulding and look for him in each borough's directory. I'll take Arthur MacDermott. Of course, they may not be in any of those. They may well have left New York altogether and be living in Dubuque, Iowa, but if we can locate just one of those men, or the woman, we'll have a chance to find out whether anything happened at that dinner after Bob Holdrup left, anything that didn't come up during the initial police questioning.'

Adele was dubious about my tactics but had lost none of her enthusiasm for solving murders. She dug into the first directory, came up empty, and grabbed the next one. In no time she let out a squeal of joy, which drew numerous disapproving looks and several shushes from neighboring patrons.

'Eureka! I found him!' she whispered hoarsely. 'In Queens. Earl Spaulding, supervisor. That must be him, right?'

'Get the Queens telephone directory and see if he's listed.'

He was.

'All right, this is great. But let's keep going. It must be your lucky day. Try Beverley Carter.'

Adele's luck continued. She hit pay-dirt a half-hour later when she found Beverley Carter, teacher, in the Bronx. She had a listing in the telephone directory too. I wrote it down carefully.

'That was an hour well spent,' I crowed as we walked out past the huge lion statues and turned down Fifth Avenue. The afternoon sun had slipped behind the skyscrapers, leaving the street scene obscured by muscular shadows. 'Two out of three is terrific. Now it's time to pay some calls on Beverley Carter and Earl Spaulding.' The Algonquin was around the corner, so we hoofed it there to use their telephone.

I had thought carefully about what to say, should we find any of the former students who ate that last dinner with Simon Landry. I didn't want to scare them off by intimating that they were under any sort of suspicion. Earl Spaulding's telephone bell rang and rang, until finally, a woman with a gravelly voice picked up the receiver.

'Hello, my name is Miss Beckett and I'm looking for a Mr Earl Spaulding.'

'This is Mrs Spaulding. Mr Spaulding is out at the moment. May I help you with something?'

'Hello, Mrs Spaulding. Was your husband a student at Columbia University a few years ago?'

'Gracious me, dearie, no. He's sixty-five and never went to school past eighth grade. I'm afraid you have the wrong number.' And before I could apologize, she hung up.

I rang the switchboard gal again and gave her the exchange name and number, Topping 2-9572, for Beverley Carter. A man answered.

'Hello, my name is Miss Beckett and I'm looking for a Miss or Mrs Beverley Carter who was a student at Columbia several years ago.'

'This is *Mister* Beverley Carter,' said a frosty voice. 'How can I help you?'

'Oh, my apologies, sir. I thought—'

'Never mind, Miss Beckett, I am quite accustomed to Yankees mistaking my name. In Virginia, where I was born, Beverley is a gentleman's name, and a very historic and aristocratic one at that. Now, how may I help you?'

'Yes, sir. According to police records, you were present at the dinner with Simon Landry on the eleventh of December 1919, the night he died.'

'That is correct.'

'The police have reason to revisit that case, and I would like to arrange a brief meeting at your home or any public place convenient to you. We'd like to ask you a few questions about that night. Would any time tomorrow be convenient?'

'With whom am I supposed to meet?'

'Myself and a colleague.'

'I was not aware that the New York City police department had hired women detectives.'

'They have not.' Although they should, I wanted to say. 'I am working with the detective in charge of this case.'

'Then you may bring said detective to my home in the Bronx tomorrow at five o'clock when I will be home from the school where I teach.'

I confirmed the address, thanked him, and hung up.

'I'm afraid Ben Quinn will be too busy to come with us,' said Adele.

'Never mind. I have another detective in mind.'

THIRTY-TWO

M r Beverley Carter, a pear-shaped man in his mid-thirties with smooth, soft hands that delivered a surprisingly crushing handshake, lived in an apartment on 176th, a leafy street in the Bronx that we reached after a half-hour subway ride and ten-minute walk through the darkened neighborhood. Adele had a meeting she could not skip, so it was Carl and me ringing the doorbell to his apartment building. No such thing as doormen here. Mr Carter himself came down to let us in.

Mr Carter glanced carelessly at Carl's proffered badge and identification before leading us up the greasy stairs to his second-floor apartment. I'm not sure what Carl would have said if the man had asked what a Los Angeles detective was doing in the Bronx, but Carl was the sort who anticipated problems and would have had a plausible response. He and I could see that Mr Carter was a music lover, as well as a fan of great literature, for one entire wall of shelves held records mixed with literary classics, stored in some kind of pattern that only he could decipher. The record player was spinning classical music that could have been Mozart – I'm no authority – but he turned it off when we came inside. He offered us a chair but not a drink. Clearly, this was no social call.

'Now, what can I do to help your investigation, detective?' he asked, ignoring me. I was content to be ignored. Carl knew what he was doing.

'Tell me about that night, what you had for dinner, what you drank, whatever sticks in your memory,' he began in his genial way.

'We were sitting at the large table in the back of Tom's, a diner across from the student residence. That was "our" table, the one we used nearly every night. Whoever got there first would take possession of the table, and anyone from our crowd who came in would sit down. There might be three students or a dozen eating there on any given night, but there was almost always someone, so you knew you'd have company. Food at Tom's was cheap and portions were large – still are, I imagine. And Tom served good beer. This was before Prohibition, mind you, but I don't doubt for a minute that Tom is still serving beer. He wasn't the type to let a little thing like the law get in his way.'

Carl had pencil and paper in hand, but he hadn't taken any notes beyond writing down the word 'Tom's'.

'I only remember the details of that night because of Simon's death and the police questioning us. Otherwise, it was like any other. Most of us ordered beef stew or pork roast or Tom's wife's fried chicken. We drank beer. Whatever he had on tap. There were six of us that night.' He raised the fingers of one hand and ticked them off. 'Beside myself and Simon, there was Bob Holdrup, who's a priest now, no surprise, he was always a preachy sonofabitch; Earl Spaulding, who was almost certainly a fag; Roy St John, who moved home to Cleveland; and Arthur MacDermott, a pretty face with little behind it.'

'You might be interested to know,' I interjected, 'that Mr St John died of cancer last year.'

'Did he? A shame. Anyway, we always found some imaginative reason to celebrate, like the autumnal equinox or the anniversary of Shakespeare's death. That night it was the Festival of the Last Class of the Semester. There was nothing the least bit unusual about the evening. Holdrup slunk out early, said he had a paper to finish. Arthur and Roy headed to another party, and the fag said he had a date with a beautiful blonde, which was so hilarious it was all I could do not to choke on my beer. That left Simon and me, and I wasn't in the mood for Simon – he could be depressingly cerebral when drunk.'

'Was he drunk?'

'Not then. But I could sense it coming. Just as the fag was about to leave, our esteemed Professor Ricks waltzed in. I had a moment of panic, fearing he was heading our way. The last thing I needed was that pompous ass pontificating about Milton and antinomianism, so I paid my tab and prepared to slip out.'

My heart beat faster. Ricks had been there! Nothing in the police report mentioned him. But he'd been there! 'Did Ricks join your table?' I asked eagerly.

Carter sent me a derisive glance, decided I wasn't worth the effort of a reply, and turned to Carl. 'The professor made his way to a corner table where he sat alone, his back to the wall, like a gangster keeping an eye out for assassins. He called good evening to us. Figuring he had not yet turned in his semester grades, I judged it prudent to respond with a cheerful greeting, then I made my way to the back door and escaped.'

'Where was Simon when you left?' asked Carl.

'Standing at the bar, ordering another beer.'

'Did he join the professor?'

'I didn't stay long enough to find out.'

'This isn't in the police report.'

'Can I be faulted for that? I informed the police of everything I've said tonight. Does that answer all your questions, detective?'

'Almost. What was your opinion of Simon Landry?'

'Simon *Laundry*, I called him. Dressed like a hobo. Brilliant mind, although it seemed the Great War had done his brain significant damage.'

'Did you ever read any of his writing?'

'Merely excerpts, nothing that sticks in my memory.'

'And your opinion of Professor Ricks?'

'George Bernard Shaw said it best: "He who can, does; he who cannot, teaches." And yes, I count myself among those who cannot. I was surprised, to say the least, when his play won the Pulitzer. I saw the play. It was excellent, I admit. There was never any indication that he had any part of excellence in him, so perhaps you should ignore my underestimation of the man since I was clearly mistaken.'

On our way out, I said to Carl, 'You know, I've always been sorry I didn't have a chance to go to school. Vaudeville makes that impossible. But if that's the sort of teacher they have in school, I'm glad I missed it.'

'Teachers are mostly the best people you'll ever find, but there's the bad apple in every barrel.'

'I can't tell you why, but I want to see this restaurant or diner or whatever it is. Across from the student residence where Simon and many of the others lived. I'd like to have a look at both.'

'If you like,' offered Carl, 'we could make our way to the university, have dinner at Tom's, and take a look around. Sometimes it helps just to understand the lay of the land.'

THIRTY-THREE

An hour later we were standing on a sidewalk littered with splinters of wood, bent nails and other debris as we viewed the rubbish-filled lot where Tom's had once stood. There would be no dinner tonight at Tom's. A man walking his Boston terrier told us that the building had been demolished two years ago.

'Old Tom couldn't make ends meet without his liquor sales, so he folded. The A&P outgrew its space and moved four blocks west, and . . . let's see, what else was there? Oh yeah, the mom-and-pop hat store closed. Don't know why. The building was old and I guess its owners decided it was cheaper to tear it down and build something new. It's been a while, though, and I don't see anything coming out of the ground yet.' He tipped his hat and wished us a good evening.

Carl and I turned to examine the building across the street, a five-story brick box, square and squat, with a flat roof and five rows of narrow windows, closely spaced – the dormitory where Simon Landry and other Columbia students lived. Without a word, we waited for a break in the traffic and hustled across the street.

The main door was open to the weather so we walked right through a vestibule and into a spacious sitting room furnished with worn but comfortable-looking chairs and sofas. Three young men were stretched out, feet up on the coffee table, reading as they listened to the jazz music coming from a large radio in the corner. They followed us with their eyes when we entered but didn't move or greet us. On the floor sprawled another young man with a bowl haircut, a boy, really, maybe fifteen or sixteen, dressed in dirty blue overalls with patches on the knees, playing with marbles. Not playing marbles, but playing *with* marbles, carefully lining them up on the grout lines between the floor tiles. He gave us the once-over too. It was obvious that he was simple-minded.

To our left stretched a hall punctuated with brown wooden doors at ten-foot intervals. To our right was a single door marked with a sign that said MANAGER. Carl knocked.

And knocked again when there was no response.

'She's hard of hearing,' offered one of the students.

Carl pounded with his fist. The door opened.

'Hello. Am I speaking to Mrs Ivanovitch?' Carl asked, raising his voice and speaking in a clear, friendly tone.

The woman nodded, eyeing us curiously. She looked to be about sixty, with silver hair pulled into a tight bun and covered with a hairnet. She wore a day dress that had seen long service and a shawl she had probably knitted herself. 'How can I help you?'

'I'm Detective Carl Delaney,' he said, flashing his badge and identification, hoping for a repeat of Mr Beverley Carter's careless inspection of the out-of-state credentials. 'And this is Jessie Beckett. Can we speak to you somewhere privately?'

A police matter? That grabbed the students' full attention. The boy continued with his marbles. Mrs Ivanovitch's suspicious squint moved from Carl to me and back again.

'Here's fine,' she said bluntly.

Carl gave her his courteous smile. 'We'd like to ask you about a student who once lived here, Simon Landry. You were the manager when he died, I believe.'

'That was many years ago.'

'Seven, to be precise. You gave the police all the help you could back then, and we are most thankful for that, Mrs Ivanovitch. But I'm new to the case, and I know you're busy, but there are some gaps in the report that I'd like to fill, if you could spare us a little of your time.'

That was Carl, so pleasant, never intimidating. He almost always got people talking. She was about to invite us inside, when the boy on the floor sat up straight and said, 'Simon. He give me gum.'

'Hush up now, Buzz. Grown-ups are talking. Now, detective, I thought that case was closed. What do you want to know?'

'I wonder if you could show us the room he rented. I realize someone else is in there now, but if he doesn't mind, we'd just like to get a quick look inside.'

Mrs Ivanovitch looked down the hall as she considered the request for a moment. 'I don't see what harm that could do. Let me get my keys.'

As we waited, I could feel the silent questions radiating from the students, who were curious but probably hesitant about getting involved in a police matter. Young Buzz had no such inhibitions.

'Simon. He give me gum.'

His mother – for I assumed her to be that – reappeared with a ring full of keys and led us across the lounge and down the hall to room 107. Buzz trailed us. After a brief knock to determine that no one was inside, she unlocked the door.

'Look all you like.'

We could not both have fit inside that tiny room if we had wanted to. It wasn't much bigger than a prison cell. The current occupant had left his narrow bed a jumble of sheets and blankets. Above it, someone had built a wooden platform that hung from the ceiling and was crammed full of miscellany. His desk at the foot of the bed was covered with piles of papers, notebooks, and books. A mish-mash of toiletries and sundries topped the chest of drawers against the opposite wall. Coats and clothing hung from hooks; boots and shoes were stowed under the bed. A small corner sink with a mirror above offered the only convenience. A miniature radiator provided heat in the winter. If you opened the single window on the back wall and the door opposite, a cross breeze might stir the air in the summer months.

'The water closet is at that end of the hall,' Mrs Ivanovitch offered, indicating the direction with a jerk of her head. 'The other end has a shower. We don't provide meals. They have to go out for those.'

'Tell me about how you found Simon Landry,' Carl asked.

'Well, as I said, it was a long time ago. I didn't know him that well. He was a private sort of lad, kept his comings and goings to himself. We don't allow female visitors in the building, but he had no visitors at all, or none that I was aware of.'

'He had a mother and a sister.'

'That I heard. Never met them myself. The day I found his body, one of the students told me that Simon hadn't been in class and their professor was asking about him. The student had knocked but got no answer. Wanted to know if I would open the door to see if he was there, maybe sick, or maybe gone home. When I opened the door, well, you know what we saw.'

'Tell me, if you please.'

'Lying in bed, peaceful as a baby asleep. His shoes under the bed with his socks stuffed inside. His clothes hung up on the hooks. A neat sort. Two buckets beside his bed made us think he'd felt sick when he lay down and put them there, in case.'

'But they were clean?' I asked. Mrs Ivanovitch seemed to notice me for the first time.

'Yep. Nothing in 'em.'

'Did you see him come home the night before?' She shook her head. 'Did anything strike you as odd?' She shook her head again.

'What did you do then?'

'Called the police, of course. The local beat cop was here in five minutes. The others came a half-hour later. The ruling was death from natural causes, since there was no indication of a fight or theft or anything out of the ordinary.'

With a final glance around the room, we stepped back into the hallway. Mrs Ivanovitch closed and locked the door. I turned and nearly tripped over Buzz, who had planted himself at our feet.

'Simon give me gum. You got gum?'

Carl patted his pockets and pulled out a packet of Wrigley's Spearmint. He handed a stick to Buzz, who tore off the paper and popped it into his mouth.

'What do you say to the detective, Buzz?' prompted his mother.

'Thank you.'

'You're welcome, Buzz. Did Simon give you gum like this?' Carl asked.

'Gum.' His smile faded suddenly. 'Simon died.'

'I'm sure you miss him,' I said, wondering just how much this boy might remember. 'Was Simon your friend?'

'Simon is my friend.'

'You were a little boy when Simon lived here. How old are you today, Buzz?'

'Sixteen.'

'When Simon lived here, you were nine. Can you tell me about that time? When you and Simon were friends.'

'He give me gum.'

'Did he play marbles with you?' No response. 'Do you remember the last time you saw him? What he was doing? He came home that night. It was dark and cold out that time of year.'

Buzz appeared to consider what I'd said. Finally he spoke. 'Simon sick. Falling down. A big man carry him home.'

'Simon couldn't walk by himself? A big man helped him walk?' He must have been drunk, in spite of what the other students had said. Someone brought him home and helped him get into bed and set out the vomit pails. A big man. Edward Ricks was a big man. And Beverley Carter had seen him at the diner that night.

'Tell me about the big man.'

'Mean man.'

'How mean? Why was he mean?'

'He say, go away, boy!'

Someone didn't want any witnesses, even one as handicapped as this child. 'But you didn't go away, did you, Buzz? You saw what happened, didn't you?'

'He have animal coat.'

'A fur coat? Made of animal fur?' Did Ricks own one of those raccoon coats that were so popular with the college men?

'He put Simon to bed. Then he go away. Then he come back with pails on fire.'

'Pails on fire?' The pails hadn't been in Simon's room already?

'Two pails on fire.'

'What did the mean man do then?'

'He push me. Go away! Mean man.'

'And Simon? Did you see Simon again?'

'Simon give me gum.'

'Yes, yes. Give Buzz some more gum, Carl.'

'Simon die and go to heaven,' he said, unwrapping the stick of gum and adding it to the wad already in his mouth.

My thoughts raced. Pails carrying fire. The old phrase, *Where there's smoke, there's fire*, played in my head. But the reverse was true too: *Where there's fire, there's smoke*. I caught my breath.

'Mrs Ivanovitch, do you remember if the window in this room was open or closed when you found Simon's body?'

'I can't say I remember such a thing, but it was December, so I'm pretty sure it would be closed.'

Simon Landry had been murdered. Now I knew how.

THIRTY-FOUR

Carl put down his knife and fork and looked straight into my eyes from across the restaurant table. 'All right, Jessie, I saw your face when she said the window would have been closed. You're on to something.'

He knew me too well. In truth, I could hardly swallow my food. I didn't want to spill my thoughts when they were still theories, but I couldn't keep Carl dangling.

'I'm not certain . . .' I cautioned.

'Try it out on me.'

'OK.' I took a deep breath. 'Do you know what dry ice is?'

He shook his head. 'I guess I heard of it, but don't think I really know anything about it.'

'You wouldn't come into contact with it, not unless you were in a play where they needed smoke or fog or a spooky atmosphere. Real smoke is far too dangerous to have on a stage – a fire marshal would have a heart attack just thinking about such a thing. Stage managers use dry ice, which is frozen carbon dioxide, when they need to make smoke or fog for a scene. It looks like white marble. You can buy it in chunks and it dissolves directly into the air without turning first to a liquid, making a type of smoke that hovers low to the ground. It doesn't rise into the air like real smoke.'

'OK.'

'Only two things make dry ice dangerous. One, if you touch it with your bare hands, it burns. Two, if you use it in a small space that isn't well ventilated and if you breathe it for too long, it can kill you.'

He could see where I was heading. 'You think Simon breathed dry ice smoke?'

'Buzz noticed a mean man bringing two pails of fire – which I think means he saw smoke coming from the pails and assumed there was fire in the pails. You know, *Where there's smoke, there's fire.* But in fact, it was dry ice in the pails.'

'And Ricks left the pails beside Simon's bed—'

'At the head of the bed.'

'Made sure the window was closed and left. But everyone said the pails were empty.'

'Dry ice leaves no trace once it evaporates. Ten pounds of the stuff would be deadly in that tiny closet of a room. It would be gone in twelve hours. Less, probably.'

'Wouldn't Simon have noticed the pails there? Smelled something?'

'He would have if he'd been conscious. But Buzz said Simon was sick, falling down. What if this is what happened? Ricks goes to the diner where his students often eat, looking for Simon. He's read the final version of Simon's play, recognizes it as brilliant, and decides to claim it as his own. I understand the students ate at Tom's most nights, so it was a pretty good bet Simon would be there. Ricks sits in the corner, waiting for most of the students to leave. He says something to Simon to invite him to his table, maybe offers to buy him a drink, maybe says he has something to discuss with him. Whatever it is, Simon sits down with his professor. They drink a beer. Ricks drops something into the beer, like Veronal or another sleeping powder. Simon gets very sleepy. He staggers a bit, looks drunk. Ricks helps him across the street and back to his room. Helps him get undressed, get into bed, and go to sleep. Then when he sees Simon is asleep, he brings in the two pails of dry ice, closes up the room, and leaves. Simon sleeps until he dies, very peacefully. No evidence, no marks, no murder weapon. No one would suspect dry ice.'

'How did you know about it?'

'I grew up on stage, you know that. I've seen many acts use dry ice. It creates a lovely mysterious aura or makes a prop building look like it's burning down. They usually put hot water on it to make it smoke up faster, but it isn't necessary. It's really not dangerous to use in a theater because it dissipates quickly. Everyone knows to make sure it isn't left in a small dressing room or closet.'

'Is it poison? How does it kill?'

'Carbon dioxide isn't poisonous. It kills by suffocation. Your lungs don't get enough oxygen. But in all my years in the theater, I've never known of anyone getting sick from dry ice, let alone dying. I do remember once when there was a lot of fog on the stage and the scene ran long, some actors got a bit of a headache which went away when they stepped out of the fog. It really isn't dangerous unless it's misused.'

'So poor Simon never knew a thing.'

'Not a thing. And Edward Ricks has his play. The only copy of it, he thinks. He waits a few years, just to make sure nothing surfaces, then he publishes "his" new work, *Rules of Engagement*. Praise and acclaim! And you know the rest of the story.'

'You need to tell Detective Quinn right away.'

'I will. But you see the problem?'

'Of course. Interesting speculation, no evidence.'

'Not quite. I do have the carbon copy of Simon's play. But it's missing the title page, which would have his name and the date and Professor Ricks's class number and whatever on it. I presume poor Allen Crenshaw gave that to Ricks as proof of what he'd found. Now Ricks has it. And he could just say the carbon copy was what he shared with his students in his writing class. No one's going to put any stock in the testimony of a slow-witted boy who saw something confusing when he was nine years old.'

'I'm convinced. But you're right, there's very little proof. Share this with Detective Quinn. Maybe he'll have some thoughts.'

'He's very new.'

'I know, you said that, but he'll have others in the department he can call on for advice. Detective work is often a collaborative effort.'

'I'll collar him first thing tomorrow morning.'

'Good girl. I'll be visiting my aunt in Newark tomorrow. That ends my days off. The next day, I start back to LA. If you're free, I'll stop by your hotel when I get back from Newark and buy you dinner.'

'I'd like that.'

'Meanwhile, how about a chocolate sundae for dessert? You deserve a reward after all that thinking.'

THIRTY-FIVE

The local police precinct station was just two blocks from the Algonquin, so I slipped over there before I'd even had my morning coffee, eager to share my dry-ice theory with Detective Quinn before he got away for the day. The station was a busy, noisy beehive serving central Manhattan's theater district and beyond, with administrative offices as well as a lockup and police headquarters. A young cop pointed me upstairs to an open room that stretched the entire length of the third floor. With its honeycomb of oak desks and identical, dark-suited worker bees buzzing about, the space made me feel as if I had flown inside the hive itself. It took a bit of searching to find the dark suit I was looking for, but at last I spotted Detective Quinn. He was on the telephone when I made my way to his corner.

'Yes . . . I see . . .' he said in a loud voice, catching my eye and waving me over. 'Yes, tell 'em to call the . . . oh good, you've done that. Excellent . . . I'll be right there.'

He hung up and turned to me, his eyes shining with something that looked like triumph.

'They found Norah!'

'Oh, that's wonderful! Is she all right?'

'She's dead.'

My hand flew to my mouth. I had been so sure Norah had run off on her own accord. The shock knocked my own news clear out of my head.

'Oh, no!' I gasped. 'What—? How—? Was she murdered?'

'I'm heading there now,' he said, pushing his arms into his coat sleeves. 'I'll find out soon enough.'

'Can I come?'

He paused long enough that I feared he would refuse. After all, I wasn't the beauteous Adele Astaire. I held my breath and willed him to say yes. It worked – he relented. 'Just don't get in the way,' and he took off at a rapid pace down the stairs I had just climbed.

'They don't think the death was suspicious, so it's probably not murder. A maid found her in her room. She's been staying in a low-rent hotel not far from here. The maid thought she was asleep and tried to wake her up. Realized she was dead. No blood. They wondered if she'd taken her own life somehow.'

'How could that be?'

'The working theory is that she was overcome with remorse for her part in Allen Crenshaw's death. Veronal, maybe. Arsenic and laudanum are easy to come by too. Mercury bichloride has been popular with Hollywood movie actresses; maybe that's true for the stage actresses too. You remember Olive Thomas, don't you? The film star? She drank mercury bichloride in Paris a few years back.'

Oh yes, Mary Pickford had told me all about Olive Thomas, or 'Ollie', as the Pickford family called her. A beautiful model and actress, she had started as a Ziegfeld Follies girl here in New York, and her torrid affair with Flo Ziegfeld was common knowledge. But when he wouldn't leave his wife to marry her, Olive got hold of Mary's younger brother Jack, who would. Miss Pickford didn't approve of their elopement, calling them 'a couple of children playing together.' Gossip columnists used words like wild, gay and brats to describe the pair. When their marriage inevitably hit the rocks, Jack and Ollie sailed off to Paris for what the motion-picture magazines called a second honeymoon. After a raucous night partying their way through the city's sleazy quarter, Olive somehow drank a quart of mercury bichloride, a medicine used to treat Jack's syphilis, and died several agonizing days later in a hospital ward. Depending upon your sympathies, she had either committed suicide when she learned Jack had given her syphilis, or she had been so drunk and high on cocaine that she didn't know what she was drinking, or she intended to poison Jack all along but he forced her to drink the solution instead. Whatever the truth, the coroner diplomatically ruled accidental death and the French government shipped the body home as fast as they could, eager to avoid further entanglement with Hollywood's biggest scandal.

I thought it prudent to mention none of this to Detective Quinn. It all happened before I'd been hired by Pickford-Fairbanks Studios, so everything I knew was secondhand. But mercury bichloride? Yes, I'd heard of starlets drinking that, and far too often.

'But Norah knew her gun fired only blanks. She had nothing to do with Crenshaw's death, except for being unjustly blamed.'

'Are you sure she knew that?'

'I think she figured it out after we talked about recoil.'

Quinn's police car arrived at the Hotel Remarque in minutes. A seedy six-story brick building with a crack in the glass of its front door and a foot-worn path through the lobby carpet, the Remarque was no longer remarkable, if it ever had been. A bargain-basement hotel patronized largely by theater types on the lower rungs of the success ladder . . . surely Norah could have afforded something better?

A uniformed cop in the lobby pointed us to the stairwell. 'Fourth floor,' he said.

Crammed inside the small room were the hotel manager, two cops, the hapless maid, and the white-haired doctor who had been called to certify the death. All deferred to Detective Quinn the moment he walked in. No one bothered to introduce me. Just as well.

Detective Quinn took out his pencil and a pad of paper with an ostentatious flourish and proceeded to fire questions at the witnesses in strict order of their appearance at the scene. Probably just what the detective manual prescribed. He began by asking the maid her name.

'Juanita.'

'Whole name,' he snapped.

'Juanita Elena Ruiz.' She pushed a strand of black hair off her forehead with shaky fingers. I wished Quinn wouldn't act as if she was a suspect, for crying out loud. The poor woman was frightened.

'Tell me how you found the deceased.'

'I come to clean room. Knock. No answer, so pass-key. I see lady in bed, so I say "sorry madam" but she not talk. I think maybe she sick. Touch arm, but she not move. I run get manager.'

'Did you touch anything? Other than the body, that is.'

'No, sir.'

He turned to the manager. 'Name.'

'Bob Clemmer.'

'What happened when you reached this room, Mr Clemmer?'

'I was in the lobby when Juanita came running. Before I went upstairs, I checked at the register and noted that a Mrs Smith was in Room 412. She'd checked in a week ago. I found her like this, saw that she wasn't breathing, and hurried outside to find a cop. Him.' He jerked his head toward one of the policemen.

'You touch anything?'

'Yeah, I looked around for anything that would identify the woman beyond her last name, Smith, which I presume was an alias.' It wasn't, it was Norah's real name, but I didn't dare interrupt. 'I found that big envelope over there with a few playbills in it, and the name common to all of them was Norah Rose. I read the papers, detective, and I know who pulled the trigger that killed that actor over at the Morosco. It made sense.'

'How so?'

'She did herself in. Couldn't live with the guilt.'

'Did you touch anything else?'

'Her handbag, over there. There was nothing helpful in it. I didn't take any money off her. I know the drill. This isn't the first death we've had at this hotel.'

While the questioning continued, I surveyed the tiny room. There was a single bed, a carved oak dresser with matching dressing table that had an array of Norah's makeup and perfumes spread on top, a comfortable chair upholstered with a pink cabbage rose print, a mirrored wardrobe, and a washstand with porcelain pitcher and bowl. Beside it was a room-service cart on wheels that carried a bucket of water (ice that had melted), a bottle of champagne and one champagne glass. Both bottle and glass looked empty. A window that opened into the room was firmly closed.

'And you, Officer . . .?'

'O'Reilly. Sean O'Reilly. And this is Officer Joseph Donovan. It was just as Mr Clemmer said. I was at the corner with Joe here when Mr Clemmer said he'd found a dead body. Joe went right away to the call box to send for a doctor. I came straight here to secure the scene and wait for the doc. When we found out who she was, Joe went back to the box to tell headquarters, because we knew there was a look-out for that lady.'

Quinn came to the bottom of his sheet of paper, turned the

page and kept scribbling. He should have said, 'Good work, officer,' or something like that, but he just moved to the grandfatherly physician. 'And you, doctor?'

'Dr Frank Pelham.' He had a warm voice and a kind face. I trusted him at once. That must be what folks call 'bedside manner'.

'When did you arrive?'

'Half-hour ago.'

'Did you touch anything other than the deceased?'

'Only that suitcase over there.' I glanced over to the opposite side of the room where a plain leather valise stood on its edge. Not like the fancy ones with shiny brass locks and fittings, but not cheap cardboard either.

'Why did you move it?'

'Because it was in my way, son. It was sitting here, beside the bed, right where I'm standing. I moved it over there, so my fingerprints are on the thing.' He sounded more than a little exasperated.

'What's your take on cause of death?'

'Too soon to tell. There was obviously no violence involved. No blood, no bruises. She died peacefully in her sleep.' That phrase – 'died peacefully in her sleep' – brought me up hard. The same observation had been made about Simon Landry. My thoughts leaped ahead. Was this another murder? Using dry ice? With Playwright Ricks as the common factor?

The doctor continued with words that echoed the ones used in the report from seven years ago. 'It could have been a heart attack, although that's unusual for one so young. She seems a healthy specimen. I put her age in the early thirties. I considered suicide but there are no empty medicine bottles around, no boxes of arsenic powder. I see she consumed an entire bottle of champagne, but that should have resulted in a hangover, not death. I'll refer the case to the city's medical examiner, Dr Charles Norris, and request an autopsy. That will give us something definite to go on.'

'What do you mean, definite?'

While the doctor was talking, I inched unobtrusively a few inches over until I stood beside the leather valise. Without drawing attention to myself, I lifted it by the handle. It wasn't as light as a cardboard suitcase, but it was leather, so it weighed a bit, even empty. A gentle shake told me it was empty.

Dr Pelham continued his lecture. 'Dr Norris or one of his men will probably be able to pinpoint the exact cause of death. You don't know him? He's our city's first trained medical examiner and a top-notch pathologist. No more of these elected coroners who know zilch about medicine. Dr Norris will look at her kidneys for lesions to see if she ingested bichloride of mercury. That's unlikely, since it usually takes five to ten days for that to kill you, but it's a possibility. So is arsenic, but that's also unlikely. Tests to detect arsenic in the organs of the deceased have been around for a hundred years, but Dr Norris and his team refined them, so if there's even a trace of arsenic present, they'll find it. No, my bet is on methyl alcohol. There could have been some in the champagne, although it looks imported and imported wines are usually safe to drink. I'll have the residue tested.'

'What's methyl alcohol?'

'Wood alcohol. "Smoke," some call it. It's all over the city.'

'I've read about that, I think . . .' said Quinn, trying to camouflage his ignorance.

'Damage from wood alcohol shows up in stomach tissue and the esophagus and in the appearance of blood in the brain. Ever since the federal government mandated putting more wood alcohol in denatured alcohol, we've seen a huge uptick in hospitalizations and deaths.'

'What?'

'You new to New York's police force, Detective Quinn?'

His cheeks flushed tomato red. 'Why do you ask?'

'Because I'm surprised you aren't aware of the enormous increase in deaths this year. Last year, the government started requiring denatured alcohol to be more poisonous than it already was, since people were still drinking it after distilling out the poison. They required the doubling or tripling of the wood alcohol, up to ten per cent, making the callous argument that anyone who persisted in drinking illegal alcohol deserved to die. Why, so far this year, Dr Norris has counted more than twelve hundred people in New York City alone who were sickened or blinded by drinking some form of industrial alcohol, poisoned by our own government. Another four hundred people died. Four hundred, and the year not yet over! Most were men from the Lower East Side, the Gas House district, Hell's Kitchen, and neighborhoods like those. Men nobody cares about. Rich folks can get hold of imported hooch.'

'No, I, uh . . . I didn't know that.'

'Just last weekend, we had eleven dead and sixty hospitalized. Two days later, another twenty-two were dead. Dr Norris fought hard against the law – still fights for repeal – to no avail.'

'How long do you think it will take for Miss Smith's autopsy?'

'Usually takes a few days. They are busy men and the number of suspicious deaths is mounting alarmingly. But Dr Norris is a friend of mine who might do me the favor of putting this woman to the head of the line if I tell him it's important. Is it?'

'It is.'

At this point, I could hold back no longer. 'Excuse me, detective. I'd like to ask the doctor, was the suitcase open or closed when you came in?'

'It was open, my dear.'

'Was there anything in it?'

'No. Evidently the lady had already unpacked.'

And left the empty suitcase opened beside her bed for a week? No siree bob, this was another of Edward Ricks's murders. I was certain of it now.

No one was watching me, so it was easy to slip downstairs, back to the hotel lobby where I asked the desk clerk if he had been working last night.

He had.

And had he brought a bottle of champagne up to Room 412 for Miss Smith?

No, but I could check with Ronald Carstairs, the teenage son of the Remarque's owners. The boy worked for tips, handling room service and other special requests. And yes, he was here this morning. He was here every day. He lived in the hotel with his parents in the apartment at the back. The clerk pointed to a dark passageway that led to their door. I thanked him with a silver half-dollar.

Mrs Carstairs had already heard about the dead woman in 412 and was eager to wake her son if he could be of any help. A trusting soul, she didn't think to question my credentials. 'Ronnie was up late last night with luggage and room service calls. He's a good boy. He'll help you if he can.'

Ronnie appeared, yawning and scratching himself and stumbling in his slippers. He seemed a bit less eager than his mother was to interrupt his sleep, but when he learned there had been a murder in the hotel, he came suddenly alert.

'Ronnie, do you remember taking champagne to a woman in 412?'

'Yeah, sure. Is she the dead woman?'

'I'm afraid so.'

'Copacetic!'

'What can you tell me about the champagne? Who ordered it, and so forth?'

'Well, I was on bellhop duty when a man stopped me on the sidewalk and handed me a sawbuck. Said would I take this bottle of real French champagne to the room of a lady named Norah Rose. Well, sure as shootin', I said. He already opened the bottle, so I didn't need a corkscrew. I got the ice bucket and a glass – just one glass, he told me, he couldn't join her – and looked her up in the register but there wasn't anybody by that name on the register.'

'What did you do?'

'Stan and me looked through it for anyone named Norah who was in a single, and we found a sheba named Norah Smith. Figured she was using an alias. Lotsa people do that here.'

'Then what?'

'I wheeled the cart on up. And she gave me another dollar.'

'What time was that?'

He scrunched up his face. 'It was dark out. Maybe seven o'clock.'

'Did she ask who sent it?'

'Wouldn't you? I said what the fella told me to say, that he was an admirer and it was too dark to get a good look at him.'

'What *did* he look like?'

'Like anybody. Tall, I guess. Wore cheaters. Had a hat on so I couldn't tell if he was bald or hairy. Sounded snooty, like some big rich guy.'

'Would you recognize him if you saw him again?'

'Maybe.'

'And Norah? What was she like?'

'Real pretty. Real red hair, long. It's a shame she's dead!'

'Did the desk clerk see the man?'

'Dunno. Ask him.'

'I will. Thank you, Ronnie. You've been a big help.'

The praise made him blush bright red. 'My pleasure, ma'am.'

Just as I returned to the front desk clerk, the one I'd tipped earlier, Detective Quinn and the cops came downstairs. Quinn saw me talking to the desk clerk and frowned. I called out that I'd join him in a moment.

'Did you notice a tall man wearing glasses and carrying a tan leather suitcase come through the lobby last night? I know that's a pretty vague description, but it's the best I've got.'

He shook his head. 'That describes most of the men staying here, ma'am.'

How Ricks had found Norah in the first place, I didn't know. How he'd gained entrance into her locked room, I could only guess. But I knew how he'd killed her, with spiked champagne that made her go to sleep and dry ice carried up in that suitcase, the same way he'd killed Simon Landry. His third murder. And I had not a shred of decent evidence for any of them.

THIRTY-SIX

As soon as we were alone in the police motorcar, I hit Detective Quinn with my dry-ice theory. Just as I'd done with Carl, I told Quinn about the slow-witted boy who'd seen the 'big man' carry 'pails of fire'. I told him how dry ice could give people headaches and dizziness, and eventually they'd suffocate. He listened as he drove, nodding now and then, his hands busy with the gears of the battered Ford and his feet pushing the pedals, making no comment as I applied the Simon Landry reasoning to Norah Rose, except that Ricks brought the dry ice in with a suitcase instead of a pail. Not until we had pulled into the parking space behind the police station did he speak.

'What's this dry-ice stuff made of again?'

'Carbon dioxide.'

'And it's poison, but they use it in theaters?'

'It's not poison and it's not dangerous in open spaces. Only when it's in a closed-up space does it cause breathing problems. It prevents a person from getting enough good air.'

'And it disappears into nothing? You've seen this?'

'Many times. When it evaporates, it turns to fog or smoke and mixes with the air, so yes, it leaves no trace.'

'How long does this take?'

'Depends on the size of the dry-ice block. A few hours, a day.'

'I mean, how long does it take to kill a person?'

'Depends on the size of the space, I guess. I don't know.'

'Norah ran away. Presumably she was hiding from Ricks because she was afraid he'd kill her.'

'She must have seen him in the wings from the platform where she stood above him, waiting for her entrance. I don't think she saw him actually firing the weapon, or she'd have spoken up right away, but he was standing there when she fired her blanks, so she must have figured out that he'd killed Crenshaw and that he knew she was a witness.'

'So how did he find her?'

'I don't know.'

'And once he'd found her, how did he persuade this woman who was hiding from him to open the door, invite him in, take off her clothes, get into bed, and lie quietly on her back with her hands folded across her chest while he opened up a suitcase and exposed the dry ice? And then he told her to lie still for a few hours while the fumes killed her. Does this sound likely to you?'

'He could have drugged her with something in the champagne first. I'm sure he did that to Simon Landry.'

'Right. Maybe he invited her to a speakeasy for a drink. Do you really think a jury is going to convict someone of murder on the strength of what a sixteen-year-old idiot boy remembers from seven years ago and this fairy tale about dry ice? I'd be the laughing stock of the force if I even hinted at this nonsense.'

'It's not a fairy tale.'

But I had no answers and he knew it.

'Look, Jessie, I mean, Miss Beckett, you and Miss Astaire have been very helpful in this case up until now, and I – we, at the department – appreciate that. As soon as the medical examiner comes back with his verdict on what killed Norah Rose – or Norah Smith, I should say – we'll have a clear path forward. In the meanwhile, I have a slew of other suspicious deaths to investigate. With this epidemic of wood alcohol poisonings, we're hard pressed to tell accidental deaths from murders, so every one of 'em is deemed suspicious until we can rule out murder. I read in the paper that Mary Pickford and Douglas Fairbanks had left for California. Will you be going soon too?'

'Thank you for the ride home, detective,' I said pointedly, as he had not driven me back to the Algonquin, but to the precinct station. 'I'll walk from here. Good day.'

The maddening thing was, the man was right. I had nothing but a pretty story, a clever guess, a theory, a hypothesis, as the scientists say. No evidence. But I'd have bet my last dollar that Edward Ricks had murdered Simon Landry, Allen Crenshaw, and poor Norah Rose Smith, one with a bullet and two with disappearing dry ice. And I had an idea about finding the proof.

I ducked inside the Algonquin to use the lobby telephone to

call Adele. I was sure she'd want to come with me to the Morosco.
I caught her up on what had happened in the case, and told her
where I was headed.

'Can you meet me there?'

'Oh, Jessie, I would kill to meet you there but I've twisted
my ankle a little – nothing much, not even a genuine sprain, but
Fred won't let me move from the sofa. He called a doctor and
the wicked man is making me keep my foot elevated with ice
on it for at least twenty-four hours. It doesn't even hurt, but I
can't go anywhere without bringing on a fainting spell from
Mother and making Fred so nervous he can't eat. I think it's a
great idea that you're going, and I am begging you to call me
later to tell me what you've found.'

So I promised her I would, and I went to the theater alone.

On the busy sidewalk in front of the Algonquin, I turned west
on 44th Street and cut over to 45th at the corner, arriving at the
Morosco in a couple of minutes. The old man at the back door
– his name was Sam, I had learned – recognized me by now and
waved me in with a cheerful greeting. I made my way directly
to the stage manager's office.

Of course, he wasn't there. I tracked him down to the apron
where he was standing over the electrician, fiddling with footlights. I tried to jolly him out of his scowl with a big smile.

'Hello, Mr Levine. It's me, again, sorry to interrupt, but I have
news you'll want to hear.'

My charm offensive didn't work. 'What is it?' he snapped.

'Maybe we could talk somewhere more private? It's important,
honest.'

He snatched the cigar out of his mouth and glared at me. 'Wait
for me in my office.'

I waited. And waited. Until at last he came, leaving the door
open as he took the one chair.

'I thought you'd like to know that Norah Rose was found
dead this morning.'

That silenced him for a long moment. 'Sorry to hear that,' he
muttered gruffly. 'She was a good kid. What happened?'

'The medical examiner is going to do an autopsy. We'll know
more then. A maid found her at the Hotel Remarque.'

'Murder?'

'She seems to have died peacefully. There were no signs of violence. The cops are keeping it out of the papers for a couple of days, but I thought you should know.'

'Thanks.'

He made to stand, so I quickly asked, 'Can you tell me where you buy your dry ice?'

'Huh?'

'I want to know where you get the dry ice that's delivered here every evening.'

A young woman stuck her head around the corner. 'Excuse me, Mr Levine. Mr Belkowitz wants to see you right away.'

'Yeah, yeah,' he replied absently. He wasn't curious about my reasons for wanting to buy dry ice, just eager to be rid of me, but he owed me an answer. So he fumbled through a sheaf of papers in an in-basket on his desk until he found the one he wanted. 'Yeah, here it is, just wanted to be sure. Eskimo Ice. Near the candy factory. We get a delivery every day except Sundays.'

'Excuse me, I'm not familiar with the city. Where's the candy factory?'

'Auerbach Candy, Forty-Sixth and Eleventh. Eskimo's next door. Most of the theaters use Eskimo 'cause they're close and they deliver.'

I thanked him and promised to keep him apprised of the results of Norah Rose's autopsy. It seemed the curmudgeonly stage manager had a small soft spot for Norah.

THIRTY-SEVEN

A s I approached the block that housed the candy factory and the dry-ice works, the aroma of chocolate made my stomach grumble. I'd forgotten about lunch; there had been no time. I inhaled deeply, hoping the lovely scent would dampen the hunger pangs, but no dice. Auerbach's factory was humming with activity as I passed, as workers streamed in and out of several doors, presumably on their lunch break. Chocolate manufacturers had expected a windfall when Prohibition made alcohol illegal. They hoped people would replace liquor with chocolate drinks, both hot and cold; sadly, their optimism was doomed to disappointment. Instead, consumption of flavored seltzer waters made by Coca-Cola, Dr Pepper, and Pepsi-Cola soared. Chocolate makers consoled themselves with the surge in candy sales. Auerbach's was one of dozens of such factories in New York alone. I guessed that the location of Eskimo Ice next door was no accident. Dry ice would come in handy when shipping ice cream. A freight train chugged past on the Eleventh Avenue tracks, adding an unpleasant, gassy, sooty smell to the chocolate. Gratefully, I ducked inside Eskimo Ice where most of the outside noise and aromas couldn't follow.

The Eskimo office held one desk and two oak chairs opposite it. A lanky, middle-age colored man wearing a tan work shirt with *Jake* embroidered above the pocket was helping the oddest-looking pair of customers I'd seen in a month of Sundays. A very tall, lean man and a short squat woman put me in mind of that old nursery rhyme about Jack Sprat and his wife.

'Be with you in a minute, ma'am,' Jake acknowledged me as I came through the vestibule. I took one of the two chairs and looked around the office as I waited my turn. A 1926 calendar taped to the wall had the picture of a scantily clad bathing beauty reclining provocatively on a beach chair. A cork board behind the desk was stuck with as many straight pins as a porcupine, and the desk itself was messy with papers. A metal file cabinet stood in each corner, drawers hanging open, and a small black safe with a combination lock sat beside one of them. The Eskimo man was dickering with Mr and Mrs Sprat about prices for some upcoming orders.

They concluded their business, the men shook hands, and the couple prepared to leave. Just as I stood up, another colored man entered and said something about being there to pay his bill.

'Please go ahead,' I said, sitting back down. 'I'm in no hurry.' He wouldn't take long, and my business probably would. More important, I didn't want anyone else in the office when I made my request.

The customer was from the Lafayette Theater up on 132nd Street in Harlem, one of the few New York theaters that let colored patrons sit in orchestra seats and not just the balconies. Everyone in the theater world knew of the Lafayette. Last year, they'd done the unthinkable – put on a drama written by a colored man, someone named Anderson. I wondered if this man was that playwright, but no, he gave another name, counted out the cash to pay the theater's bill, and bid us good day. Jake made some notes, opened the safe (taking care to position his body so I couldn't see him dial the combination), deposited the money, and turned his attention to me.

'Good afternoon, Jake,' I began, with a smile and as much charm as I could cram into each sentence. 'I'm Jessie Beckett, here on an errand for Detective Benjamin Quinn, who is investigating the suspicious death of an actress from the Morosco Theater. I know your company supplies dry ice to the Morosco – Bill Levine, the stage manager, told me how pleased he is with your product and your delivery service – and the detective would like to know if you sold a small quantity of dry ice yesterday, Tuesday, to a customer by the name of Edward Ricks. Do you know that name?'

'Ricks? Sounds familiar. You said yesterday? Lemme just take a look here.' He fished out a folder from under a pile of papers. 'We call 'em walk-ins, folks that come for a one-time order. We had a lot of 'em Sunday, it being Halloween and them wanting something spooky for their parties. They buy our small blocks cut in two-foot squares. But yesterday . . . let me see . . . yep, it says so right here.' He held the paper toward me as he pointed to a line in the middle of the columned page and read out loud, 'E. Ricks 20 pounds.'

I was so intent on the name – and so thrilled to have found some hard evidence at last that I could hardly contain my excitement; I was scarcely aware that the door to the vestibule behind me had opened. Jake glanced up, however, and looking past me said, 'Be right with you, sir,' but then I heard him gasp. 'Oh, my lord, mister, we got no money here but what's in the safe, and they don't let me know the combination.'

I spun around only to come face to face with Edward Ricks himself, holding a pistol in his right hand. A pistol identical to the one Norah used at every performance. The one he used to shoot Allen Crenshaw from the wings.

'I'll take that, if you please.' He held out his hand for the Tuesday customer list. Jake was no fool; he gave it up.

'You got what you want, now, mister, you can go.'

'You!' he spat, looking into my eyes with a glare that shimmered with liquid hate. 'You are the cause of all this. You are the reason Norah is dead. You and your meddling. Well, you're done now. You'll pay the piper. Now go!' And he pointed with his gun to the door at the back the office.

'There's nothing back there, mister, no money; nothing but warehouse and garage,' protested Jake.

'Shut up. Both of you, go!'

Jake opened the door with a reluctant look backwards at me, as if he was sending me a message. I couldn't read his eyes. There was nothing to do but follow him into the cavernous warehouse, a vast expanse of concrete floor with a ceiling as high as a theater stage. Ricks and his gun stayed at my back. He was going to shoot us, deep in the bowels of this manufactory where no one would hear the gunfire. When the police eventually arrived, it would look like a robbery gone bad.

The warehouse was poorly lit by a few high windows and some naked bulbs dangling overhead. To the right I spied a huge metal door that looked like something out of a bank vault, impregnable and thick. When Ricks ordered Jake to open it, I realized he was familiar with the layout of the place, probably because he'd been here more than once in the course of his theatrical career to make arrangements for dry ice.

'Open it up, boy!' he snapped.

With a metallic clang, Jake wrenched the door handle and pulled open the thick door. It was the dry-ice storage vault, a walk-in cooler. He wasn't going to shoot us; he was going to lock us inside to suffocate.

'Well, damn it all to hell,' Ricks swore. 'Where the devil is all the ice?'

Darkness obscured the far end of the vault, but clearly the space was empty. Whatever dry ice that had been stored there was gone now.

'It's usually empty this time of day, mister.'

'Where's it gone?'

'On the trucks for delivery.'

'Then let's go have a look at the trucks.'

The size of the plant astonished me. I'd thought Eskimo Ice consisted of the office and maybe a back room for storage. I had no idea they actually manufactured the stuff on the premises, but the presence of an assembly line of boxy steel machinery connected by a maze of pipes drove home the realization that this was where they created the solid dry ice from liquid carbon dioxide and pressed it into blocks for sale. The warehouse space stretched from one end of the block to the other, from 46th Street to 47th, sandwiched between Auerbach Candy and a carpet cleaning business. At the far end of the garage, a fleet of Ford Model TT panel trucks waited to make the day's deliveries.

Our footsteps echoed on the hard floor as Ricks marched us toward the trucks. The eerie silence of the warehouse was broken by distant clattering sounds coming from Auerbach's next door. So near and yet impossibly far away. I tried to lag behind Jake a bit, to get closer to Ricks, thinking maybe I could knock the gun out of his hand, but he never let me come within striking distance. Measuring the distance to the door at the far end of the warehouse, I considered making a dash for it, hoping that Ricks's shots would miss a moving target, but then I remembered that he'd hit Crenshaw in the heart from all the way across the stage.

'Open up one of those trucks, boy. Lemme see inside.'

'This won't work, Ricks,' I said, foolishly, since it was obvious his plan was working quite well. 'Detective Quinn knows where I am. He's planning to meet me here. If you leave now, you can probably get away before he and his men arrive.'

Ricks paid me no mind. When Jake got the truck door open, I saw the blocks of white ice stacked inside, full almost to the top. As soon as the moist, warm air hit the ice, wisps of white fog swirled out.

'No good. Open the other. Quick!'

Jake slammed the door shut.

The trucks, six identical Fords, had been modified with enclosed backs, turning them into delivery trucks. The second truck Jake opened was similarly packed to the gills. The third one held less but still didn't meet Ricks's needs.

'Listen, Ricks, don't be a simp,' I said. 'The cops know all about Simon Landry's murder. And that you stole his play and called it your own. We've got the carbon copy for proof. And they know you shot Crenshaw. A witness has come forward. You still have time to get away if you go now.'

I may as well have been talking to the wall.

The fourth truck was only half full. Just what he was looking for. 'Get in,' he ordered, and when I wouldn't move, he came closer to shove me. Before he could push me, I dropped to a crouch, under his gun hand, and launched myself against his knees. I tried to hit hard enough to topple him, but there wasn't enough momentum behind my thrust to do more than shake him. I grabbed one of his legs and pulled.

'Help!' I shouted.

Ricks fired one shot into the air to freeze Jake and brought his gun hand down on me, smashing my shoulder and driving me on to the floor. I hoped he would reach down to grab me and give Jake a chance to tackle him. Instead he stepped back out of my reach.

'Get her up,' he ordered Jake, waving the gun. 'Get in there, both of you.'

My shoulder exploded in pain. I kept to the floor, making it hard for Jake to move me.

'Get inside or I'll shoot you in the head right now. And don't think I won't.'

For a small man, Jake was strong. He practically lifted me into the back of the truck and deposited me on the floor. Ricks slammed the double doors shut, threw the bolt, and padlocked us in the dark tomb.

THIRTY-EIGHT

Dry ice is far, far colder than regular ice, so much so that you must use special gloves to handle it, so naturally the interior of the panel truck was freezing cold. A thin white haze obscured the ice blocks, making it hard to avoid touching them. I was wearing my jacket, but Jake had no overcoat and was immediately shivering like he had the Spanish flu. My shoulder throbbed. I wondered if the cold would kill us before we had time to suffocate.

What I knew of dry ice would fill a thimble. Jake, on the other hand, was an expert. His analysis wasn't a happy one.

'How long do we have?' I asked bluntly.

'No telling for sure, miss. In this small space, it'll be fifteen minutes, maybe, before you start getting a headache. That's the warning to get into some fresh air. If you don't, nausea and breathing trouble come next.'

'When will the drivers get here?'

'Not until four o'clock.'

It was about two. Unless one of the drivers arrived very, very early, we were doomed.

'Is anyone else around? Anyone who would notice you're missing?' He shook his head. 'Would a customer come in here, looking for you?'

'Not likely. Still, it don't hurt to make some noise.' He put on a pair of gloves he had stuffed in his pants pocket and began pounding on the metal door. I almost told him to stop, in case Ricks was still outside, but realized it was highly unlikely the man would stick around. And so what if he did? If he had any smarts at all, he would return to the Morosco and make sure lots of people noticed that he was far from the Eskimo Ice factory on the afternoon that two people died in a panel truck. And he'd burn that sheet of paper that showed him buying dry ice the afternoon before Norah was murdered, just as he had no doubt destroyed the incriminating title page of Simon

Landry's carbon copy. There would be no evidence whatsoever that pointed to any involvement by Edward Ricks in the three theater murders.

It took no time at all to ascertain that there was nothing in the panel truck that would help break us out. No crowbar, no ice tongs, not even an extra pair of gloves. Nothing but white blocks of dry ice stacked almost to the roof, filling the front half of the truck.

But there was a small oblong window on the front of the truck, a window that let the driver peer back into the cargo hold. 'What about that window? Can we break it?'

Jake stopped pounding. We couldn't even reach the window, let alone try to smash the glass, not until Jake moved the blocks of ice one by one from the front to the back of the truck. I couldn't help him – touching the dry ice would burn my hands badly and Jake had only the one pair of gloves. My head hurt, and soon my temples were throbbing so much I forgot about the pain in my shoulder. Fear is a great motivator, however, and Jake moved the ice in record time. He reached the window just as the first symptoms of nausea washed over me. I swallowed hard. This was no time to throw up.

He pounded the glass with his gloved hand. It didn't crack.

'It's pretty thick,' he said, and turning sideways, he tried bashing it with his elbow. Again and again he threw his weight behind the blow, but the glass held tight. 'Wait, I almost forgot. I have this.' He drew a pocket knife out of his trouser pocket. Two blades, one about three inches long, one shorter, came out of one end, and a dull, short blade that looked like it might be useful as a screwdriver came out the other end. With that blade, he tried to pry the window open at the edge.

It snapped off.

He tried the smaller, sharp blade, but that broke off as well.

Finally, he grasped the closed knife in his fist and hit the glass with the butt of the knife handle as hard as he could. It cracked.

'Halleluiah, Jesus!' he cried, striking the glass with everything he had. And again and again. Each time the cracks multiplied, until at long last, the glass shattered, scattering bits of glass on to the truck's floor and through to the seat on the other side.

Putting his mouth to the opening, he gulped several deep breaths of fresh air, then motioned for me to stand in his spot and do the same.

'This will keep us safe until the drivers come,' I said with relief. Jake shook his head. He wasn't so sure.

The reprieve dissolved some minutes later when my vision became blurry. I blinked hard, trying to clear my view, but nothing worked. With my nose and mouth at the broken window, I sucked in as much fresh air as I could. Jake watched me a while before offering his verdict. 'It isn't enough. The outside air isn't coming in fast enough to reduce the amount of carbon dioxide.'

I was feeling dizzy, and nothing focused, but I could make out the familiar dashboard on the Ford. I had learned to drive a Ford Runabout back in Oregon, and this panel truck was nothing more than that same Model T front with an enclosed rear end in place of the passenger seat. I recognized the gears and few of the buttons. More important, I knew where the horn was.

'I think I can reach the horn. Maybe someone will hear us honking, even if they couldn't hear your pounding.'

I stretched my arm through the window, cutting my underarm on the jagged glass. Before I could bleed to death, Jake pulled off one of his gloves and stuffed it between my skin and the glass. 'Here, can you reach now?'

Stretch as I might, I couldn't get my fingers all the way to the horn button on the steering pole. 'My arm's not long enough. You try.'

Gingerly we switched places again. Jake wasn't a big man, but he was bigger than I was, and his reach was a good four inches longer than mine. With groans and pants, he pushed his arm through the little window until his shoulder got stuck in the opening, but he managed to touch the steering pole. 'I got it! I got it! Just let me feel around for the button now . . .'

And there came the welcome sound of a sharp horn, honking long and loud, again and again.

'Try S-O-S. Do you know that? The Morse code signal?'

'No,' he grunted.

'Three short, three long, and three short. Then pause and do it again, three short, three long, three short.'

Echoing throughout the cavernous garage came the international distress signal in endless repetition: S-O-S, S-O-S.

'Surely someone will hear that,' I said. My head was swimming now and I was shivering uncontrollably. I would soon fall down if I didn't sit, but I couldn't sit on the ice. I had to risk sitting on the truck floor, with only my clothing between me and the freezing metal.

With Jake's arm completely blocking the window, there was no fresh air at all coming in. I was already woozy and sick, and no longer any help. Jake was a little stronger, but we had only as long as he could hold out. If someone came into the office, or if someone outside heard the S-O-S, we would have a chance.

This was all my fault. If I had only told Detective Quinn where I was going. If I had only left word for Carl, Jake and I wouldn't be in this mess. But no, I charged ahead, independent as always and overly confident in my ability to deal with whatever problem came my way. I could picture Carl coming to the Algonquin to say goodbye before he left New York. He'd ask the desk clerk where I was. He'd become concerned when I wasn't in my room, then frantic. He'd track down Detective Quinn and learn that he didn't know where I was either. Carl knew me well enough to know I'd not given up my quest to prove Edward Ricks's guilt, and he'd realize I was alone and probably in trouble. He cared about me, probably more than anyone else. But he would be helpless. Out of his element in a strange city. He'd know nothing more until after four o'clock when the drivers came and found Jake and me dead in the truck. Carl would figure out what had happened and who had done it, but he'd be as stymied as I was when it came to evidence. I'd let him down. He really cared for me. He'd be devastated, and it was my fault. Carl was not going to appear in the nick of time to save me from my own impulsive investigating.

Edward Ricks may not have been a great playwright, but he was very, very good at murder.

The last thing I remember before I blacked out was Jake's honking the Morse code signal over and over and over and over . . .

THIRTY-NINE

I blinked back into semi-consciousness to find myself lying on my back on the cement floor of the Eskimo Ice garage. Two anxious young men wearing white were gently slapping my hands and cheeks. A woman in a white apron held a bottle of smelling salts under my nose and I jerked and gasped.

'Wake up, lady. There you go, wake up now. She's coming around, I think, Ethel. Hey, lady, come on, wake up.'

For long minutes, I couldn't figure out where I was, but gradually, images of the dry-ice office, Jake and Ricks, the panel truck and the Morse code crept back into my head. Fuzziness stayed with me for some time, but at least I knew I was alive.

'What happened?' I croaked.

Jake was sitting beside me on the concrete floor. He couldn't speak, but his nod toward the young men told me a lot.

'We were working the chocolate-almond-bar wrapping machine,' said one. 'We share a common wall, and luckily, it was thin enough that we heard this SOS noise from somewhere.'

'At first,' said the other, 'I brushed it off as someone tapping out a joke, but when it kept going, I said to Paul here, I said, "Let's just go look outside and see what's what." Well, there was no sound outside, so we came into the office here to see if you folks had heard anything, and there was no one there.'

'But the sound was getting louder,' said Paul, 'so we followed it into the factory and saw the panel trucks, and, well, here we are.'

All I could do was croak, 'Thank you.'

'Aw shucks, lady, t'was nothing. Paul and me, we served in the navy during the war, and we all knew Morse code.'

'We should call an ambulance,' said the women.

'No, I'm fine. I don't need an ambulance, do you, Jake?'

Jake stood up on shaky legs. 'No, missy, I'm fine. I didn't conk out, like you did. I just need some time to clear my head.'

'Please, call the police,' I told the woman. 'Ask for Detective

Benjamin Quinn and tell him that Ricks nearly murdered two more people. He'll come right away.' To be honest, I wasn't sure he hadn't washed his hands of me entirely, but it was worth a try.

The mush in my head began to settle like the fog from the back of the truck. The woman in white determined there was nothing more for her to do and returned to her assembly line. The two former sailors, enjoying their moment in the limelight, wanted to wait for the police to make their rescue story official.

'Jake,' I said. 'How long have you worked here?'

'Nearly nine years.'

'Has your job always been the same?'

'Sure has. I take care of the office and help in back with the ice manufacturing and sometimes with the loading.'

'How far back do your records go?'

'Twenty-four years, to the start of the company. When it was just regular ice.'

'Are you feeling steady enough to look up another date? Eleventh of December 1919. Same name, Edward Ricks.'

Eager for the results, I wobbled my way back to the office with Jake. His files were in order, so it took only a minute to pull up the sales for December of 1919. Lo and behold, Ricks was there in black ink on white paper, having purchased twenty pounds of dry ice that very day he killed Simon Landry. Evidence at last!

But I wasn't going to kid myself again – it was weak evidence.

At that moment, Detective Quinn pulled up outside the office door in an official motorcar with a uniformed cop driving. He looked very unhappy.

'What's the story here, Jessie?'

'Detective Quinn, this is Jake, the office manager for Eskimo Ice. I came here to see if Edward Ricks had purchased dry ice the day Norah Rose died, and Jake found evidence that he had, indeed, bought twenty pounds of the stuff, just the right amount to fit inside a suitcase. But Ricks must have overheard me when I was asking the stage manager at the Morosco which dry-ice manufacturer they used, and he figured out what I was looking for. He followed me here and jumped us with a gun – a gun

identical to the one Norah used every night – and took the daily
sales list. Then he forced Jake and me into a panel truck packed
with dry ice in order to kill us. If we hadn't been able to signal
to these two gentlemen working in the adjacent factory, we'd be
dead by now, and Ricks's murder count would total five.'

Quinn looked at the two candy-makers, who were nodding
their solemn agreement. He took down their names and stories
and dismissed them.

'There was one thing Ricks forgot. He'd bought dry ice here
seven years ago, the afternoon before Simon Landry's death, and
that piece of paper is right here.' He scrutinized the ledger Jake
handed him.

'So he did. That's evidence all right, but evidence any lawyer
would dismiss as coincidence. A second coincidence would carry
more weight, but you say Ricks took that away?'

'And has surely destroyed it by now.'

'Maybe not. Anyway, we can arrest him for two counts of
attempted murder. That should get him a couple of years in the
pen, unless a crooked lawyer gets him off on some technicality,
which could well happen considering he's famous here in the
city. I know that's not what you want, Jessie, but it's likely all
you'll get.'

'What happens now?' asked Jake.

'We'll pick him up at the Morosco Theater or, if he's not there,
his home.' He picked up the telephone on Jake's desk and called
the police station to ask someone to look up Ricks's address,
which he jotted down in his notebook. Then he requested backup.

'Can I come with you?'

'I'll drop you at the Algonquin when we go past, but I don't
think it's a good idea for you to be there when we arrest Ricks.'

Ricks's address turned out to be a ritzy apartment building
near Park Avenue and East 64th, making it a waste of Quinn's
time to go far out of his way to take me home first. He would
go to Ricks's place, and I would stay in the motorcar while he
and the other cops arrested the man, if he was there. If he was
not, they would drop me at the Algonquin and descend on the
Morosco to pick him up.

That was Quinn's plan. It wasn't mine.

FORTY

E dward Ricks owned a lovely four-story brownstone on East
64th, purchased, I presumed, recently with money he'd
amassed from his hit play. His street was one of the
quieter ones, with young trees in front, girls hopscotching on
the sidewalk, and a pretty church steeple on the corner. A woman
walking a cocker spaniel sent a curious glance as the two police
cars pulled up to the curb in front of his house, but she didn't
pause to inquire about their business.

'Stay here,' Quinn ordered, checking his Colt police revolver
and putting it back in its holster.

He and two uniformed cops walked up the front steps. A
fourth man circled around to the rear by way of a narrow
passageway between buildings to make sure Ricks didn't scoot
out the back. I watched a brown-skinned woman in a starched
black uniform answer the front door. The bachelor's housekeeper. As she invited them inside, I sprang from the back seat
and scurried up the steps in time to slip in behind them. Before
she could close the door, I was inside the narrow entrance hall.
Quinn, his attention fixed firmly in front of him, didn't notice
anything amiss. I hoped that by the time he looked over his
shoulder, it would be too late to shoo me out.

Quinn led the way into the living room, where a startled
Edward Ricks stood up, a newspaper in hand. I hung back in the
hallway out of sight and listened to him say, 'Edward Ricks, you
are under arrest for the murder of Norah Rose and the attempted
murder of two persons at a factory this afternoon. Please come
with us.'

Edward Ricks had spent decades as a writing professor, years
as a playwright, and months as a high-society man-about-town,
but for all his association with the theater, he was no actor. His
exaggerated facial expressions and hand-wringing could only be
described as high melodrama.

'What?' he cried, dropping his newspaper to the floor and

raising one hand to his cheek in mock surprise. 'How can this
be? How dare you? Do you know who I am, young man? I've
been here all day. And last night. Luisa will vouch for me, won't
you, Luisa?' He turned to the housekeeper.

'Yes, Mr Ricks. You been here all day.'

I wondered whether he'd heard the word 'attempted'. Did he
realize Jake and I weren't dead? I wasn't sure. He could hardly
exclaim, *What? Are they still alive?* Then, as everyone turned to
look at Luisa, they caught a glimpse of me, standing behind
her at the edge of the living room, trying to melt into the
wallpaper.

'You!' he exclaimed, turning bright red with rage. No acting
here – this was genuine fury at its highest volume. 'You miserable little whore! This is all your doing. I had nothing to do with
Norah's death, detective, and this liar's word is worthless. I wasn't
anywhere near Eskimo Ice today.'

'No one mentioned Eskimo Ice, sir. Thank you for clarifying
that you were there. We have two credible witnesses, your
intended victims, and we also have enough evidence in Norah
Rose's death to charge you with murder.'

'This is preposterous. I'm going to call my attorney at once.'

I couldn't resist adding my two cents' worth, nor could I help
inventing some evidence against him in hopes he'd blurt out
some sort of confession. 'You were in the wings that night. You
shot Crenshaw because he was blackmailing you, and Norah
Rose realized it when she understood that her gun had been
shooting blanks all along.'

'Ridiculous! It was Wesley Crenshaw who switched the bullets.
The police found the proof at his house.'

'Sure, a box of shells with your fingerprints on it.'

'That's not possible. I—'

'What? You wore gloves? Not carefully enough, it seems. Then
you killed Norah the same way you killed Simon Landry, with
dry ice; only this time, there's hard evidence. The leftover champagne will show which sleeping powder you used to drug the
poor girl. The bellhop who delivered it has identified you. And
the desk clerk remembers you carrying the suitcase upstairs. You
may have destroyed yesterday's ledger at Eskimo Ice, but their
records go back more than twenty years and they still have your

name on the ledger from eleven December 1919, when you bought the dry ice you used to kill Simon. And all for the play you stole from him, your own student.'

'I didn't steal anything. I wrote that play.'

'We have proof it was Simon's. He was in a critique group and the members remember him writing every word.'

'You think that early draft is evidence? He wrote that with my help. Mine was the idea!' His voice rose with each word until he was almost screaming. 'Everything that boy wrote was under my supervision. I made all the suggestions, all the revisions. It was a brilliant work. He didn't deserve it. No one that young deserves that much success. He hadn't paid his dues like I had. After he died, I was the one who turned dross to gold. The play is mine! I'm the victim here!'

'No more of this, sir,' said Detective Quinn. 'You'll need to come with us quietly now.'

Ricks looked about the room frantically, as if searching for something he'd lost. Then he heaved a great sigh and calmed down.

'All right, detective, but wait a moment, if you please. I'm going to telephone my attorney and tell him to meet me at the police station. Then I'll come with you.'

He took a few steps toward the telephone sitting on a table by the window, and then stopped. 'His number is in my office, upstairs. You can come with me if you think there's another way out of the house, but I assure you, there isn't.'

'Go with him,' Quinn muttered to one of the cops.

The cop followed Ricks up the stairs and through a doorway.

There came a sharp shout, then a crash of shattering glass and the sounds of a scuffle. Quinn reacted first, rushing to the staircase and pounding up the stairs. As he reached the top, a single shot rang out.

'Don't nobody move,' ordered the cop who was left alone with me and Luisa. He pulled out his Colt revolver and headed toward the stairs. Luisa gave an anguished cry and crumpled to the floor, sobbing, 'I lied, I lied. I am so sorry.'

'There, there, no one blames you.' I tried to comfort her.

After what seemed like hours, Detective Quinn came to the top of the staircase. Looking down on those of us in the living room, he said, 'Ricks shot himself. He went for a pistol in his desk, not a telephone number. Don't come up. It's not a pretty sight. He has his pistol in one hand and a newspaper in the other. The paper with the article about him winning the Pulitzer.'

FORTY-ONE

'After all the adulation,' I said to Carl later that night, 'he preferred death to the shame of being exposed as a thief and a fraud.'

He had invited me to dinner, but I was clearly in no shape for anything that public. 'I can't possibly eat anything,' I told him, so Carl brought a box of crackers to my room and ordered hot tea with honey from the hotel. As I sat with my feet up on a cushioned chair, he encouraged me to take in some nourishment and drink some tea, which, as the British say, cures everything.

'He must have realized he was facing a long, humiliating murder trial and a death sentence. Taking his fate in his own hands must have seemed preferable.' Carl bit into a room-service sandwich. 'His student's play was his ticket to fame and glory. That meant more than life itself. His own and others'.'

'You know what, though, a Pulitzer doesn't make anyone that rich. I mean, it's money, but it doesn't make you film-star rich or royalty rich. Why kill for modest riches?'

'It was the type of riches that mattered to him – literary immortality. He could put himself in the same category as the giants he taught year after year: Oscar Wilde, Victor Hugo, George Bernard Shaw, and the rest. It must have rankled that he had taught for so long at Columbia University, the very university that administers the Pulitzer Prize, where no one recognized his genius.'

'So he stole someone else's genius. And then he convinced himself he deserved the prize, that's what astonishes me. That drama prize rightly belongs to Simon Landry.'

'I overheard someone say that the Pulitzer jurors would doubtless review the award and the university would make the correction.'

'That would be so gratifying for Sarah Landry. And for Simon's friends.'

'Detective Quinn gets credit for solving all three murders. That was good of you to throw everything in his lap.'

Carl's praise felt warm. I realized how much his good opinion meant to me. And I realized something else.

There are different kinds of love. Everyone knows that. There's the respectful love you feel for your parents or for those who raised you, the people who tried their imperfect best in an imperfect world to nurture a child into adulthood. I felt that love for my mother. There's the love for a child that is greater than any force on earth, that brings parents to sacrifice anything for that being they created. While I've not had children, I believe I know what that love is for having received it.

But between a man and a woman there are also different kinds of love. The love I felt for David – magnetic, fierce, blind and intensely physical – was entirely different from the love I felt for Carl. With Carl, love meant respect and trust, and two minds so much in tune that silence often substituted for conversation. There may be other kinds of love that I am unaware of, but I can say I experienced both of these, and when I had to choose, I chose Carl. Maturity over childishness. Love over infatuation. I'd always known that my romance with David was going nowhere. He'd told me often enough that he wasn't the marrying kind. And he'd told me often enough that he was going to go straight. With a jolt, I realized that when David said goodbye and sailed off to Havana, I hadn't been devastated for more than a few hours. I hadn't seen him in over a year, and during that year while he was in prison, I'd written him every week. He'd written me once. Prison turned a hard man rock hard.

David was a boy. He would forever be a boy. I wanted a man.

'What time does your train leave tomorrow?' I asked.

'Eleven fifteen. Are you going to come wave me off?'

'I'm going to try to get a seat on the same train.'

His eyebrows shot up. 'I was not expecting that, Miss Beckett.'

'Well, I'm not needed at a trial. And Adele and Fred leave for England in a couple of days. There's no reason for me to stay in New York any longer. If you don't mind having company for the trip home, I thought I'd get a ticket to LA in the morning on the same train.'

'I can't think of anything I'd like more,' he said, reaching across the table to give my hand a quick squeeze.

AUTHOR'S NOTE

The first thing I want to know when I read a historical novel is how much of it is true. If you share my passion for history and historical accuracy in fiction, you'll be interested to know that Queen Marie of Romania did visit New York during October of 1926 with her two children. Princess Ileana was a teenager, and I surmise that, like most teenagers of the day, she enjoyed watching American silent movies, which were widely available throughout Europe. Prince Nicholas was indeed a young officer in the British Royal Navy, serving his mother's country on a light cruiser. He was given leave to accompany his mother, an English princess, on her trip to America. I invented Prince Nicholas's interest in the Crenshaw murder – since the murder itself is fictional – but his mother was a good friend of the First Sea Lord and could easily have applied to him for information. Queen Marie was truly beautiful – just google her name and you'll see a picture – and she was a staunch advocate for women's voting rights throughout the world.

Dry ice is commonly used in theatrical productions and for parties and other social events. It is not dangerous except in enclosed spaces, where it can kill. A recent bit of news provided sad proof: in 2018 an ice-cream salesman's wife and mother suffocated to death in their enclosed car when fumes escaped from four coolers of dry ice.

David's appearance in New York was timely, as the New York mob, known to the public as Murder Inc., expanded its tentacles to Havana, Cuba, that year. The gangsters I mention – Lucky Luciano, Arnold 'The Brain' Rothstein (who did indeed fix the 1919 World Series) and Meyer Lansky – were vicious killers who led the organized crime syndicate in New York. By the 1950s, the New York mafia had come close to controlling all of Cuba. Castro's Communist revolution of 1959 closed their nightclubs, casinos and brothels, putting them out of business.

It's hard to believe, but the US government did deliberately poison industrial alcohol by making suppliers add a heavy percentage of wood (methyl) alcohol, even though everyone knew very well that people were drinking it and many would die. The program began in 1926, when this story is set. New York's medical examiner, Dr Charles Norris, and his chemists and staff protested long and hard, to no avail. Deaths from drinking 'smoke' (as slang called it) mounted alarmingly. Deborah Blum's fascinating book, *The Poisoner's Handbook*, provides details.

And finally, Adele Astaire is little remembered today, but during her heyday, it was *she* who was the star of their vaudeville and stage brother/sister act, not Fred. She retired from professional life in 1932 when she married an English lord. Fred Astaire went on to worldwide fame through the movies. Today he is widely acknowledged as the greatest dancer in film history.

Whenever possible, I use real locations. For instance, the Algonquin Hotel, Mary Pickford's favorite, is still on 44th Street – I've stayed there and recommend it highly. The Astor Hotel is gone, but the famous, elegant Plaza sits across from Central Park. The Morosco Theater on West 45th was torn down in 1982. Detailed street maps of New York in the early 1920s show what sort of houses and businesses existed in those years, for example, D. Auerbach and Sons Candy factory were on Eleventh and 46th and the railroad that brought their supplies ran conveniently along Eleventh Avenue. Eskimo Ice is fictional, but there were many such in New York, then as now.